©Background Digitals Publishing GmbH
All rights reserved
ISBN 3-9807328-1-9
Printed in Germany

Herstellung: Libri Books on Demand

The Meaning Creator
Hela Bog

Chapter I.   -Ronda`s World -

In the year 2013, when I was eighteen years old, I escaped the Belgian home-nest of Ronse. Born in Ronse, I was called Ronda, which supposedly my parents meant nothing in particular with. In 2014 and 2015 I saw Ronse again, to celebrate Christmas with my parents. In 2016 they moved to Liege.

Out of curiosity, I organized a class meeting with the old schoolmates a few months ago. More than thirty years after graduation but it was amazingly simple to find the data of the old buddies. They were all registered in an unprotected data base. Almost all came, but it was disappointing. We met in the old school-pub. Of course, the pub still exists as does the school. Many had remained in Ronse. „Becoming stones on the Commu-Sofa", as I call it. The Internet and television may prevent us from silliness, but it has nothing to do with real life. Some had even studied and become teachers or lawyers, but despite their formation, they were totally boring - almost dead -.
I had much to tell my old pals, but they didn`t have any interest. I believe, a few even got annoyed, having exchanged their Commu-Sofa for the chair in our school-pub, presumably, they were missing at that moment an interactive-show on the Internet-TV. We drank a few glasses of dark beer and tried to remember old stories and teachers, but despite all attempts to brighten things, it was a total flop.
My best friends from the old days, Zazo and Michel, did not come. Zazo had to rewrite a computer-program, and Michel was hanging in Italy between two olive trees in a hammock, apparently.
After this hopeless evening, I got the idea to write my story as a script. Admittingly, a certain missionary spirit drives me, but I am sure, a skillful producer will film my story so that

thousands could be torn from their petrifaction.Anyway, I had to write the book, but for another reason.

Therefore, 2013, I was 18, my brother two years older and my parents harmless. They constantly tried to organize harmony, however with naive methods. They tried to manage the contradictions of life by concentrating on the so-called „good" pushing aside the „bad ", whenever possible. For this purpose, they constructed some practical drawers, in which life was sorted. Order, diligence and: „what you don't want done to you, don`t do to others", came in the good drawers, whereas chaos, aggression and doubts came in the bad ones. Of course I was bad when I went at 18 to Paris, the criminal, fucking French capital.

There, I, like my parents and millions of other unemployed people, lived from the state-welfare, distributed by the French government and the EC, respectively · enough for a grey life. Now and then you had to do some stupid work for the authorities. In Paris, rubbish collecting in the suburbs`meadows and forests was popular. At home, in Belgium it was renovating factory-ruins and weeding. But where in the regular tracks of Belgium boredom and depression drove Ralley, in Paris I was genuinely challenged. Here, everyone wanted everything from everyone in every sense. Of course, there was a certain gloomy atmosphere also in Paris, because here too, maybe even more than in the small protected towns, the majority of young people had no perspective. They were unemployed, functionless and notionless on what kept life connected. But there was less control and therefore more survival-training. It certainly was the bad drawer.

After a few weeks, my life in Paris assumed direction: in the suburb of St. Denis they alloted me an apartment in the block of flats >Taurus III d <. For sleeping, the grubby bachlor apartement of 16 square meters was minimally better than the bridges and demolition-houses, that had housed me until then. In St. Denis the streets were in the hands of black gangs.

Innocent as I was, I came back to Taurus III d the first night singing. Tipsy, unknown and white skinned, that could not go well. They sent forward a dwarf in order to test me. A popular game, as I found out later. This boy appeared in front of me and explained that the toll was 100 Euros, upon which I shoved him out of the way. The gang, that came after him, was not so easily shoved out of the way. But I fought bravely.I kicked at least three Mullahs straight into the hospital. Unfortunately, I also ended up there. My stay at the hospital lasted for two weeks and as a permanent reminder of a sneaky knife-sting, I still have a scar on my stomach, which hurts when bad weather announces itself.

After convalescence, I began investigating this gang. That`s simply the way I am. Whoever does bad to me must reckon with revenge. Quite carefully, I asked around, used children and elderly in our block of flats in order to find the track of the local Matadors. It didn`t last a month,I then knew the gang. I knew, when and where they met and that they called themselves „Jungle Noir " -how imaginative-!

Because I had always had a technically skillful tiny hand, I installed a small bug in their boiler room-meeting point, which betrayed their plans and ideas. The boss was respectfully named „Moraine " by his subjects and was just as vicious. A collosses of a man, hands like griddles and eyes, quick and greedy. He was a beast of prey. Strangely enough there are always these bosses. And always running behind such heroes are hordes of stupid men full of fervor. For Moraine, a human life was a piece of dirt, „fly-dirt ", he said and just walked all over people. I held him and his brutal blood personally responsable for my injuries. The more I knew of him, the more my decision to teach him a permanent lesson ripened.

Because I was always a circumspect human being, I approached the matter systematically. I wanted to grill Moraine slowly but certainly. For more than two months, I collected information about him and his troops. Then, I took the first step. As they decided to do a supermarket, I gave the cops an anonymous tip. My astonishment was great when I noticed that the cops did nothing. My small transmitter told me the reason: the cops were shitless-scared, furthermore the local social-cop was in their hands because of some sex-things.

But now Moraine knew that somebody had betrayed him. Of course, he suspected the traitor to be in his own ranks, which was o.k. . Part two of my grill-party began. Moraine put pressure on his boys. He took one after the other and tormented them all. Nobody admitted to betraying him. All swore eternal fidelity. Moraine was furious and helpless. For the next coup, he announced single-conversations, the old confidentiality was gone. At intervals, he practiced miscellaneous tests and tricks, as with: „now I know that you did it", and pointing the pistol at the temple, created new mistrust and animosities. It finally came out that Moraine trusted his crony Franque the most. With him he schemed on how to find the traitor. Also, he mentioned to Franque, that he intended to form an alliance with the neighbouring-gang >Cool Devils <, which is why he wanted to eliminate each risk in his own ranks. The Cool Devils were a weak troop, that controlled only two blocks of flats. Moraine simply wanted to swallow them up.
My next move was a cool anonymous message to the Cool Devils which indicated that the Jungle Noir was having leadership-problems and Moraine was no longer man of the situation. I let the Cool Devils know where Moraine was going to eat next Sunday with his sub-chieftain Franque.

Furthermore, I hinted in my cool letter that it would not be unwise to leave Sub-chieftain Franque intact, since he could achieve good services for an expansion of the Cool Devils. It didn`t take long for the answer to show itself. The Cool Devils served dessert on Sunday and clearly for longer than me, Moraine went for five weeks into hospital. His transportation into the clinic was the optimal entry-situation for me.

I found the homeless jungle-brothers –where else-but in the computer-animation-gamehall. I played the benefactor, and with some games and drinks, the boys learned to like me. My generosity and my spirit of invention was very useful to me. I knew what they wanted: money and adventures, and that was exactly what I gave them.
I had found out about some optimal break-in possibilities into luxury villas and went in small groups with the orphaned jungle-brothers on tour. There was hardly anyone, who didn't like my ideas. As Moraine came out of the hospital, his boys had begun trusting me. It turned out that, despite the short time I had a better deck of cards than Moraine. Nobody wanted to go back to Moraine, even though I had made it clear to everyone that I would not be vicious in case they returned. They had noticed that I was more clever and probably more successful than their boss was. Of course I had optimally prepared the boys mentally and organizationally for Moraine`s return.

Moraine`s hate for Franque and the Cool Devils was unspeakable. Of course he had created, in the half-coma, the idea that only Franque could be the traitor, because only he knew about the Sunday meals. Also he, the intelligent Moraine, had realized, despite all the Sunday-meal-turmoil, the Cool Devils had hit Franque in a strange way quite reservedly. The matter was plain and Franque in Moraine`s language-jargon: „dd " (declared dead). For security reasons, Moraine finally wanted to take care of the Cool Devils, although, he needed the other boys. Therefore, as Moraine started collecting the old cronies, we set an evil trap again. The details are somewhat embarrassing for me today. I want to say only so much: Moraine`s imagination hardly ever went beyond the physical. We therefore administered him, together with the Cool Devils, with which we cultivated a peaceful neighbourship, a recent vehement beating. Furthermore, I took care that Moraine vanished for a half year in quarantine in the tropics-desease hospital. Moraine later went to Marseilles and from there got on a ship to Africa. As of that time, he didn't matter to me.

In this way I had become by chance the chieftain of a suburbian gang. Because the next chapter of my story is a bit dim from a present-day point of view, I would like to get rid of some information as my justification.

In my Parisian time, the goods of the world were unjustly distributed. There were the so-called „mega-rich", that did not even amount to 5% of the population world-wide, but possessed more than 70% of all values. These people automatically became richer and richer which was in France no different from the other industrial states. The most mega-rich sat in America and the fewest in the so-called „developing countries". On the other hand, there were more and more unemployed people, because more and more work was taken over by robots and computers. The reason for both: the growing unemployment and the growing wealth of the mega-rich, was the so-called >shareholder-value-principle<. The world economy worked on this principle. Business-profits were absolute priority. With a constant climbing tendency, unemployment was actually 40% in Europe but officially at 20%, because the governments tried to hush up the fact of the scarce work through activity-programs. The masses of young people had no perspective. Just like my jungle-brothers, without any orientation they danced through life. Okay, there was sex and sports (usually fighting and weight-training), but if that is the only meaning, frustration and imbecility are not far. Politicians were politicians, because they were power-hungry, and they received this power as puppets of the mega-rich. They justified their impotence with „objective forces", because, where the politic doesn't obey, the mega-rich with their productions and values, go where they find better „basic conditions ", which means better puppets. As I said, the most fatal effect of the shareholder-value-principle was the constantly growing use of ever more perfect robots and computers. Because of this more than half of humankind lived in poverty. All were helpless. Not me. I used a part of my troop to fight against the injustice, namely against the alleged mega-rich.

The jungle-brothers were my camouflage. I went with them on small tours and helped the local police with their tasks. We lived quite pleasantly, and those blocks, which were under my control, had no worries. My resourcefulness and the physical fighting-strength of my boys gave us a remarkable reputation. Just after one year, we were undisputed market-leaders in the blocks from Taurus to Aries with over 50 active fighters. The street-gang, which we showed outwardly, was, as I said, only the half truth. The gang was a perfect camouflage for a small, internal special-troop. The most clever minds of my troop I made into the „Insiders ", an elite-troop, whose members nobody knew, besides ourselves. We Insiders acted rarely but effectively. Our specialty was the mega-rich. Troops like ours sprang up at the same time in Amsterdam, London and Berlin, without any agreements or contacts. It was just the signs of the time. Paris, anyway, gave us respect. The Parisian police formed a special-unit to fight us and the press called us „Mistral ", because we came just as unexpectedly and severely. With that name, we were in competition with a car-mark. Nobody, not even our wives, knew, who was behind „Mistral". For them we were the >Jungle Noirs<. With >Mistral< I became the Parisian Robin Hood. Where ever the rich were to be caught, we caught them. We plundered their villas, set fire to their cars and motor-yachts and let them pay well for their own protection. The money was directly alloted to kindergartens, soup-kitchens and youth-centres in the slums. So we had no trouble with the unpleasant transfer-problem. The poor liked us even though the press did everything to demonize us.

Retrospectively, I must admit to having acted incorrectly. Although we never applied force against people, even acting as „Insiders", today I know that force always generates counterviolence and doesn`t make things better. At that time the topic force was nothing special for me. Force was everywhere and necessary. At least, if one like me, lived on the street. There was always someone coming along, who wanted to play the big boss. Of course those guys had to receive a bit on the ears. Furthermore, there were thousands of maniacs, that had watched too much tube and believed, that shooting and hitting makes the hero. Force reigned the street, at least in our quarter of Paris. At that time, after I shot my first candidate in a shooting, I wrote a poem about force. Here it is. Whoever doesn`t like poems, like myself, should skip it.

Force

Jesus told his enemies:
>I don't fight back,
and turn the other cheek.<
He was nailed on the cross.

I said: >I fight back.<
And shot the man,
who wanted to shoot me
into the grave.

Jesus forgot the stupidity of the masses.
I forgot my own cleverness.
The question is who was the most stupid,
the idealist or the activist.

Whoever wants to avoid victims,
should remain at home,
the meeting with reality
is always brutal.

Okay, it doesn't rhyme. But nevertheless it is a poem. Force in any case, as I know today, does not change things for the good. If somebody attacks me now, I am clever enough to act insane, to run away, or to discuss from person to person, depending on whoever comes. In politics, the last years have proven to be the same: the change to a more just world could only be arranged peacefully and democratically.

Going back to the Insiders. Furthermore, we made the mistake of not distinguishing between such rich people, that became wealthy from their own strength, and those that only administer their super-heritages. The necessity of this differentiation I learned through the Global Justice Movement later on. Also, at the time I didn`t know that the truly mega-rich outwardly acted rather modest and left the shine and glory to the new-rich. One time, however, I certainly caught the mega-rich, when we crashed a party of the Spanish king at the Ritz. We carried off so many precious jewels then, that we only could get rid of them, by getting them cut apart in Antwerp, with lots of trouble. The echo on this coup was huge. From all over the world, special-units were sent to take care of us. We put the Insiders in a deep sleep at that time.

In the winter of 2014, I found time to act on the Internet more intensively. There, a political development was growing, which went well with my Robin Hood philosophy. It was about the foundation of the French Global Justice Party (F-GJP).

At that time throughout Europe and North America, global justice parties (GJPs) were established. Beyond this stood the idea of the Global Justice Movement (GJM). The idea originated from a small novel and spread like fire. It was a scientific and such a plausible idea that it was clear even to the most stupid; the most brilliant political idea for centuries. It put an end to ancient injustices. The GJM became possible through the Internet, because almost all GJPs established themselves over the Internet. On the Net, people could discuss, find truths and spread the idea uniformly world-wide. I came upon it, with a tip from my newsvendor. He gave me a paper, on which stood the address: www.global-justice.org . „Have a look" he said, „it could be of interest to you". When I think about it, this newsvendor was probablly decisive in my later life. Maybe he knew more about me than I thought.

Therefore, I looked under: www.global-justice.org on the Internet and the following page appeared. I had it printed out right away.

GJM = Global Justice Movement

We determine with world-wide validity:

Justice means to create a fair starting-position for each human being, enabling them to achieve human work, that had become scarce through machines and robots.
It means to distribute the resources of the earth so that those who cannot work in the market economy or don`t want to work in it, are provided for, in a global welfare-system with the essentials and fair education in exchange for minimal work.
Justice means, to leave earnings to successful people and at the most tax one third of it.

Justice means that it is only allowed to inherit per life-partner (at most two people) and per child at most $ 1,5 million U.S. , and furthermore any other inheritance (maximum three people or institutions) at most $ 100.000 U.S. each. The remaining amount of money is to be used for the creation of the Global Justice System according to the principles of the GJM.
Justice means that all political principles are determined by democratic processes.

We further determine:

Neither the European Union, nor the NAFTA, nor the ASEAN, nor the MERCOSUR or the single-states of this earth are able, alone or in alliance, to organize justice after the principles of the GJM, because
The power of the mega-rich, that amounts to less than 5% of the population world-wide, but who own more than 70% of all productive assets, rule present-day world-politics, why
Only the organization of completely new parties (Global Justice Parties) that are strictly prescribed in the principles of the GJM will be able to alter this, with what
These alterations have to happen world-wide so that via democratic processes GJPs will come to political power in hopefully all countries, so that by legislation any possibility for the inheritance of the mega-rich to escape is prohibited.

At first I did not understand the meaning of these sentences. I thought: „again such radical-political cheap-talk", and already wanted to click to the Webside of a really sweet honey, when I, more out of solidarity to my newsvendor clicked on the button >discussion<. I was very surprised, to find a highly interesting, vehement discussion on the guiding principles, and little by little it became clear, that perhaps there was a real world-revolution in the making. If they used the inheritance of the mega-rich for a world-wide basic-care, the world would change. It would become, for the first time in the history of humankind, a global planned economy. The mega-rich fought back of course. They wanted to inherit more than $ 1,5 million U.S. per child and life-partner, so they engaged the best scientists in order to prove the impracticability and the disastrous effects of this idea. It was about a lot of money. An American Harvard Professor had calculated that within the next twenty years at least $ 8.000 billion U.S. would be for the Global Justice Movement (GJM).

Concerning the inheritance-limit of $ 1,5 million U.S. , there were highly scientific examinations that this amount must be freely inheritable at least to hold sufficiant incentive in the market economy. The whole system would not work without the market economy. It was written in the program of the GJM, that the free coming inheritance money should be given to a supernational organization, such as the United Nations (UN), in order to realize the global distribution. The democratic, world-wide growth of GJPs on the basis of the >Global-Justice-Idea< should provide the individual states with corresponding laws. As simple and plausible as the idea was, it still proved very difficult in the discussion. Statisticians and experts of constitutional law from the rich countries enumerated how much life would lose, if people became addicted to this „crazy idea". Economists quarreled about the effects on big and small businesses, the world economy, the stock exchanges, public finances and so on.

I don't want to be boring with details, but for two reasons, the discussion on the Internet became important for my personal story.

The people, who quarreled about the feasibility of the global justice-idea, were highly intelligent specialists. People, like me, could only be amazed with the kind of arguments they threw at each other. With luck, a few French and German students had furnished a service for mere mortals, where the most important discussion-results were clearly summarized, once every week, in French, English and German. Under: www.global-justice-party.org they published their service. Strangely, it was always students of one of these countries who influenced decisively the course of history. I watched the development of the GJM for a few weeks and came to the conclusion that it would fit me as the Parisian Robin Hood to join the French GJP. From my point of view, it was sure that the idea was realistic. Neither multi-national concerns nor smaller enterprises would break down. They would implement tax offices of the single states in order to seize inheritances and to uncover tricks. As an equivalent a part of the inheritances would come to the single states. They would restrict the basic-care to basic-foods, minimal-living space, energy, water, medical basic-care and basic-education, and in doing so, leave enough space for the market economy. Specialists calculated that 60% of the total-economy would be covered by a well working market economy.

Everywhere, the GJPs drew large crowds. In America, they tried to prohibit them with constitutional law, which failed because of the liberal American constitutional judges. We in Paris printed fliers, distributed them in the city and publicized our GJP everywhere. We simplified the matter a bit, but we mobilized the masses. Our fliers looked something like this:

In the present day market economy, half of humankind has no chance anymore.
70% of the instruments of the market economy are possessed by the mega-rich, which is why the market economy is useful for them above all.
$ 1.500.000 U.S. per child and life-partners is enough as an inheritance!
The Global Justice Party wants to bring the world into equilibrian again.
Earth bears enough for all people.

We are for the market economy, but where it gives no chances, the essentials should be distributed over a global planned economy.
Therefore, vote for the French Global Justice Party.
Info under: www.global-justice-party.org

Unfortunately I don't have a flier from that time, so I can write only from memory. Anyway, we have successfully advertised for the GJM with our big talk.

Concerning the discussion on the Internet, I was only an observer until then. This passiveness ended when they had on their panel what to do with $ 200 million U.S., spontaneously given, by some rich that liked the idea of the Global Justice, to the GJM, respectively the different GJPs. On the Internet, they discussed how they should use the money. It was clear that it should not ooze away in the several parties. They wanted to do spectacular things with it. What the brains babbled about on the Internet, was from my point of view, rather short-sighted, however. The majority of the specialists had voiced agreement to give the money to the United Nations, so that the realization of the Global Justice Idea could be worked on there. The general secretary of the UN had, just like some other high UN-officials, steered the discussion in this direction. Admittedly, also in the GJM-program, the UN had been mentioned as the possible provider of the global distribution, but from my point of view, the UN was not exactly a reliable candidate. Not, that I was a UN specialist, but a certain notion told me that one had to be careful with this club. I thought about how I would, as a mega-rich, defend an attack of the GJM and came to the conclusion that I would organize a trap. The United Nations admittedly had honorable goals, but they had been a game-ball of the rich countries for decades. Their finances and leadership positions were not by a small amount under the control of the rich countries, that is, of the mega-rich. What would happen, if the UN collected the money and then

14

delayed everything and babbled about. Maybe they would organize UN-decisions, that softened the GJM-aims, so that it would be bearable for the mega-rich. As I said, it was only a notion. Therefore I sat down and wrote a letter, that I finally sent into the discussion-forum: www.global-justice.org . The letter was as follows:

Dear ladies and gentlemen,

I am only a simple human being, but I ask you to think about, concerning the award of the GJM-money, that the United Nations is possibly not really willing to represent a 100% of the idea of the GJM. From my view, it would be irresponsible, to entrust the United Nations GJM-money only on the personal vote of its president and some high representative, without an official, unambiguous vote for ,,100% pro GJM". Perhaps one has to call for securities despite such a vote.
Yours Sincerely,
P1
Copy of this letter goes to my party, the GJP-France, Paris.

So far so good. The answer didn't take long. The executive of our French GJP congratulated me by e-mail on my clever observation. Even in the discussion of the specialists, first hesitatingly, then increasing, the opinion reinforces that this ,,P1-objection" was not so stupid after all. They wrestled through, to demand an official, 100% confession from the UN to the GJM-principles.

And now the ralley began. The United Nations divided. The representatives of the poor countries and the UN Secretary General fought for the GJM. The American government signalled that all UN-subsidies would end for ever and ever if the members of the UN would voice agreement with the GJM. Some European countries thought that the so-called ,,development-help" would be enough to turn things for the good. In the end the opinion prevailed, that such honorable institutions as the United Nations must remain independent and should not connect its fate with daring experiments à la GJM.

That „P1-objection " –called like this everywhere- had taken. They celebrated me as a saviour of the GJM-money. Admittedly, I was proud. What came a few days later, resembled a push into cold water. In my mailbox, I found the following letter:

Sender: Coordination-advice of the Global Union
Address: P1 at this time Paris, Rue de la Galette, France

Dear „P1 ",

We would be very happy if you would join the new established coordination-advice. The coordination-advice was formed after the United Nations decided in their session of the 02.03.2015 not to be a provider of the inheritance-regulation of the GJM. We want to establish as global providers of the GJM, the Global Union (GU).
The GU should become the provider of the Global Justice-Movement. The coordination-advice will work out the details. Please contact us at: http.gu-koordinationsrat.579.gb. Please don't relay this address since it is given only to a known, selected circle of people, in order to guarantee the balance and effectiveness of our discussion.
With the best greetings
GU-coordination-advice
Serena Costa

So should I become a member of this coordination-council, to organize the construction of the „Global Union (GU)". I looked under: http.gu-koordinationsrat-579.gb and found the discussion in full swing. Here a departure from the protocols, that I had had printed at that time:

Professor Bouvier (from Paris): „The idea of the Global Justice was born to solve the problem of world-wide unemployment. It would be only logical if we did something symbolic for this problem with the first money. Symbols move the world. We should build as a symbol of a new era the centre of the Global Union. A monumental building ".

John Darwell (American): „Symbols have always been destroyed until now. Build a symbol and somebody will blow it up into the air."

Prof Kent (Germany): „First of all we have to strengthen the idea of the GJM, that is: we must promote the GJPs. In many countries, the GJPs don't have the money to organize themselves neatly, even less to make available computers for their members for the Internet. In some countries, there are no GJPs. The first money should be used, to clear the way for the GJPs."

Isma Mbumara (Nigeria): „On our continent every minute two children die. If you really want to achieve importantance, then give them medicine and food."

Mrs Iljakowa (Russia): „As well as a symbol as a source of food I propose to buy the first wheat-fields. Everybody should see, that the GU is serious with the idea of the basic-care ".

Mr. Wright (England): „Where ever we talk about distribution, we talk about greed. With absolute priority it is necessary to develop an unmanipulatitive computer-system, that organizes the cultivation, demand-investigation and distribution".

„We must first establish an executive and a parliamentary advisor for the Global Union", Jose Maria Lopez from Brazil wanted to know.

With the most different arguments, they fought, and I sat before the screen again amazed. Finally, I printed out those suggestions, which pleased me the most. From this collection of clever thoughts, I formed symbioses, as well as possible, that I brought as solution-suggestions. So I didn't admittedly turn into the father of new thoughts, but I had probably given one or the other thought-impulses, however. Specialists sometimes wander around in their think-tanks unable to see the light covered by their specialization. I was one of the few people in this coordination-advice, whose home was the street, better said I was somebody, that dared to open his mouth, despite of low origins. A woman, whose name was Mrs. Dreyer, and which I did not suspect at the time would eventually become quite important to me, encouraged me by e-mail:

„Dear P1, you say that you come from the streets. Be proud of it. Your practical thinking has already rescued us once."

We had discussions for one month and finally came to the following decisions: We bought 80.000 acres of wheat-fields in Southern-Russia and ordered GUGLOBE. In comparison to today, GUGLOBE was at that time a tiny computer-installation. GUGLOBE would steer the global planning economy. In its characteristics, we wanted the program even now to be prepared for all its later tasks. By that we killed two birds with one stone: On the one hand in the year 2018 the Global Union could harvest for the first time food for the worst emergencies by themselves and on the other hand we had a real test-possibility for GUGLOBE. We wanted to check out in practice whether the system worked. Everything had to be operational if the GJPses were successful in the parliaments and got the inheritance-money for the Global

18

Union (GU). The tests proceeded easily, so that as a third effect, one year later, we had a nice advertisement for the GU. After these first decisions of the coordination-advice, there still remained enough money to build the first GU-healthcare-centre in Lagos/Nigeria.

The work of the coordination-council lasted longer than planned, as the more people saw the idea of the Global Justice becoming a reality, the more people joined the GJPs and donated money. We chose a GU-board, but who did not have much to say. GUGLOBE`S area of authority at that time was already so long range that there was hardly any room for human decisions. GUGLOBE pulled its data out of dependable sources, it analyzed scientific statistics, research, population-development, medical data, weather-influences, satellite-pictures and much more. From all these data, it developed decision- and action-suggestions for the development of agrarian-surfaces, housing, hospitals and energy-providers. The board mainly had to prove the plausibility.

Membership in the coordination-advice was an honorary office, that is, we received no money for it. Also the officials of the GJPs received no money. The Global Justice-Movement wanted to differ unequivocally from the usual political parties. I no longer knew how long I had discussions on the Internet, but it must have been for about two years. The more money the GU received, the more decisions we made. GUGLOBE and the new board adopted our work after a thorough testing-stage only in the year 2019.

Something, we had also pushed in the coordination-advice, and which the new board put into action later, was the story with the meaning-givers and meaning-creators. I want to briefly talk about the backgrounds, because it has to do my personal fate in it:

There is the saying >Humans don't live from bread alone, souls also want to be fed<. This saying even at that time became more and more important. In primitive times, when humans were after wild animals with stones, soul needs were rather unimportant. People had to deal enough with bodily needs. Within the centuries one or another philosopher and religious founder sprang from the human race, which gave a bit more spirit to the earthlings. Nevertheless, till the third millenium, work was the most important thing, as it was the continuation of Stone Age hunting. Day in and day out, one had to fight for bread and butter, in other words, he had to work. Then came computers and robots. They adopted the work and many people became free. Suddenly they had more time and no work. Some couldn't cope with it and became unhappy. Some people were genetically or through education so very much fixed on performance and work that they couldn`t find anything similarly satisfying. Leisure time didn`t offer any sense-alternatives. I was born in this time and with me my Jungle Noir and millions of other frustrated youngsters. The so-called establishment held franticly to the solid ideals of „success through performance and work". For them the maintenance of the old order and above all, power was tops. For this purpose the media- and film-production used them. In there, indefatigable, they sang the holy song of the market economy. Human spirit of invention and human work were put forth as attainable ideals. Single states and power-blocks competed in growth and market-shares. The attempt, to organize human life via the market economy, even though most work was done by machines, could logically only lead to a successful result for half of mankind. Only those people who succeeded in shaping computers and robots more effectively were really successful.
That however,only accelerated the changing-process.

We, living in the streets of the cities, knew exactly that this high-tech-world had no place for us. We were not sufficiently qualified. We were only bouncers and loafers and, who now and then qualified ourselves as paper-collectors. We were the meaningless, like the underprivileged of the so-called developing countries. We were dependent exactly like them on the mercy of any state-organs. Yes, it was a mercy, to be brought through as an unemployed person in this society, organized by the market economy. The definitions were these, and therefore we were the frustrated meaningless. Actually, they would have expected more from us. And because we were failures anyway, the one or the other atrocity did not matter at all. Worse could not happen. If we sat a few weeks or months in the slammer, it was O.K., then we were among us and had a regular routine, maybe even a touch of meaning and work. I knew some frustrated that hated everything so much, that their own life was worthless to them. They risked their tiny life by jumping onto driven container-trains or had vehement shootings with other frustrated.

This development had assumed absolute ludicrous forms in America. Nowhere was competition so glorified, as there, and one ran amock constantely somewhere. The state enforced one death penalty after the other and was surprised that people`s contempt for life increased constantly.

For these reasons, we decided in the coordination-advice to help the unemployed of the world not only materialisticly but also emotionally, at least in the beginning. We were confident that the GU could help the unemployed better, than any other organization. After all, the GU was completely free from market economy ideals. Namely even churches tried at that time, to found >profit-centres<. The bacillus-profit-maximus had almost infected the entire globe, but only almost, because we existed. Life could also be healthy for us independent from supply and demand. We wanted to put aside the youngsters of the cities those „meaning-givers" that preached no ideals. In contrast to traditional meaning-mediators, we sold no dreams, neither from fair chances in the market economy, nor from any religion. Our program was different. They could find something with us, that actually seemed to be lost forever, namely an ideal-typical world, beyond performances and competitions. While the ideals of the market economy were called „fight and profit", our topic was „justice". We had a real ideal. Who could deny that „performance and competition " had more to do with „fight and Stone Age" than with desirable advances of civilization. Our concept of justice let the soul-hearts beat higher. Besides that for the half of humankind „performance and competition " was an illusionary ideal anyway, because objectively there was too little human work.

Therefore we turned the skewer. We turned the losers of the market- and competition-world into the winners of the new justice-world. We made it clear to everyone that the market economy for half of humankind was an unattainable dream, and that there could originate with the idea of the global justice a second new world, a just distribution-world. We created the planning sister-world of the market economy. We needed no competition and no performance pressure. We needed ideal support and confident people for our idea. Whoever helped us helped themselves, and the only ones, that suffered damages through our idea, were the heirs of the mega-rich. However, even to them we left so much that they had no cause to worry. We newly discovered the planned economy. After their dictatorial disaster in the former Communist states, they were pronounced dead. We made the planned economy to the democratic second part of the world economy, to that part where the losers of the market economy could live in fact without the feeling of being denied, or parasites. We asked the youth of the world: „Help us build a new world. The market economy needs a strong sister". Admittingly, the slogan simplified the matter a little, but in essence, it illustrated that it went beyond building a new world of justice.

I had been advising and discussing all this in the coordination-advice. In particular I had given advice on the formulations of how to speak to the youngsters of the cities, in order to make our idea plausible. Exactly on this topic, they asked me for advice again and again. I was finally a specialist in the area of >street-children<. Nevertheless, I was not badly amazed, when I received the following e-mail from the board of the GU:

Dear P1,

In the past you have proven yourself to the Global Union with incalculable services. Your know-how and creativity earn admiration. Since you have a natural access to the youngsters of Paris, we would like to offer you the position of the first meaning-giver of Paris. Conditions and further details please discuss with Mrs. Dreyer: .
Cordial congratulations.
With the best greetings
Global Union
–the board-

Spontaneously, I refused. „that`s out of this world", I thought. Me and law and order! O.K., meaning-givers were not police, but nevertheless I was rather the opposite. Even if I had given some tips to the coordination-advice, concerning meaning-givers, I belonged to those that meaning-givers should convert. I was the boss of Jungle Noir –just to be silent of the Mistral/Insiders-.

Of course they wanted to reward my participation in the coordination-advice with this offer, which is why my cancellation had probably shoved the board of the GU away. That didn't matter to me. Law and order or social work- such stuffiness didn't go with me.

I had almost forgotten the meaning-giver offer, when the before mentioned Mrs. Dreyer –not stupid- tried to find contact to me via Ben, our poor social-cop. Dreyer, the name seemed familiar to me, but I couldn`t place it anymore.

I will never forget my first meeting with her. It was in December 2018. Finally after so long Paris had snow again and the Christmas consumption-carousel, centrifuged human goodness.

She immediately seemed nice to me. Approximately 50 years old, with eyes, that could not be more lively. She had tied up her white hair into a braid. So, as she faced me, she constantly seemed to smile inside. All kinds of small things filled her with enthusiasm, and what was strange and annoying in life, amused her more than got her angry. If there exists something like positive people, she was one. For her visit with me, she had chosen a butchy appearance. Long brown leather pants and a thick fur-jacket gave her the touch of a Canadian rancher. We sat in my favourite cafe when it became clear to me that this woman came from the board of the Global Union. She said: „You didn't want to visit me, therefore I came to you." I tried making clear to her, that her visit was useless. „In case you are trying, to make a meaning-giver of me, I am sorry", I said. „I will be an employee for nobody, because I love my freedom too much ".

She smiled leniently, which in other people I would have accused as arrogance. In her case it was different, she knew, she would win, and I suppose, I also suspected the same from the beginning.

Her way of talking was mild and mighty. With no word, she was reproachful, but nevertheless she exposed my small selfish ego. She made clear to me that I understood my life as a fight- and desire-mission. I agreed with her; because according to my conviction it`s all about love, money,

24

acknowledgment and district-fights. I in fact was selfish and with conviction. Within three hours, she proved that life was more. She taught me, so to speak, a basic lesson in matters of meaning-finding. First, she built me up: „You have charisma and a good head on your shoulders. You are not accidentally the boss of a street-gang. With your gifts, you already are responsible for several people today. Your Jungle Noir are your charges, and if you are honest, that doesn't overtax you in the least. Could you tolerate more activities, or not"? Peculiarly slyly, she grinned at me, and I wondered, whether she knew something about our „Insiders". But she wanted to get at something else. She emphasized –which I already knew by the way-, that the Global Union is a very special organization. Not comparable with anything past. „We melted many ideas of justice," she explained to me and told pompous things of freedom and equality, of historical sizes and responsibilities. I finally became perceptive when she told me about her idea of life.

She explained: „Each human being has two strength-centres, that are equally strong at birth: the material and the mental strength-centre. Normally, the material centre wins the game. This material centre deals with desires: hunger, thirst, sexuality and recognition-urge. It mobilizes enormous strengths. How many things we do for money and love...! The cause of these desires is our material existence, our body. Almost constantly, it cries for more, more meals, drinking, money, power and sex."

All this was not new to me. She continued: „The material centre is your main strength-source, but you also carry this second, unattended source in yourself, the strength-centre of the soul. Your spirit tries to give food to your soul, too. Music, pleasure of nature, friendships and good art is the same food for the soul like philosophy and religions. The soul wants to elicit more from life, than just simple instinct-satisfactions. Souls want to grow and want to perfect themselves. They anticipate truths and cause intuitive actions. I believe, they are the divine part in us humans."

Mrs. Dreyer laughed: „Isn´t it funny, for the material part of us, which will die soon anyway, we struggle so much, and for the soul, which is divine, maybe immortal, we do so little."

I asked her, whether she belonged to a certain religion, and she answered astonishing things: „Religions are, as I said, the beautiful attempt, to give food to the soul. Whether it is Christianity, Islam, Hinduism or Buddhism, all religions are good likewise. I believe, there were many messengers of God on earth, not only Mohammed, Buddha and Jesus. If one sees life, without personal desires, from the view of the soul, one would get the idea that we humans are on vacation on earth.

„On vacation "?, I looked surprised at her. „Why on vacation?" –„On vacation of spirit," she answered and laughed heartily. She enjoyingly slurped her milk-coffee. „Imagine, if souls are truly divine, maybe immortal, then they live on, after the end of our material existence, in a mental world presumably without bodies. No human being knows what this world looks like. But try to think of a world full of souls. There are only mental activities. No material. No fragrances of flowers, no sea, no tenderness of the skin and no taste of sweet milk-coffee or salty cashewnuts. Don't you believe that souls have a great mind on all these material deliciousness one day? Always mental food and never nougat-chocolate? Someday the souls rustle to God or to the divine vacation-official and submit a vacation-proposition: Gender-vacation on the earth. It certainly is especially popular."

„And what about the thousands who starve, what about the children who are shot in the war? They certainly have no fun on vacation ". –„That, " so Mrs. Dreyer said, „is the problem of self responsibility. We humans are responsible for our actions. Imagine if God would immediately intervene when injustices or brutalities happened. There admittedly were no injustices and wars anymore, but what would be the price? If God would correct each injustice, we would wonder again and again why things happen differently than natural laws say. And if the bad guys suffered directly from God`s punishment, they wouldn`t exist anymore, because of fearing automatic punishment. It would be a world without self responsibility and without freedom, a strange world. So our world is fortunately different. In our world, the natural laws are valid, and because that is so, we are free in our decisions. We must, or better said, we are able to choose what we do. We choose between justice and injustice, between brutality and meekness, war and peace. And if people lead wars and kill small children, then they can do that, because they are free in their decisions. Presumably, their souls must answer for it. And if people starve, although the earth has enough food for all, then it is possible because people are free in their decisions. Presumably, the souls of those, who are responsible for such a distribution, have to answer for it. Maybe, it could be that the decisions between >justice< and >injustice< or >good< and >bad< belong to the vacation. Maybe, we are not only in a gender-vacation but also in an educational-vacation for the soul. An educational-vacation, maybe on the topic >good and evil<, who knows?"

The idea of understanding life as a vacation filled me with enthusiasm. It was the opposite of what most religions preached. There, people went on vacation, the paradise, only after a God-just life. Mrs. Dreyer`s paradise already existed today, here before my eyes. This idea was –though I didn`t believe the whole religious crap anyway- more appealing to me, than the idea, of having to behave well and having to slave away, before being –after death- treated well. For a long time, no idea had pleased me so much. Spontaneously, I mentioned that now I was sure, knowing about the galactic vacation-theory, that my soul needed a vacation and not work. Mrs. Dreyer laughed heartily. We discussed the pros and cons of her theory with much fun, and the longer we spoke the more it became clear to me that this explanation of life was more plausible, than all other theories and religions. Mrs. Dreyer took advantage of my enthusiasm shamelessly: „Of course you are free like all the others to fight for a more just world, or not. If it suffices you to grab the next bread with cheese or the next pretty woman, then don't complain about the bad quality of your holliday resort."

So, when Mrs. Dreyer asked me, whether I knew someone - not wanting to do the job myself– who could become a meaning-giver in Paris, she nearly had me buttered over. „This first meaning-giver will be a symbol in Paris. The whole of France will look at him and will measure the Global Union by him. He will show what the GU can do. We must find somebody, who has the strength for this job and furthermore the trust of the youngsters. Do you know somebody, capable of that?" She had pulled the right strings, and I discovered a new quality in me: >idealism<. Of course I didn't want to give up my freedom completely, therefore she conceded that I still remained boss of the Jungle Noir. Also, I could quit the meaning-giver-job at anytime. So, in 2019, I became the first meaning-giver of the GU in Paris. It was the first time for me, that I earned money through regular work. Meaning-givers earned $ 3.000 U.S. net monthly at that time. Incidentally: the idea, that our life on earth is a vacation, still influences me today.

Afterwards Mrs Dreyer invited me to go skiing for three weeks in Canada. She was too smart not to betray to me that an educational-centre of the GU awaited there for me. I had never stood on skis, therefore I accepted the invitation joyously. One month later I sat in an airplane to Toronto –my first flight-. Toronto was cold, minus 20 degrees Celsius. Luckily, I had my fur-lined leather-jacket with me. From the airport the fast-train went to Saracuse and from there the bus continued further on in the direction of Telton. After a two hour trip, there was only to be seen forests and snow outside, no houses, and no human being; a dreamy beautiful winter landscape, amidst the Apalachens. Thousands of ice-crystals glittered with the sun, like diamonds. At the last stop, Jeff, the ski instructor, waited for me between a few wooden houses. With a ski-doo, we rushed through the glittering snowy forest; everything seemed very surreal to me. Only a few hours before, I had been sitting in the Parisian Metro and now: this wild world of nature.

The training centre consisted of log cabins, in the middle of the forest. In a big cottage was the restaurant with a meeting-area and in another twenty-one smaller cottages there was accomodation for the seminar`s participants. Furthermore, there was another log cabin with a sauna. Seventeen future GU-co-workers from Asia, Australia, Europe and America were invited. Besides myself there were seven further meaning-givers, the others were „paper-tigers". We called them this, because they didn`t come from the streets like us, they were theoreticians, and everybody could see that. We meaning-givers were from other stock. Somehow our feet were more solidly on the ground, which did not apply to skiing, however. We were all equally successful in involuntarily mortale somersault on skis. It was great fun. Unremittingly, Jeff pulled us up the mountains with the ski-doo. From 15 o'clock, we collected wood for the ovens, and from 16 o'clock, we discussed the GU-philosophy in the meeting-area with mulled wine and small snacks. Small translation computers made the English language into the communication-basis.

GU-philosophy implicates a huge quantity of science, economics, psychology, political science and so forth. After three weeks, I could ski fairly well and virtually explain the justice theory of the Global Union just as plausibly as Mrs. Dreyer. The end of this snow experience -with lasting mind-images- came much too quickly. After this pristine nature I saw France and especially Paris with other eyes –a little bit more distantly.

In my lifestyle things didn`t change much with this meaning-giver-job. I remained the boss of the Jungle Noir in the Aries- and Taurus- blocks. At first I converted my frustrated. Yes, as a meaning-giver, I was a missionary of the GU. I publicized the justice-theory and made clear to my frustrated that they were not failures. I explained to them that there is, anyway, too little work for all people on earth. I explained to them the propaganda of the mega-rich and their television institutions. I gave my first prepared speech to at least one hundred youngsters from the blocks of Taurus and Aries. And I was good. Almost all joined the GJP afterwards. The crib for this speech I still have today. Here it is:

People,

You know, you can rely on me. And even if I am now a meaning-giver for the Global Union, that can only be of use to you. I have learned many matters from the GU. For example, that millions of youngsters throughout the world are without work, and that all these people are no failures. We are the fighters of the streets, which everyone knows, and we are proud of it. Whoever treats us as outsiders of society, has not understood that the high-tech-society only has chances for every second. For half of the Parisians, there are no jobs, no stylish houses, no cars and no vacations. It looks even worse in other parts of the earth, there whole populations live just like us, and even worse. What do we do in a world, that has so little work? We won`t pretend it`s our fault anymore. We no longer will play the underdogs. We will climb out from our boiler-cellars and build a more just world. Throughout the world, GJPs will be founded and some of them are already in parliament. In a few years, the GJPs will build a world-wide inheritance law, that will provide a just distribution. It is not that we won't grant someone his success. It is not about envy. It is not about wanting to prevent that someone looks after his children. $ 1,5 million U.S., people! Whoever has so much money, doesn`t have to worry, at least not then, if he keeps his money wisely. If all of you had inherited $ 1,5 millions U.S., you would have happier faces now.

People, that is, what the GU wants: only the heritance, that exceeds $ 1,5 millions U.S., to be collected and put in a global planned economy with a minimum basic-care. It fits the bill. What a few families had too much of for generations, is enough to organize a world-wide basic-care for the jobless. You ask: why world-wide? I say: Why not? Each state for itself, as it has been until now? I tell you, therefore world-wide, because the jobless-problem is a world-wide one, and besides that, the mega-rich would play hide and seek with the poorest and the most helpless. There would be no starvation anymore on this earth, only because of a few families swimming in money. All jobless people, also those in Africa and Asia would be minimally looked after. And minimal basic-care means: only the minimum, so that one has basic-food and a roof over their head, but doesn`t revel in good feelings. There must be the incentive, to leave the sofa, to take care of one`s life, to be creative, to improve their own living. But it should also be a matter of course, being looked after in a world without work. And there has to be equal opportunity, the children must receive school-computers and teachers. People, let us do meaningful things, for us and for the justice, let us support the idea of the Global Justice. Whoever wants to take part will receive all information from me. And you will receive even more. You will finally receive a meaningful task. You can all become fighters for the idea of the Global Justice. We will be the first to turn the word „globalization" to the good and not apply it with concern-politics but with justice. Whoever wants to fight for the idea of Global Justice, for them, I will provide the necessary knowledge and training. Trust yourselves, people, we live in a departure-time, let`s move!

So, that`s how things were, at that time. We meaning-givers were real summit-stormers. While the governmental „resocialisation-colleagues" still tried, to manage resocialisation with human work, we from the GU were logically a step ahead. Maybe I can sum it up by saying that humankind at that time, due to market economy propaganda, was too stupid to realize that slowly but surely other meaning-contents were necessary other than human work.

By the way, the United Nations tried in this time a kind of counter-propaganda. After they had renounced the global justice-idea, and in particular, after they saw how many young people streamed towards the GJPs, they gave a hell of a lot of money, especially the USA, to build up the so-called >aid developing projects< for the >Third World<, mainly in order to implicate the young people. The diversion didn't work, however. The difference was too obvious between the GU and the UN. With the GU, not only the poor countries but also the youngsters knew that it was about a fundamental change in the distribution of justice. Our idea let the losers of the market economy no longer be dependent on the winners. With us there was an equally entitled parallel-world to the market economy. The jobless people of the world, primarily the poor of Africa, were no longer petitioners of the rich dispatcher-countries. They did not have the feeling any more, to be losers and people of third class (the explanation „third world", still used at that time for such poor countries, already said everything). Everyone knew: The Global Union would build a world-wide planned economy for the losers of the market economy and, just as important, GUGLOBE was incorruptible. Justice got a chance independent of personal relationships.

As a meaning-giver, I had a big rush. In the course of years, thousands of youngsters came through me to the GJP and to the GU. My Jungle Noir organized >LA RUE<, the first street-newspaper of the French GJP. The newspaper was a hit, because our tips for cheap buys, good parties and insider news was always first class. My people were the first that were allowed into the GU camps. More or less alone my people built the GU camp in the Southern-Russian wheat area. Some even found a new home there. Lara, my wildest frustrated became a nurse in the GU hospital in Calcutta. Television teams came, that wanted to report about the Parisian meaning-giver and his >Ange Noir<, so they named my Jungle Noir. We, fighters of the streets, would have never dreamed about such constructive life contents. But as a meaning-giver I also had to fight. The most vehement attacks came from fascists and from the press. What concerned the fascists, we had no problems. Even as these fools moved their troops from all over France to Paris, in order to clean that multicultaral dirt, we played cat and mouse with them. We let them run carousel in Paris and admittedly, in the somewhat narrower alleys, we also hit them on the mouth now and then. Things were more difficult with the press. On television and in the highly polished youth magazines we were characterized as communists, as destroyers of the world economy and satanic sect-members. They left nothing untouched to make us look bad. And that, even though in the year 2018 the French GJP had already received more than 25% of the votes in the parliamentary elections, by the way quite similarly in Italy and Germany. The attacks of the press made our LA RUE newspaper even more popular. Mrs. Dreyer got for us notable scientists, that clarified in general comprehensible articles and gave clever answers on stupid questions.

My particular hot-line to Mrs. Dreyer helped me very much. Whether it was about information and arguments, or about support for my people, she always had an open ear for me. In 2020, she became the first meaning-creator of the GU and with it officially responsible for us meaning-givers in Europe and North America. She was our contact, if we had requests and worries, and every year, she organized a supervising in

Canada. I believe, she loved the nature there just as I did. Beginning in 2020, regularly every six months, we meaning-givers met in groups of 20 in the Canadian forests. In summer, we paddled with canoes, in winter we skied. The actual supervising was, Mrs. Dreyer having long-hour single conversations with each of us. She wanted to find out if we were happy in our jobs. I was totally, but there were others, who had real problems. Maria from Rome for example, educated Catholic had come full of idealism to the Global Union. After she had become a meaning-giver of Rome, the Catholic Church and the Italian Mafia wore her down. The church accused her of having betrayed Jesus, and the Mafia bothered her parents. Or Pierre, meaning-giver in Marseilles, he was too sensitive for the job. His personal kindliness didn't come plainly with the hardness of the street. Mrs. Dreyer found a solution for everything, she was brilliant.

Apropos of the Mafia: especially the Russian Mafia had tried to stop the GU. Their bosses belonged to the mega-rich and according to old Mafia manners, they wanted the heads of the GU „switched off". In the winter 2020 with our first supervising of meaning-givers, Mrs. Dreyer told us that two Russian scientists, members of the Russian GJP, had been murdered. „Russia is a difficult country," she said, and I prophesized that there would be a revolution in Russia, in which I was right. The Russian people voted for the GU idea of justice, that was clear. It was also clear that politicians and elections were manipulated. Internet-connections were the exception in rural Russia. Fliers, word-of- mouth propaganda and prominent athletes spread our idea. The message was luckily short and simple: „Take away the inheritance of the mega-rich and let the GU build with the money a world-wide sister-economy to the market economy, a global planned economy. That could be understood by everyone. One says, political history is inclined to repetitions. So, it also was in Russia. The Mafia bosses had divided among each other the former state-companies and mineral resources, police and military got their part of it. When with the GJP a serious political force appeared they tried to prevent democracy with brutality.In 2023, the people swept them away, the second big Russian revolution happened. In the following democratic elections the Russian GJP got over 50 percent straight away. At this time more than half of Russians were unemployed. The Russian parliament decided, to hand over to the GU the property of gigantic mineral resources and estates. Russia became a country, in which the GU had to make hard efforts to convince the population that it did not want to abolish the market economy. For the GU here opened an upside-down world. While they normally mostly had to do with building up the planned economy, it was in Russia, the same as later in China, different all around. Here they had to help the market economy get on its feet. It seemed as if the Russians wanted to turn back time and introduce the planned economy as a cure-all. With lots of difficulties the Russian GJP and GU encouraged the Russians to set up themselves and establish their own small businesses. GUGLOBE passed another test. It calculated that the Russian market economy had to increase by one third in order to come into the balance with the necessary planned economy. GUGLOBE also calculated that the push-funding for this one third could be easily derived from GU-funds.Besides the GU, there were only a few organizations and concerns that wanted to give the Russian economy another chance. Therefore in Russia the GU acted as a sponsor of the market economy. And that was consistent, because in the previous decades Russia had only suppression instead of support for independence. But the GU theory of justice required a balance between feasable market economy and necessary planned economy. Mafia bosses, who had survived the revolution in foreign countries, were radically pursued, locked up and properties reposessed. Nevertheless, it lasted for twenty years until a normal market economy had grown in Russia.

In the winter-camp 2021/2022 I met my future wife. Me, loving freedom so very much, got married. It was the same dilemma as it was with the meaning-giver-job: I wanted to be free but bounded myself nevertheless. Admittedly, the job as a meaning-giver was great. On the street, I was in my element and thanks to the GU-support, I could give vent to my creativity. Besides the usual activities as a trainer of motivations and founder of ideas, I organized parties, bike-ralleys, match-makings and so on. Logically, I met a lot of pretty women, well, in any case more than the average citizen. I wasn`t too shy either, to come closer to the sweeties and bring them into the pleasure of my tender soul and my hard body.

Julia was different. Yes, it is like that. It is always those, who are different. They reach, what others don't reach. Julia was not only pretty, she had humor, more than any others before her. With her instant wit, she surprised me without mercy. Quite often, I stood in front of her, fighting for words. She was strong and I succumbed to her. The nights with her were highlights in my life. Julia! Five years younger than myself, more sensitive and stronger. She grew up in Luxembourg and wanted to become a GU-manager. Mrs. Dreyer organized an educational place for her in Paris. A new world opened: I wanted to be alone with her, instead of grand parties. Romantic nights were newly discovered, I became jealous, went through everything, that concerns it. We wanted to live together and wanted to stay with each other. She was rigorously monogamous and warned me: „If you decide in favor of me, then exclusively. Absolute trust and security, not to be deceived, those were her conditions." Just as she said it, I also wanted it. I wanted to be just as exclusively sure of her. She found our common apartment in Aubervilliers, third floor with a view to the St. Denis Canal. With a consierge, just like in the old days. There, we lived and wondered how quickly time passed. It became winter, summer, winter, and we didn`t find out the reason why everything went so quickly.

I took care of my job sovereignly, in the meantime I got some routine. In 2026, Julia became pregnant. We had practiced contraception only half-heartedly, maybe with the hidden wish to conceive a child. We didn't want to abort, so we became a small family. We called our son „Paul". He took our time and gave us much more joy.

Then came the year 2029. Everything became different. For 10 years I was a meaning-giver, 35 years old and I felt grand. Bodily and mentally I could not be fitter. With Julia and 3 year old Paul, I was in the zenith of my life. Almost insolently by strength, I took care of my job as meaning-giver with a certain high handedness. It was spring 2029, when a group of bad skilled guys, I guess, they were religious fascists, had badly abused a girlfriend of one of my frustrated. We knew exactly who the violators were. We also knew that the fellows would wriggle out of the police. Therefore we had to give them a reminder. Obviously, our action was not legal and really I was not allowed to participate in illegal matters as a meaning-giver. Nevertheless, I took twenty of my best guys into the district of these scum and grasped the guilty. More exactly said: we kidnapped them. I don't want to go into detail now, but after our action, the fellows were tamed like lambs and with their nerves on end.

Two days later, a telephone call came from the GU headquarters in Toronto. I was asked to go there as soon as possible. Flight ticket and hotel reservation were deposited. „Well clear", I thought, „someone has squealed on you." In the meaning-giver training they had pounded into our heads a thousand times: „No illegal activities! The consequence would be ·booted out·!" O.K., on the one hand I was a meaning-giver and felt quite well in the job, but on the other hand I would never become as gentle as a lamb, like I had to be as a meaning-giver. Full of defiance I thought: „If they throw you out, it doesn't even matter. Then, I am free again. I will also get Julia and Paul through life without the Global Union. I would never play the repentant sinner."

At 19 o'clock, the plane landed in Toronto. The reception of the „Harrison Hotel" gave me a message from Mrs. Dreyer: >I expect you tomorrow at 9 o'clock in headquarters at the Atlantic Square. I wish you an agreeable night!<. She had written this by hand on the back of her calling card. Badly tempered I drank some beer from my room bar but nevertheless I slept badly.

The next morning, at nine o'clock I grimly climbed up the stairs to the GU·centre. Mentally, I wasn`t a meaning-giver any more. I was free and would always remain so! I saw the GU headquarters for the first and probably the last time. Like a gigantic egg of glass, the building struck out into the heavens. Computer technology checked irises and fingerprints at the entrance and opened the way. In the middle of the foyer was the reception desk, surrounded by cafeteria. The reception ladies were kind and greeted me by name. I got a blue chip card. „The card will show you the way to Mrs. Dreyer," they said. And actually, when I got into the elevator with that blue card, the loudspeaker croaked: "third floor, room 3029, Professor Dreyer", and zoomed up to the 3rd floor. I had barely entered the corridor, when yellow arrows with the room number >3029< lit up on the walls and pointed me in the direction. Finally, I stood in front of a blinking doorsign. >Prof. Dreyer, Department: Special Tasks< it flashed in blue/yellow/ blue/yellow. I didn't have to knock, because the visitor system had reported my arrival in the room before. The door rose with a jerk. „Hello Ronda, come in." That sounded amazingly kind. The size of the area surprised me. Three venerable figures sat at a conference table, that was built for at least twenty people. Alertly, they sized me up. It seemed to me as if they were thinking about how to best punish such a scoundrel. Mrs. Dreyer did her best to lighten up the situation. She introduced the three

Jurors to me: „Mrs. Breitenbach, one of our best psychologists." · „of all people a psychologist", I thought and hoped, they would not try, to make me out as a psychological misdirected. Mrs. Breitenbach was approximately 60, with roundish red cheeks. She grinned cheerfully at me. „Moving on I would like to introduce Mr. Irving to you, our best economic-expert for micro-economics and Mr. Suzuki, a philosopher by heart. I was surprised. What did an economic expert and a philosopher have to do with such a court-martial? Seething as I was, I sat down, and before I could make sense of all that, the bomb dropped. Mrs. Dreyer explained in her typical direct way: „Dear Ronda, you`re for sure wondering, why we have fit you in. To make things short: we want to promote you. It is an honor for us, to offer you the position of a meaning-creator. When she said that, I had the feeling, of being witness to an error, a victim of a mix-up. Me and a meaning-creator? That was unimaginable. There were maybe forty meaning-creators for the whole earth, altogether highly educated and Mrs. Dreyer was the only one of this sort, that I knew. From her I knew that meaning-creators had access to all inimaginable data. They have their own headoffice and are initiated into all GU-secrets. Their task is not only the supervising of meaning-givers, but in addition each meaning-creator has another very particular task. Mrs. Dreyer for example quarreled with the Jewish religion and their representatives. In their field of speciality meaning-creators were influential GU-managers and direct co-workers for GUGLOBE. They earned the tenfold of a meaning-giver. I must have probably looked rather flabbergasted, because the four were amused with me. „I see, we have succeeded in surprising you," Mrs. Dreyer said. „Before you spontaneously say >No< again, like you did last time, when we wanted to make you a meaning-giver, please first look at a documentary, that we have prepared for you.

I leaned back. It spun in my head. „forget about freedom," I thought, „here the exact opposite is happening to you."

The documentary was about the formation of the Global Justice Movements up to the Global Union. To my shame I had to confess that I pursued the development of the last years only half-heartedly. The meaning-giver job had rather seized me. The film showed statistics, it reported what percentage of the population in which countries had already chosen the Global Justice Parties, and where they had tried to undermine the Global Justice Idea. My homeland, of course had played an inglorious role again. There, an old civil party, the Social Democrats of Belgium, had completely taken over the program of the Global Justice Movement and renamed themselves >Social Global Justice Party Belgium<. In the Global Justice Movement the political pros saw their chance to resurge. Primarily their aim was to rescue their old party, because in past elections, they had lost half of votes. It was plain that such an attempt had to fail. These lobbyists were not suitable for the idea of the Global Justice. They had sense for posts and relationships, but no idealism. They were obligated to this one and that one and wanted it right for all. Quite soon, they had diluted the idea of the Global Justice in infinite discussions. They had delayed the start of a real GJP in Belgium with that. „Typical Belgium style", I thought.

The film also showed the activities of meaning-givers and meaning-creators. I could hardly believe my eyes, when I saw myself in close-up, as „the first meaning-giver of France". One of my speeches for the frustrated was represented as an exemplary action, which admittedly let me sit up a little bit higher.

In the course of the film it became clear to me: the Global Union had done it. There were 178 states on earth and in 173 states Global Justice Parties had established themselves. In 135 states, the parties of the Global Justice had pushed through the uniform inheritance law. The Global Union ran millions of acres of farmland. In Africa and Asia gigantic solar-installations desalinated sea-water and watered GU-country. Crucial was the 11th Global State Conference, which had taken place one year before. There, the >big hip-swing< had taken place, which means the introduction of the uniform inheritance law world-wide. At this 11th Global Conference the GU and 135 single states had found an agreement. Since then, the tax office-computers of 135 states were switched equally. There were several accompanying laws, that would cause the remaining states to join the agreement. It began to show world wide that no inheritance passed by the GU any more. The 11th Conference had fixed it, so that 25% from the free coming inheritances went to the respective single states and 75% to the GU. The single states performed the bulk of work in investigation and collection of the inheritances through their tax offices. Furthermore, the single states adopted the care of the unemployed in the first two years of unemployment. The GU was responsible for the >long-term jobless<.

After the >big hip-swing< thousands of new tasks rose for the GU. The film brought GUGLOBE`S calculations and a future vision of a world without need. 3000 meaning-givers and 120 meaning-creators would be hired.

The film however, also showed problems. Some years before, GUGLOBE had calculated unexpected excesses. The GU board and the meaning-creators had adjudicated to distribute the excess, which means to raise the quality of basic-care. By that, the quality of life for the long-term unemployed became so good, that people had less and less drive to qualify, be it for work or a self-continuous activity. In warmer regions of the earth it was like in the old times, laziness and dawdling were in full swing again. However, the Global Justice needed a functioning market economy beside the planned one. Otherwise, a social standstill and cultural decline would be pre-programmed. The history of humankind had proven again and again that societies that were too well taken care of, became automatically needy after a while. Healthy societies need ambition and qualifications from generation to generation in order to maintain current technologies and make advances in development. What else could the GU do but tighten the belt more narrowly again. The basic-care was measured so strictly again that it hurt, and because of that gave enough incentive, to achieve something. Of all these problems, I was aware of none.

Mrs. Dreyer mentioned, that as a meaning-creator I would probably have to deal more often with such pompous political conflicts. An idea, that at first glance, didn't please me, in the least.

The film also showed some spectacular technologies in whose development the GU was involved, for example, a new propulsion for space-gliders. Time neutral trips seemed almost possible with the technology of repelling energies. Even with projects of this type, meaning-creators, besides the technicians were asked as advisers.

Mrs. Dreyer explained after the film: „As you can see, we meaning-creators have spread widely quite well. Whenever it is about important things, we are one of the party, which probably has to do with our responsibility within the GU for the giving of meanings. The GU, as you know, has no profitable intentions which is why our particular meaning-assessment is especially in demand. What do you mean? Do you want to belong to the meaning specialists of the earth? You will get excellent training of course..."

From the released meaning-giver to the >top of the tops<, a meaning-creator, and all that within an hour. That was too quick for me. About Mrs. Dreyer's question, I could only think of a counter-question: „Why me"? Her answer was stunning: „It has to do with your youth." –„With my youth? I am almost forty "! –„With your youth I just mean the time twenty years ago", she amused herself. „You had a very special friend at that time. A man, who you will deal with again as a meaning-creator."

I brooded –twenty years ago I was a student ... a friend from this time? I had only two real friends at that time: Michel and Zazo. Two people, who could not be more different. I was torn between them · like Goethe`s Faust between good and evil. Michel, the perceptive one. Who could listen. To who everyone opened their heart, who loved humans. And Zazo, the genius, that surpassed all. Who could do everything better, who was even feared by the teachers. With preference Zazo amused himself with the stupidity of others and unscrupulously took advantage of his strength. I admired them both and tried to copy each one once. In comparison to them, I always had been only mediocre. After diving into the Parisian street scene, I had lost contact with each of them.

Mrs. Dreyer solved the puzzle: „Do you know, what has become of Zazo?" – „No." It was therefore about Zazo. What could he have turned into? Into a successful businessman. „He became leader of the Looni eight years ago. Do you know the Looni ?" – „Yes, a sect." – „Whether it is a sect or a religious community – this will be your first task as a meaning-creator to find out."

The four looked at me as if I had won the lottery. I looked back just as spellbound. They expected a reaction, but I was cool. The street had made me into a pokerface. And because my adrenaline level had reached a high peak for over an hour, I was automatically cool. I thought of Zazo, the old fighter, and imagined having to deal with him as a meaning-creator. Our old rivalry would surface again. With Zazo, there were only rivalries. Like in former times he would try to make me look stupid. However, in Paris, I had also learned some things.

Mrs. Dreyer asked: „Before you decide, whether you assume the task, please listen to our specialist of micro-economics, Mr. Irving. Or do you already know you will refuse?" I shook my head which elicited a relieved smile from her.

Mr. Irving arranged the papers lying before him. For his small figure, he had a rather deep voice. „Dear Ronda, you have heard that the single states help us with the investigation of the normal inheritances. Nobody helps us with the question of the sects and religious communities. Maybe, you can still remember your discussion on this topic in the coordination-advice?"

I could remember it. In the coordination-advice, that time, was mainly about the Catholic Church. An English professor had calculated that the Catholic church had brought together their fortune to more than three quarters by robbery and extortion. His suggestion was to apply the new inheritance law rigorously to the Catholic Church. Finally the comming inheritance law would have to shuffle the property cards anew and remove historical injustices. The discussion had interested me only in the beginning.

Now Mr. Irving presented the results: „In the 11th Global Conference it was decided that religious communities and sects had to declare their fortune every forty years. For each registered member, they were granted a tax allowance of $ 3.000 U.S.. The rest went to the GU. For religious communities however, an elementary exception was applied: they could keep everything, which only served meaningful, nonprofitable purposes, that is: active churches, kindergartens, universities and so on. Finding this compromise with the major world religions was not easy. Above all the Catholic church had big fear of being impoverished." Mr. Irving had to laugh heartily about his humorous insole. „That`s for religions. Things are quite different with sects. Please understand, that with the term

>sect< I also include cults. So in this sense, we don't want to protect sects. They don't become acknowledged as >of public use< and don`t acquire a particular status. Besides the tax allowance of $ 3.000 U.S. per member, sects are taxed every forty years radically. Do you understand? Your friend Zazo has a very particular interest, to get his Looni acknowledged as a religious community. If you examine this question as a meaning-creator, Zazo will leave nothing untried, to influence your decision. You will ask now, what distinguishes sects from religious communities? Or differently asked: what can a religious community do better than a sect? This question was also answered in the 11th Global Conference. The most important criterion is the >freedom of one`s own will<. Whoever visits a Catholic school must remain unaffected even if he converts to Islam. And a student of an Islamic university, which criticizes a religious leader, shouldn`t be rebuked. Tolerance is crucial! A religion without tolerance is degraded to a sect. >Idealistic life goals< are the second crucial criterion. Only something which pursues positivity, be it proximity to God, to harmony, to love, or simply to the good, can be a religion. We don't protect Satanists, people worshippers and magic circles. So far so good. Now to the essentials, the economics. In the same way, that we have to decide by ourselves the question: >sect or religious community?<, we also have to organize by ourself the confiscation of sect fortunes. Of course the state tax offices and police organizations will help us, but the delivery of factual findings for evasion, and the lists of people, we have to realize ourselves. In our assessment, your friend Zazo has amassed a fortune of $ 30 billion U.S., I repeat: $ 30 billion U.S. with his Looni. One can move some things with it. Zazo would never give up such a fortune voluntarily. There are at least 10 million Looni in 38 countries. Zazo has brought about these numbers with the snowball system. Do you know the principle: one doubles a number, the result becomes doubled again, and so on. With the Looni, each member is committed to recruit at least one new member each year.

There is no Looni, that doesn't fill this task, because the Looni offer excellent service. Mrs. Breitenbach and Mr. Suzuki will present this to you. It firmly stands, that the memberships and the fortune of the Looni double at least each year. We considered mathematically, starting with 40.000 Looni eight years ago and a minimum property of $ 3.000 U.S. per each member, today 10 million members and a total of $ 30 billion. Presumably, the actual numbers are much higher. According to our calculation, Zazo can continue these increases for at most 5 years. World wide he would then have 300 million members and $ 900 billion U.S. in fortunes. The Catholic Church is not much bigger. It is for sure that Zazo will turn into a global player. If you have to fight against him, he will be Goliath and you David." – „It was always like this," I interrupted, which interested Mr. Irving less than Mrs. Breitenbach, the psychologist.

Mr. Irving reported on the context between GU-care and Zazo`s economic circle: „Almost all Looni are unemployed GU favourites. As you know, the GU had paid, until recently, money to the long term unemployed. Zazo has collected this money and saved a pretty penny through bulk orders. With this money and the savings of the Looni, he bought agrarian land and built cities. He particularly has influence in Argentina, Paraguay and Chile. Gigantic Looni plantations are located there. With Looni money Zazo has sponsored election campaigns, and made presidents and ministers. Ever since the 11th Global Conference the GU doesn`t disburse money anymore but instead distributes monthly valid basic-care coupons. Zazo will still handle the supplies for his Looni centrally, but he will not obtain as high excesses anymore, like before. Since the 11th Conference, Zazo switched over to parcelling out the plantations into 23 acre lots and transfer them to single Looni members. He obviously wants to take precautions in case we classify the Looni as a sect. In which case there would exist no sect fortune anymore but only single properties below the inheritance limit."

Then Mr. Irving explained the meaning-creator`s world: „You will have an annual budget of a maximum $ 2 million U.S.. One can get more only as an exception. Every six months, you will report on your activities on GUGLOBE`S forms. Your travelling expenses in all means of transportation are free and, if necessary, you can also have your own space glider. Your access-code entitles you to the absolute utilization of all GU-facilities. You are a member of the meaning-creator conference and twice a year you decide on elementary questions of the GU board. These breaks are used by most meaning-creators to meet their meaning-givers afterwards. As you know, Mrs. Dreyer practises this regularly in the Canadian snow desert." Mr. Irving again thought this formulation to be extremely funny. In the beginning, you will take care of twenty, and later up to forty meaning-givers. As for yourself, you will be supervised by Mrs. Dreyer. I think, that`s it on the whole. Details will follow later."

I leaned back. What I had heard, was heavy stuff. I knew Zazo. If I were to take the job, I would have the fight of a lifetime ahead of me. Obviously Mrs. Dreyer saw it the same way, carefully she asked: „Deterred?" Again, I shook my head and she smiled. Then, she asked Mr. Suzuki to introduce me into the world of the Looni philosophy just before lunch.

Mr. Suzuki, as said his name, was of Japanese descent. However, according to his look, his ancestors were African. He distributed a manuscript which reasonably simplified the matter for me. Mr. Suzuki obviously loved to do reports, because while talking, he, with huge pleasure, swung his upper body back and forth, almost like my budgie when becomming hyper. „We philosophers are strange people. We interfere in everything and try to find components for eternal truths everywhere. In doing so, we are skeptics. We want to know, we don't want to believe. My specialty is the >wholistic-harmony-doctrin<, which goes well with our topic, because the Looni have adopted many principles of this theory. As an example here is a sequence of arguments:

All changes implicate the search (of nature, of being, of God) for balance and complement, which means for harmony.
Only the end of all changes, which means complete harmony, can lead to wholistics.
All material existances, therefore can only be an expression of this quest, but can never can be wholistic.
Because the truth is wholistic, human thinking could only approximately reach it in paradox (change causing contradictions).
Because of that humans need the freedom, to think and accept contradictions.

By luck, everything was written in the manuscript, where I could look these sentences up. Mr. Suzuki waited patiently until I was ready. „You should know Ronda, the Looni complete this theory quite skillfully, if it is about God and harmony, they shorten it to about freedom and contradictions. This is typical for an organization, that wants to have their members in a grip. In this way Zazo has tinkered a building of thoughts, that is solid as a rock. Some religions could make an example of it. Looni actually concentrate on their souls. They consequently pursue >purity< and >harmony<. All secular things, and above all financial issues are transfered to the organization, so that their souls are >free< from it. They live in Looni-cities and have their own closed economic cycle. By it Zazo reaches a well-known phenomenon of the group-dynamics: community creates meaning. Meaning, completely in the sense of wholistics and harmony. The Looni actually live together harmoniously. Nobody owns a considerable personal fortune, so hardly any envy exists. Disputes about love and sex are rare, because the Looni live by the principle of absolute openness.They live in strict monogamy, as soon as they get married . They name absolute openness >purity< and mean by that a life without lies and self-deception. In other words, the Looni are loyal to their partners, more than anyone else. Their aim of higher and higher >purity< is pursued with mind-machines and >supervising<. We all know that mind-machines can be useful, especially if it's for deep relaxation and computer-supported learning. I have recently taught myself with a mind-machine a new political economic theory while sleeping, so to speak. Things change if mind-machines are used for thought-control and brainwashing. We name such mind-machines >destructive<. Whether the Looni use destructive mind-machines, we don't know. Your task would be to find that out.

Mrs. Dreyer explained that mind-machines even within the GU were becoming a big thing. Even in the education of meaning-creators, they would be used. They could save three quarters of learning time.

Then, Mr. Suzuki got under way again. His upper body fluctuated to the topic >freedom<. I would never have thought that someone had so much to say on such a matter. „Freedom has much to do with welfare," he explained. „We constantly strive for conditions, in which we feel as well as possible. We understand the possibility to do this as freedom. Without the quest for well-being, there would exist no freedom. Because of this the Looni are not completely wrong, if they claim: >freedom is the possibility to experience as much as possible of that, which makes one happy, and not trying out as much as possible<. For the Looni freedom is the ultimate satisfaction of needs with minimal frustration, what usually would also be defined as >happiness<."

For me this was too much philosophy. Luckily, Mr. Suzuki soon became more concrete: „that also goes with your tasks, Ronda," he said, for him it was clear, that I would accept the job „The Looni believe that their leaders, who they call >chiefs<, are purer and more soulful through God than others. They give up their individual freedom to the big collective Looni freedom. Zazo admittedly doesn't practise any personality cults, as the Catholic pope did until recently, but the chiefs, which means those, who do the >supervising< of the Looni, are sacred to them. If a chief says, that it will be advantageous to go to China, then one goes to China. And if a chief proposes a certain partner, then one is convinced that this is the right one. The chiefs operate the mind-machines and take care of the single blocks. These chiefs are supervised by >3rd–Chiefs, which on the other hand are under the control of >2nd-Chiefs<, and those of >1st-Chiefs<. The >1st-Chiefs< are directly under Zazo. Each Looni has the chance, to climb up the purity ladder, and to become a chief, yes even 3rd-, 2nd-, or 1st- chief, with help from supervising and mind machines. If it should turn out, that mind-machines brainwash the Looni, which means freedom is taken against their will, there would be no chance of being ranked as a religious community. The problem would only be, that if the 3rd-, 2nd-, and 1st- chiefs were also brainwashed, Zazo would probably be the only human, that wandered around with a clear mind and saw through all the tricks.

„Would be typical for him," I said, and again Mrs. Breitenbach looked interestingly at me through her steel-rimmed glasses.

Mr. Suzuki worked himself up. He gave a brain twister to all present: „Let's assume the Looni would offer courses for >wholistics<and >harmony<. In these courses, >love< and >altruism< would be the goal. Individualism, that deviates from these goals, would be wiped out. The course would be in increasing the >us-feeling< and weakening the >ego-feeling<. Individual freedoms would become untrained. What do you think? Would we have to condemn that? Would we have to classify such an organization as a >sect<?" – „An evil trap", Mr. Irving noticed, „one could condemn some Islamic and Christian educations as well." –„The question is, what does the untraining look like", Mrs. Dreyer said, „is brainwashing or

force part of the game, then for me it would be a sect." –„It would be bad, if toddlers were indoctrinated from the beginning", Mrs. Breitenbach said, whereupon Mr. Suzuki countered: „That toddlers are severely educated religiously Christian or Muslim, had still not disturbed anybody until now. Where is the border to brainwashing ?" All were silent, and Mr. Suzuki declared: „ As you can see Ronda, we are at the start of an interesting discussion. There are no solid guidelines, but that is nothing new. You know that. You have always been a man on top of things." He spoke about the coordination-advice and about the fact, that there would be no GU without me. In the end, he thought that it would be best to give vent to common sense. Furthermore, I would probably have enough experience with sovereigns and subjects.

Obviously Mr. Suzuki alluded to the power struggles of the streets which again reminded me of my last revenge job. How had I come to Toronto? With the defiant feeling of the sinner, and how is it I stand here now? As a hero? If these naive theoreticians here knew, how tough as nails I was, and how far away their official moral passed me by the ass, they would think twice about electing me to meaning-creator. I was on the point of mentioning the matter when Mrs. Dreyer anticipated, almost as if she could read my thoughts.

She said: „Dear Mr. Suzuki, I thank you for your input. With you philosophers we always have to listen twice before we know what you mean. Particularly excellent for me was your appeal to the common sense at the end. About: Sometimes, our common sense is a bit clouded. You know that, Ronda! One does things controlled by emotions and forgets some rules of reason. I`ve been thinking of your vengeful action in the second district recently.". I was blown away, talk about naivity, they knew everything. Mrs. Dreyer added: „We know about these things, and although we don't approve of them, we don't interfere. One cannot deny a certain morality with you. It will be different if you become a meaning-creator. As a meaning-creator, you will stand fully in the limelight. There a >certain moral< won`t do. You would be one of the highest representatives of the GU and would be subject to an intensive control by the other lead members. We are really a little elite group, and something we don't control ourselves, will be controlled by our enemies the more. You will be surprised at how many people would suddenly like to criticize you. Not only the Looni will be very imaginative in this relationship. For us is valid the principle of absolute tidiness even if sometimes we would like to burst of anger because of legal impotence. As you see, life at the top is not always enviable. But now I would like to invite you to lunch, because I can hear some stomachs already growling."

The dining room was in the glass cap of the egg, on the 22nd floor. The entire dome was made from glass. Movable paper walls provided a Japanese flair. A small area was divided for us, directly in front of the glass wall, with an eternal wide view over-looking Toronto. The table was covered festively for five people, classical music with added bird chirpings, it was nicely done. Mrs. Dreyer pointed to a ball, that hung three meters over the table: „With this we can screen ourselves accustically from the neighbouring tables and especially add to our table, music, nature-sounds or information. In the midst of this big canteen we were completely undisturbed." Then, the meal came. Never, had I such feelings in the mouth. Real fish, codfish, in a way delicate, with cream-dill-sauce, butter-dumplings and broccoli. With it white wine: Chablis, first class. Had I not been so full, I would have been able to eat more for hours. „The fish is a rarity", declared Mrs. Dreyer, „we ordered it specifically for this day. Our intelligent computer knew that you would like to eat fish, Ronda. Normally, of course we dine on the basic-food of the GU, which by the way is prepared tastefully." Mr. Suzuki philosophized about the topic of >work<. He was fed up with work. „Finally more time for private life", he wanted, „to visit

52

art- and sports- clubs, meditate...", he reveled in. „You got too much accustomed to working", Mrs. Breitenbach tried to stop him. „Forget about getting accustomed! A philosopher gets used to nothing at all !" –„That`s what I said", was the cool answer of the psychologist. The four pleased me more and more, and after an expresso with whisky I was in an optimal mood. Until then I didn't know, whether I should take the job, but now I thought: „Why not "! It would be a real challenge, and all the advantages, that the job would bring, were much too tempting. At that time, I did not yet know the trick with the perfect business meal. Later, I, myself accomplished a lot with it.

Back in the conference room it was for Mrs. Breitenbach to inform me about Zazo and his disciples. She went far back: „As well concerning politics as our own little luckiness we would like to know, what is right and what is wrong. But who really knows that? As Mr. Suzuki has determined so aptly, we are not capable of grasping the whole truth with our minds. We always catch only a tiny little corner of it and unnecessarily must reckon that the opposite corner on the other side is true as well. What a frustration however, as we would gladly like to know, in which direction it goes. Maybe Mr. Suzuki was right, and all truth consists of contrasts. Who, however, can become happy with such shaky information? To the stupid, or better-said the ignorant, it doesn't matter, they live on vigorously. The intelligent suffer from contradictions more easily, they just think more about it. Those more intelligent people are ideal candidates for Zazo`s Looni philosophy. It is the more clever, that Zazo convinces, which primarily speak on his behalf. More precisely, it is the clever sensitive ones who end up with the Looni. They are not robust or sufficiently strong enough, to stride alone through the chaotic life. To them Zazo offers hold with his proximity to God, to nature and to being quintessential.

How does he do that?

The proximity to God and to being quintessential, the Looni experience through purity and meditation. What does purity mean, we have just heard. With meditation, Zazo continues a century old tradition of the Buddhists. In the meantime some Christians have adopted the meditation. Concerning meditation experience, I would not like to present it here, but that`s for sure: many people who are to be taken seriously are convinced, of having come through meditation to higher consciousness.

The proximity to nature Zazo arranges for his supporters by hard work on Looni plantation, of course in connection with meditation.

According to Zazo`s theory, one can only be and feel wholistic, if one is in harmony with God, in body, in soul and being quintessential. The way to there is through purity, meditation and working in nature. For our sensitive, clever Looni this means an endless occupation until the end of their life. For us from the GU the unknown dimension of purity is of particular interest. We don't know the mind-machines of the Looni. We only know, that each mind-machine is connected with a data line to a central-computer and receives certain impulses from there. Whether these impulses cause destructive manipulations of thoughts and brains, we don't know. Nobody, besides Zazo himself knows the code of the impulses. The mind-machines themselves –we succeeded once in grabbing one- gave us no information about it. And who as an unfaithful Looni could be found out by us, knew nothing in particular to report. There were incidentally only two or three unfaithful Looni, and that was some time ago. They went back to the Looni again later on. All Looni are, to their own conviction, happy and content. That was it for this group of Looni, those sensitive clever ones. They cover approximately 50% of the entire Looni, with a tendency to climb. From them Zazo recruits the 3rd-, 2nd - and 1st– chiefs.

There is also however, quite different types of Looni, in fact those, who think the protection of their basic needs is the most important. Ideals don't matter to them. As long as they are well taken care of and are sure of being in a group of similar-minded people, they are content. They don`t suffer from existential miseries, like our sensitive clever ones. They are structured rather simply. Do you know the old Looni advertising? The slogan: >You`re finally searching for a home? Find it with us!< or: >You`re looking for work? With us you have the choice< and >You`re looking for the right partner? We have it for you!< ? These slogans aim at those people. For them Zazo has cultivated housing construction and match-making. He has organized education to become bricklayers, carpenters, electricians and much much more, further more he let them build traditional beautiful natural houses under the motto >we build with nature<. They have raised very beautiful cities in this way and still continue to build them today. The busy drudgery, interrupted by regular purity sessions, stands under the motto: >with natural work to wholistic<. For the match-making, Zazo applied his central computer and successfully organized partnerships under the dictation of purity.

Since the 11th Conference some things have been changing. It is rumoured that in the meantime basic-needs are secured by the GU. Zazo had already foreseen this development several years ago and reorganized the Looni propaganda. Today it says: >Authorities give you bread, we take care of your soul< and: >Watching TV isn`t really helpful? Find the true insight with us!<. A long time before the 11th Conference Zazo had foreseen the new time coming. By the way, although, through the big hip-swing some fears and insecurities of the unemployed have been erased, paradise has not been reconquered. We psychologists prognose, that completely new problems will arise, such as increasing aboulia and depressions. But that was only incidentally. Back to Zazo and his characteristics.

What I will tell you now, is my own personal assessment. The GU cannot afford such an assessment because of lack of proof. Zazo has never faced any test and is hardly ever seen in public. You can only compose a puzzle from some circumstances and logical conclusions.

So: Zazo possesses brilliant intuition. Intuitively, he can rightly size up not only historical developments but also the potentials in people. He intensively takes care of qualified and gifted co-workers and guides them where they can best apply their abilities. With this he is useful for the individual as well as for the entire organization. He is not so much after personal wealth, but after power. He could have retreated with hundreds of millions of dollars, long before. But he wants to expand the organization and with it his power. In doing so, he is enormously creative. He organizes informative trips, educational seminars and musical festivals in order to bring his Looni closer to the goal: each year a new member from everyone! One of the unfaithful Looni claimed, Zazo was striving for world supremacy, in my opinion a somewhat exaggerated view. We know however, that in certain states of South America he determines politics. Zazo is rigorous. Whoever gets in his way seriously, is crushed unmercifully. There are cases, in which Interpol is looking for missing opponents, gone without a trace. I suppose he has no moral borders. Like a Mafiosi, he eliminates his opponents. What do you think? Am I wrong? You presumably know him better from your common youth than any other person on earth."

After listening for hours, I was glad, to finally have the opportunity to talk myself. The memories of Zazo were fresh as if I had been together with him only yesterday. „He always was brutal ", I said, and told a typical story from our hanging out pub: „Our favourite pub was not a students' pub. Student pubs were just too trivial for us. As trivial as those pimply students themselves with their girlie wet dreams. We went to

56

>Bouvier<, that redneck pub with table-soccer and girlie-flip. There, we spent half of our school days, Zazo, Michel and I.

One day, a slightly drunken fellow, approximately in his fifties, stood at the bar. Michel placed himself beside him to order our beer. The guy attacked him: „hey, you twit ! Playing hookie again, eh?" Michel spoke to him, and the guy, two minutes later, poured out his heart. I believe he even cried. The guy then paid our beer. It was my turn to order the second round of beer. The guy critically sized me up and not a minute later I had to quarrel with him. Of course I had to pay our beer myself. The third round was Zazo`s. He cooly countered the attack of the guy: „Old timer, you`ve passed your life by, guzzle on and shut up." After some more tough bragging, the guy tapped him on the shoulder with respect and paid our beer.

Mrs. Breitenbach could hardly calm herself down from laughing. „I believe, I would have suffered the same fate, as you", she said. Further on I reported on an IQ test, that I had just done for fun together with Michel and Zazo: Michel 110, myself 135 and Zazo 178. She said: „With that man one probably has to be careful."

In the late afternoon, Mrs. Dreyer said farewell to me with the words: „Consider carefully, whether you would like to exchange your intact meaning-giver world for the hard job of a meaning-creator. Mrs. Breitenbach winked at me. We agreed to make the decision the next day, 16 o'clock, room 3029. I would keep the blue chip-card until then.

The evening at the Harrison Hotel looked much friendlier than the morning. Everyone smiled at me, and I seriously wondered whether they knew about the meaning-creator thing. However, I was probably only in a better mood.

Julia didn't want to believe the story. „You, and a meaning-creator? Then I will soon become a member of the GU-board," she said. In her well sorted bureaucratic head, she could not imagine things like that. Meaning-creators, above all Mrs. Dreyer, were the maximum for her. Of course for her there was only one possibility: „Take it! Go, go, go!"

That night I went on a bar crawl. I am like that, if my head is too full, I have to romp it clear. Until three o'clock I was in a discotheque. Then I jumped from place to place with a really hot blonde and finally boinked her in her city-car. She wanted my address and to become acquainted with me. For her I was Gerome, her name was Miki.

I got out of her car at a container terminal and went for a walk. Finally, it was already getting light, I luckily caught a taxi to the Harrison Hotel. They were already serving breakfast. After that, I took off into the centre of the city, for shopping. For me I bought Canadian leather boots from buffalo leather of the finest quality, for Julia a silk dress and for Paul a children's computer. After dropping off the things at the hotel, it was 15 o'clock. Time for Mrs. Dreyer and the Global Union. I had squandered so much money that, only because of that, I had to accept the new job. No, seriously, that thing was decided without being able to explain the arguments. My intuition told me to do it.

Mrs. Dreyer had not expected something else. She solemnly handed over my certificate of appointment. They gave me three months time to train my successor for Paris. After that I had to build up my own new office, „wherever you think it's best, it doesn't matter where on this globe." But first, Mrs. Dreyer thought, that I should go for a week on vacation to celebrate the event. With a wink, I asked her: „Maybe in Canada, with a continuation course in the mountains ?" She delightfully amused herself. With her farewell, she gave me a communicator, that fitted into each trouser pocket. With that apparatus I could reach her anywhere at anytime. The thing was fantastic. It was a camera, computer, telephone and laser-projector, all in one. It worked via satellite. Digital lasers recorded 3-D films, storage capacity: three hours. Those could be sent within seconds. The implicated projector bounces received picture-data in 3-D into the room, irrespectivly having received it as a film, Internet pages or life pictures from the other end of the earth. The access to the GU knowledge data bank was fixly stored. There was no better data bank, because the GU had access to all university- and governmental data banks. The code was a combination of my fingerprint and my iris.

„You will become a good meaning-creator, Ronda, I know that", Mrs. Dreyer said and: „Oh yes, I almost forgot: we would like to know within the next two years whether the Looni are from your point of view a sect or a religious community." Back in the hotel I had such a good snooze as I hadn`t for a long time.

In Paris, St. Denis, I had to break gently the news of farewell to my frustrated. I tried it the nice way and organized a fat good-bye party. Into one of our dead end streets, I carried mountains of Tortilla chips and barrels of beer. Joe, my successor, also was one of the party. In muscles not as fit as me, but with lots of humor. The dude was right for the job. My frustrated accepted him right away. Some however, almost moved me to tears. They tried to convince me that it would be better to remain a meaning-giver: „What`ya want? Becum meaning-creature? It`s not your thing, buddy, believe, way too crappy. Stay here, is better..." Others asked me, when and how often I would be in St. Denis. In their own cool way, they made me understand that they would miss me. And I felt the same.

Julia was happy and pregnant with our daughter Lilo. She allegedly had always known that I would turn into something special. We thought about where to live. City or country? Europe, Asia or America? Zazo alternatively lived in San Francisco and Tokyo. I had no desire for Tokyo's human crowds. Julia would participate in everything. After the good-bye party, we drove on vacation: North Sea, Germany, Wangerooge, my favorite island. One week, only relaxing, long sleeping, long breakfasts, strolling along the beach. It was autumn and the beach deserted. I love that. No tourists and walking for hours by the waves, packed into thick sweaters, rubber boots, rubber-jackets and rubber-pants. Having hot punch, after the walk, in the pub behind the dike. A lot of reading. Divine.

After the vacation, I still worked for a few weeks in St. Denis with my successor. I introduced him everywhere to everyone, explained connections and initiated him into the tricks. By doing all this, one day, I got the idea to move to San Francisco. I wanted to be in Zazo`s proximity, furthermore California`s climate was quite nice. And after all San Francisco was not as square, as the rest of this screwed up America.

How would Zazo respond if I called him? Should I play with an open deck from the beginning? Anyway, with his ingenuity, he would see through each hostile act. Why did I think of hostile acts? Was I biassed or did my instinct tell me that I would not make it without fighting. Zazo would hardly tell me the full truth. Presumably, I would have no chance to see behind the scenes. How could I hand over a credible statement about the Looni, without having known their true life? What else remained to be done but become a Looni myself?

Julia didn't like that idea so much. She had heard bad things about the Looni. „Who goes there, will never come back, people say. They presumably practise brainwashing. If they found out, you are a meaning-creator, you would be finished! Many people, supposedly have already got lost there! Maybe, they manipulate your thoughts?" She pushed me to call Mrs. Dreyer.

For some days I mulled about the idea, then I called Mrs. Dreyer. I told her my intentions. She liked the idea of becoming a Looni. „In all honesty, we already had considered something similar. You would be the first undercover agent of the GU. Of course, it is not without risk. But in the meantime there exists a vaccination against destructive mind-machines. A drug indicator is injected. Destructive mind-machines namely activate bodily endorphins. The drug-indicator would track down the endorphins and cause corresponding reactions. Recently, there are admittedly destructive mind-machines, that don`t activate endorphins, but these appliances need accompanying drugs for its effectiveness. And these drugs also activate the drug-indicator so that we are always on a certain side."

I wanted to know exactly what would happen and she explained: „Whenever they would try to administer drugs to you, or to manipulate you with a destructive mind-machine of older construction, you would be blocked through the vaccination. You would simply be powerless for two days. That all makes sense, if we arrange one duty communication per day. That is: if you don`t report on a day, we will know that something is wrong and you would be immediately pulled out." – „In that case my career as an undercover agent with the Looni would be finished, for sure." – „That`s probably true. But it`s still better, to be an unemployed undercover agent, than a brain manipulated one. Furthermore, we will certainly think of something new in order to get at Zazo and the Looni."

Mrs. Dreyer gave me a contact address in Amsterdam for the vaccination and as a hiding place for the communicator, she got shoes for me with a detachable sole. She said that the communicator is untraceable because it contains no reflective parts of metal or similar things. After this conversation, I was sure to have the matter under control. Julia had now also calmed down.

So it became certain: I would become a Looni. Julia finally also agreed. After that we also decided to look for an office and a home for us in San Francisco. By e-mail, I informed Mrs. Dreyer of my decision: >office and new home in San Francisco ! Are there still any rooms?< Just one hour later I received the reply: >office address: Adelaine Street 7, San Francisco / secretary: Corinna Vand / reserved flight: 01.11.2029, No.: 2041, at 14:25, Paris-Le Bourgè, air Moustique – please confirm by tomorrow 20 o'clock. Private-home: on your own initiative, recommendation: house rent in the sea-side quarter, real estate agent: Top-Reagency, San Francisco, limit of rent: $ 2000 U.S. mthly. / removal organized by GU<.

I was impressed. The GU-organization worked professionally.

At the same time Zazo and Demian sat together. Demian was Zazo`s pupil, 28 years old, arrogant, member of the beautiful people, intelligent, with a cleverness, that even impressed Zazo. „Boss, a friend of your youth, Ronda, has become a meaning-creator. Special assignment: Looni, department >special task<, which means no playing around." Demian was proud. The Looni`s early warning system was his work. „My old friend Ronda," Zazo contemplated, „he was always kind of naive." Our contact in Toronto reports that Ronda has decided to become a member of ours", Demian reported further on, „by that, he hopes, to become more familiar with our organization." – „As I said, naive !" –„What shall I do? Eliminate him?" – „Eliminate? My young friend, you do have a lot to learn." – „Why boss? Gone is gone. In the long term it will take away their desire to explore us." – „At what price? That they annoy us with controllers and police, and we, at the end are classified as a sect?" –„They don`t have a snowball`s chance in hell, boss, let them come." – „Demian, why should we saddle ourselves with such unpleasant work if we on the other hand could have so much fun with Ronda?" – „O.K., boss, let`s send him to the training centre of Helsinki." – „I think, Copenhagen is adequate." –„Copenhagen! That`s nothing at all !" – „For naive Ronda it`s enough." Demian protested.

Until 2031, the Looni ran in Helsinki their centre for obstinate cases. There, problematic cases became >harmonized< : renegades, traitors, despotics and know-it-alls. They all came back gentle as a lamb, harmonized for life. In Copenhagen, it was for more harmless cases. Here, melancholians, pessimists, jealous guys and nonbelievers found their way back to harmony. Also newcomers from Northern Europe were brought to Copenhagen. As in Helsinki, in Copenhagen the Looni brought into action their mind-machines, in order to offer the special service of an elaborated personality analysis. Finally, they wanted to help everyone individually. Mind-machines, that promote relaxation, are known to everyone. The fact, that mind-machines like this are used in tests, is nothing special. They help to relax and by that, they help to come closer to honest results. According to the first appearance, mind-machines played a secondary role with the Looni. The Looni for example didn't use them as a method of learning. In fact, Zazo`s mind-machines could absolutely generate particular convictions and fears. Sometimes Zazo backed the treatment with depth hypnosis, but in most cases only a few >exercises of relaxation< were enough to bring people back on their way to purity.

These apparatus were their own developments with the newest technology. They did not need any accompanying drugs. Because of their strongly manipulating effect, they definitely were >destructive<. Their use was illegal, because the concerned had not agreed to such a treatment, furthermore an objective medical control was not guaranteed. The applications were administered by the >chiefs<, who did not know about the manipulating effect. They were manipulated themselves often enough, to be convinced, they were doing good. Zazo was the only one, who knew the contents of the central computer, from where all mind-machines were supplied with data. Even Demian didn't know the code. He indeed suspected that hidden behind the mind-machines was more than simple relaxation- and concentration- support, but despite all demands, Zazo had always assured him, that they caused no manipulations. Demian avoided, being anywhere near a mind-machine, and Zazo loved to tease him with that.

All in all, Zazo had much fun with his Demian, who still tried to convince him, of sending Ronda to Helsinki instead of to Copenhagen. Was there something involved like jealousy? And indeed, Ronda was the last person, whom he had conceded to a certain emotional proximity. Once, he had even cried because of him – from fury and disappointment ·. It was the last time, he had cried at all. At that time, Ronda had enticed away a girl from him, and had done it, in not such a nice way. Today, something similar could not happen to him, anymore. On the one hand he had lost his romanticism, concerning women, and on the other hand he had become more clever, in which he was sure that the first fact arose from the second. Where Ronda was concerned, he secretly had to admit to himself, that the thought of meeting the old schoolmate warmed up his heart. Would Demian`s legendary instinct have recognized that? But what would it finally mean? He could not say, that today Ronda would still be his friend. Although some kind of bond might have remained. However, he certainly would be clever enough, to control such emotions. What would >friendship< really mean in the end? Since the classical antiquity, best friends had betrayed and murdered each other, if they only had spent some more time together. Zazo knew that relationships between people were more similar to the education of animals or to the chess game, than to a romantic winter fairy tale. Women were admirable, as long as they were young and pretty, otherwise one could only admire oneself, at least, if one`s name was Zazo. If he was in a bad mood, which rarely happened, he hated people. Then, to him, they seemed like snakes, with their greedy egoisms, and only the stick could do justice to them. Mostly however, his humor prevailed, or better said, his sarcasm. He loved, to make fun of the mass of little assholes and their squared self-interests. He played cat and mouse with them, he flattered them, shocked them, disgraced them, just as it pleased him. Now, there was no difference, coming alive again with Ronda, an amusing part of his youth. There was not a bit of sentimentality. For him, Ronda`s appointment by the GU was a pleasant diversion in a life, that had nearly become routine.

Demian was less mellow. He was young and aggressive. He wanted to go up, there, where Zazo was, his big role-model. He admired him more than anyone else. He imitated him, and his deepest subconscious lurked for the day, on which he learned so much, that he could push his man and master off the throne. Pure ambition drove him through life. Power was his and Zazo`s common goal, and there was nothing, which could distract him from it. Women, family, free time, things like that and similar nuisances were all the same to him. Concerning the urge for power, they were similar, in matters of cleverness Zazo was always one step ahead.

Zazo knew his ambitious student better than he would ever know himself. In superior style, he played with Demian`s feelings: „Demian, could we find a compromise by handling Ronda leniently? I must admit that there are some sentimental memories that let me hold on to my old schoolmate. Upon Demian`s desperate facial expression Zazo responded with clear amusement: „Have no fear, the time will come when you can oppose Ronda. Seriously, Demian. By the way, I`ve already mobilized one of our best weapons against Ronda." –„What? Which kind of weapon? Since when have you known about Ronda?" Demian was shocked, his boss was already one step further again than himself. „Demian, the early warning system is still under my control, isn`t it?" – „Okay, boss. If I may ask a question: which weapon?" – „She is blond and pretty, Demian, you wouldn`t have a chance against her." Zazo amused himself delightfully at Demian`s stupid expression. –„Boss, I really don't want to be a know-it-all, but the guy is a meaning-creator and happily married." – „She really is very blond, Demian, and she is very pretty." – „All right, boss. So, what should I do "? –„The most important thing is that you convince Ronda of our reliability. You know the decisions of the 11th Conference against sects and religious communities. Ronda is our chance. If we win him over, we have won. In other words: you will make Ronda our best agent at the GU." – „Great, boss. That sounds brilliant. That`s the way, we`ll do it."

In Copenhagen, things were prepared for the arrival of the novices. This time everything shall be especially nice, was the slogan of the 2nd- chief. The Copenhagen Looni centre was in a distance of approximately 18 kilometers to the old part of downtown, situated on an artificially raised island in the Oresund. Anyway, the reception rite was sufficiently solemn, so nothing needed to be altered. 250 novices would be admitted simultaneously with Ronda into the Looni, which was clearly more than normal. Furthermore, an impressive wedding ceremony would be organized. From the beginning, Ronda ought to know what kind of a great troop the Looni were.

III. Chapter   -Ronda with the Looni-

My flight to San Francisco lasted 4 hours. The office was situated in the centre, opposite a consumption temple, in which one could get lost. I entered the new office and was surprised. The office equipment was from the finest: leather chairs, tables made of real wood, designer lamps, the most modern technology, on first gaze everything seemed to me a bit too stylish, even the secretary, Corinna Vand. She looked like she had escaped from one of those television series, in which the crucial roles are played by money, power and love. At that time, I didn't suspect how quickly one can get used to luxury. Corinna was friendly and she was a professional. She had taken care of everything. The office was her work. Furthermore, she had equipped the small kitchen with champagne and snacks, had installed the communication systems and become acquainted with the neighbours. I had allowed three weeks time for San Francisco, after that I wanted to become a Looni. I told Corinna that I would visit a GU course, that would last for two or three months. During this period, I asked her to elaborate the data of the meaning-givers, assigned to me, as completely as possible. I wanted her to find everything, she could: documentary films, personal records, writings, actions. Immediately after my return I wanted to organize the first meeting and prepare myself for each individual. She smiled at me enchantingly.

Over the Internet, Julia and I put three houses on the short list. She wanted to see the houses >live<, therefore she flew with me, very pregnant to San Francisco. We left our son Paul with her parents in Luxembourg. Finally we decided in favor of an old, renovation- needing villa with two baths, seven rooms, view on the Pacific and $ 1.600 U.S. rent monthly. Renovation had to be done by ourselves. That meant, carrying buckets of paint, selecting tiles, installing bathtubs. We did almost everything ourselves because then things

68

would go more quickly, being still in training from our Parisian apartment. In the end, however, that action was maybe a bit too exhausting, because exactly while polishing the parquet flooring our little daughter Lilo was born. I could hardly bring Julia to the hospital. After having successfully settled all these existentialist things, I flew to Toronto. Before the Looni job, I wanted to talk to Mrs. Dreyer again.

In the meantime I was well acquainted with the GU glass egg, and the same with Mrs. Dreyer. She considered it advisable, to fit me with another identity for the time with the Looni. An „airtight" one, she said, because she assumed the Looni made examinations of identities for their own protection, a guess she would be right about. Johan van Vel, that would be my name. A name that pleased me, having always wanted to have a Flemish name as a Wallone. For the first time in my life I had to submit to a mind-machine treatment with depth hypnosis. „In order for the identity to have really sunk in," they told me, and on my inquiry of possible side-effects, Gil, the responsible GU doctor answered: „Later we can easily turn back the wheel again. All this made me conscious that up until now, I had lived in a simple world, despite of all fights in the streets and actions with the Insider. This playing secret agent was just another number. My stakes increased.

After the mind-machine treatment, I felt completely normal. Actually, it was different. They showed me a video of Julia and Paul, and I didn't recognize them. I was sure of being Johan van Vel, journalist, single, born in Antwerp. On the other hand, my awareness was unimpaired. Later, after the annulment of my alias identity, I would be able to remember all the details of the Looni world. The question, if the Looni robbed their members of mental freedom, would be fully answered by me. The daily duty communication was inoculated into me as the worried demand after my old mother. In the evening my flight went to Amsterdam, because there, the history of the Looni candidate Johann van Vel would begin.

Demian had not lost sight of Ronda since his takeoff from San Francisco. Each step, each telephone call, each word was shadowed by him. When Ronda, alias Johan van Vel entered the Looni information centre in Amsterdam on the 30th of November 2029, it was Demian personally, who welcomed him at the information desk: „welcome from the heart to the Loonis'. How could I be of help to you?" – „I would like to be informed about your organization. Good and bad things are reported about you." – „That`s the same with all things, exceeding the usual. By the way, even the Looni are only humans, which means material carriers of spirit, and only because of that within themselves full of contradictions, good and bad things at the same time." – „I have heard about your theory of contradiction." – „The theory of contradictory wholistics is acknowledged by many scientists and therapists, even from those, that have nothing to do with our religious community. I`m just thinking, as an example, of the psychologists, who have derived the ambivalence theory out of the theory of the contradictory wholistics. Are you interested in science?" –„I´m more interested in the question, if there exists something like enlightenment or God." – „Our religion is complex. We resemble Buddhism a little bit. With us, the road to cognition leads over several steps of consciousness. To climb these steps is not easy. Our religious community achieves support in doing so." –„I`ve heard many things about this support." – „Yes, I know, contradictory things! Do you feel like having the time to form your own opinion? We offer introductory courses. It`s free of charge, including return flight, it lasts two weeks, and we offer a general overlook into our activities." – „I might like that idea." – „Next week we start an introductory course in Copenhagen." – „And how do you finance all that?" – „There exist 40 million Looni world wide. Many of them are wealthy. We finance ourselves exclusively through voluntary donations. So don`t be shy. If, after the course, you`re not interested anymore nobody will be mad at you. Also, you won`t receive any bill from us." Ronda, alias Johan smiled and Demian inquired after: „May I write out the ticket for Copenhagen?" Johan nodded.

In Copenhagen, housings were prepared for 258 novices. The reception ran after the usual scheme: friendly Looni hostesses gave as a present, to the newcomers, blue silk shirts with a golden sun on the breast and on the back. A golden sun on a blue background –the insignia of the Looni-. In their centres, all Looni wore such shirts. Champagne was handed out, which lifted the mood quite soon. A friendly old gentleman in a blue shirt held a heady lecture about life in general and in particular with the Looni. Radiant with joy he related, how much strength the Looni way had given to him, and indeed, with his more than seventy years, he made a thoroughly, healthy, powerful impression. The old man said: „ There are no lies between us. We are honest to ourselves and to others. Only in this way can we really meet ourselves and become happy. Nature is important to us, we respect it and live together with it in harmony. We have no plastics, no genetic food and no genetic manipulated children. Johan felt the first enthusiasm with the novices. Nothing was done up artificially, the Looni all together radiated a natural happiness. Life here seemed to be heavenly. The old man emphasized, the most important thing in life would be the proximity to God. All his lifetime he had run after all kinds of dreams until finally, thirty years ago, he realized that true happiness comes from inside, from the proximity to God. Here with the Looni, he had found the way. The applause at the end of his speech seemed to have no end, and when the old man invited the audience to put on the blue shirts, Johan didn`t see anyone not doing so.

After the lecture, the novices were asked to the table. The dining room, with its long wooden benches and wooden

71

tables reminded me of a rustic beer tent. Johan could not remember anymore, where he had already seen something similar. Rare delicacies were standing on the tables: real asparagus, cooked ham and buttered potatoes. Many novices didn't know asparagus. It was green asparagus, that melted in the mouth and tasted divinely. Earthen jugs with white wine stood on the tables and at the end of the meal Irish Coffee was served. The general well-being could hardly to be surpassed.

After that, computer examinations were offered. Each novice could, if he wanted, work out an initial, strictly confidential analysis of his personality. All data would be evaluated: previous activities, origin, learned abilities, talents, wishes, goals, ideals, just as if it was about an application in the highest economic circles. The friendly hostesses pointed out that it was to enable all novices optimally, in finding the proper way through life and perhaps the ideal partner. Since the Looni had introduced the >match making< service, more and more people came to them, only because of this. It was rumored that with the Looni there existed the best chances in finding someone, that matched. High-tech was applied, which means the newest computer programs filtering reliable, mutual sympathies out of opticals, smells and mental things. In consideration of the immense number of people, being Looni or wanting to become so, the probability was good, in finding a matching partner.

Johan didn't want to be conspicuous as an outsider, therefore he joined in. He actually did not like the idea of such an analysis. In all, he was surprised, at how willing all the other novices took part in everything and felt at home in their blue shirts. They seemed to him like a flock of sheep. Many of them were already willing to fill out the reception forms, lying around everywhere, and to become a member. Had they come to such a decision in such a short time or had they already come here with the intent of becoming a Looni?

When one got involved so hastily in something unknown, their previous life could not have been of real worth to them. Ronda, the meaning-creator, knew about dreary life contents. Johan van Vel didn't remember his time as a meaning-giver. He only knew that he, as inconspicuously as possible, wanted to find out whether the Looni took away their members' free will. But what does >free will< really mean? That, after a lecture, some glasses of wine and a computer-analysis, people leave everything behind and become Looni? Something similar could not happen to him, he was an individualist at heart, skeptically against mass events and leader personalities. How could he find out, where that >free will< existed, which was to be protected? What does freedom mean to these people? Had they ever had some? What freedom could they lose? Johan started brooding.

The results of the computer analysis were discussed in the afternoon. Most were surprised how apt their personal strengths and weaknesses had been recognized. There were given recommendations for suitable occupations, hobbies and relationships. Everyone recognized themselves and were flattered. Who had ever been offered before such an extensive computer analysis? Each novice was taken aside by a Looni for evaluation. Johan was joined by Mandy, a nice, young woman in a blue shirt. „Are you happy with the analysis? Do you see opportunities to alter your previous life? Why have you come to us?" These, and other similar questions she asked of him and Johan answered in a sovereign way, evasively. Obviously she knew his data, because she knew him as unemployed and single. „You know, we have wonderful possibilities to come to a meaningful life. We find the meaning of life namely step by step, which also implicates successful experiences in profession. But our specialists will explain the theory of contradictions much better to you than I. You`ll stay with us, however, won`t you?" Johan nodded. >Profession<, this expression he had not heard for a long time; today people only talk about >jobs<. Profession, that reminded him of the good old days.

The Looni terrain resembled a big city. Shops, restaurants, their own harbor, a fish-farm, workshops, everything existed, which was needed for a well working social system. However, there was one essential difference from a normal city, and that was the masses of blue dressed people. Mandy led a bistro where fresh salads and bread were offered on buffet tables. They ate and they drank as much as they wanted to. Paying was not needed, because money didn't exist. „We normally don`t consume alcohol," she said, „we want to live healthy. We drink alcohol only on particular occasions." – „For example, if new candidates are arriving", Johan supplemented. The fact that people could receive everything they wanted, without coupons or money fascinated Johan. Could something like this go well? Wouldn`t people collect all sorts of things as a reserve or for their own benefit? „You can`t take anything with you", Mandy explained, „we have a closed system. We need nothing from the outside and we give nothing to the outside. Furthermore, we don't incriminate our soul with such things, like property and money. There are more important things, things that provide more joy. As you can see, we live well. Anyway, better than those only receiving GU basic-funds, and a lot better than the miserables, squandering away their life with greed and money. Johan had the impression that her opinions were not so wrong. In the evening, Mandy led Ronda to his housing. All Looni housings were standardized. They lived modestly but stylishly. 20 square meters were available for each person: a room for living and sleeping with 16 square meters and a bath with 4 square meters. The interior was made from real wood in a shapely, round design. So, everyone had their own comfortable privacy. For couples there existed larger units, depending on how many children. Mandy offered herself to spend the night with Johan. „Because you may feel a bit lonely on the first night", she innocently said and supplemented: „For me, sexuality is one of the steps up to the realization of God and nature. We Looni namely practice sexuality just as natural as eating and drinking." - „I have heard, that you are absolutely loyal", Johan said, and Mandy explained to him: „That's correct. If I had a solid partner, I would not make this offer to you. Furthermore, our computer was of the opinion that we would fit quite well together. Johan had no objection, because Mandy was exquisitely pretty. She sweetend his first night with the Looni, and the computer was right, they matched truly well.

Within the next days, the novices toured different Looni projects. New houses, a new fish-farm, a shipyard in construction, the Looni town widened and increased everywhere. Here was work for everyone, because people worked traditionally. Within the closed Looni system, there existed no competition and no robots. Real craftsmanship was in demand. Marc Jerom, the leader of the Copenhagen centre, a 2nd- chief, was especially proud of the growing independence of the Looni system: „I`ll tell you, within the next ten years we won`t need a cent from the GU anymore. We`ll become more and more independent. Each half year, people from the tax office come and estimate the value of our work. We become better from year to year, which admittedly means decreasing GU support, but it shows on the other hand, that we are on the right way. Whoever works for us, doesn't receive money or bonuses, as in the free economy. We don`t stand in need of such things. We work, because it`s fun for us." Johan liked the system. He took a particular fancy to the joiner`s workshop. Drafting and constructing furniture could be the right thing for him. He met Mandy in regular intervals, they understood each other very well.

One morning, it became serious. A >brain-check< was on the program. The two weeks, getting acquainted phase, were finished, and whoever wanted to stay with the Looni, received the first serious >assistance for the right way<. There were only a few, that flew back to the normal world. „Who leaves us, usually is addicted," Mandy explained, „you cannot find alcohol or drugs with us." Mind-machines were put into use with the brain-check. They would serve as relaxation, in order to be able to determine in the most frank way people´s own possibilities and their individual way to God and nature. Here, of course all results were also handled confidentially. For Johan, the brain-check was a risky test of his alias identity. If the Looni found out, that Ronda was behind Johan, they certainly would think about reacting a bit unpleasantly. Johan himself didn't know about his alias identity. He only felt an intuitive aversion against this brain-check.

Zazo manipulated the mind-machines with his central computer. The usual treatment had three steps. In the first, fractious energies were localized, which in the second were eliminated, while in the third Looni ideals were implemented. Concerning >Johan van Vel<, he had instructed the central computer to avoid any manipulating effect. Not that Zazo acted out of old friendship, he had rather found out that Ronda, alias Johan, had received a vaccination against destructive mind-machines. However, Ronda should become his best agent with the GU, and not proof of a forbidden action. He forgot about Demian.

Demian sat at breakfast in San Francisco and looked forward to the brain checks of the novices in Copenhagen. For „Ronjon", as he named Ronda, alias Johan, he had made up a particular treatment. In the long term, he admittedly wanted to win Ronda as a sympathizer of the Looni, just like his boss had said, however, he had considered it appropriate to bring the trouble maker under better control. He also could not deny a certain jealousy. What would happen if the old friendship between those two was revived? Zazo had made a strange emotional impression, by saying that Ronda was incorruptible. „Never Demian", he had said in a solemn sound, „never will this man be corrupt. So don`t even try it, at all. Actually, the Copenhagen computer analysis had confirmed that exactly. The man was incorruptible. Would Zazo take again pleasure in the old friendship, in someone, who would honestly give him a piece of his mind, Demian`s influence on Zazo would be automatically weakened. He wanted to get this man under control. Long and hard he thought about what he could do. Then, he remembered Raja, his best specialist for hypnosis. Hypnosis, that was the solution. In a few minutes, Raja would sit vis-a-vis Ronda, alias Johan, and make sure, that everything would go the correct way.

Like all novices, for the brain-check, Johan was led into a >meditation lab<. The ceiling and walls of this tiny room were covered with sound-devils, creating the atmosphere of a sound studio. Absolute silence prevailed. A comfortable leather chair stood in the middle of the room. There was no space for more. The brain-machine was installed onto the rear of the chair. It looked like a simple model, purchasable in each department store. Technically seen, it was composed of a helmet with integrated three dimensional video-goggles, real-surrounding-sound, and some electro-stimulators in the upper helmet area, which were needed to stimulate particular parts of the brain. The Looni, who would help Ronda with the helmet`s adaptation, would arrive at any moment. Johan knew of brain-machines, he knew, that he had already tried such a thing, but he just didn`t know, when and where. Indeed, such subdued power of recollection sometimes seemed strange to him, but the feeling of this strangeness passed within milli-seconds.

Raja, Demian`s specialist for hypnosis was an Indian. He had carefully prepared himself for the meeting with Johan. He was very clearly aware of Demian, having a particular interest in this case. Raja knew about his own charismatic aura and from the computer analysis he knew Johan had a similar strong personality. Such a constellation of two strong people, could be an advantage, especially if mutual sympathy was given. Completely different things behave with antipathy. If he were to play his charisma in such a case, nothing would work out at all. He therefore, as a precaution, decided to act devoutly. For clothing, he had chosen a gray pants suit with a green shirt, the appearance of a craftsperson. He knocked before he entered the meditation lab. „How do you do, Sir. I was sent to assist with adapting the helmet." Johan nodded shortly: „Hello". –„Have you ever used a mind-machine before?" –„Yes, but a long time ago." – „Then I would like to explain things again." The conversation proceeded precisely as Raja had anticipated. He put the helmet on Ronda, fiddled around at the electrodes and explained that the whole thing would be a wonderful relaxation with beautiful pictures and soft music. „Things will work out for the best, if you relax completely. Let your arms hang down and let your legs stretch out." Johan followed his advice. Calmly and a little bored Raja continued: „Your arms and legs hang down comfortably and will become wonderfully soft and heavy. Breathe calmly and deeply. Your head will become heavy, your thoughts peaceful. Relax and let your eyes follow the pendulum of the clock on the wall." Johan just now noticed the small pendulum clock on the wall and followed the pendulum with his eyes. „You'll become calm and relaxed." Not five minutes later, Raja put Johan under hypnosis.

Mrs. Dreyer just wanted to sound the alarm, when Johan reported from the Copenhagen centre. Johan considered Mrs. Dreyer his mother: „Please excuse the delay, mother, but this stupid mind-machine action lasted longer than expected." – „And did you like it?" – „Quite comfortable, soft music and beautiful pictures." Mrs. Dreyer became alert. Ronda's answer was clearly too positive. „Do you remember something in particular?" – „No, actually not." –„Who assisted you with using the mind-machine?" – „Some kind of caretaker." Mrs. Dreyer intuitively suspected something was not correct. „We do have a bereavement in the family, Johan. Please be so nice and interrupt your stay for one or two days. Aunt Edith has passed away, there are some things to organize." Johan spontaneously agreed: „All right, mother, I`ll come."

Zazo was cross: „Didn't you have orders to leave Ronda alone?" – „Boss, I only arranged a harmless depth hypnosis, nothing bad, at all." –„What kind of hypnosis?" –„We`ve programmed him on the word >Bengal-sheet<. With that word, he falls back into hypnosis. Then we can easily experience his plans, and if necessary, put some influence on them. Is that really bad?" – „Bad it is, if the GU works it out." – „That would probably be true. But how could they work it out ?"· „Ronda is already back again on his way to Toronto. Why is that so? Because he was so pleased with us?" – „Boss, I really was surprised myself." – „Oh, you really were surprised yourself? You fool, I`m not surprised about anything anymore. Think well about voluntarily visiting the GU to apologize. I´ll be awaiting your answer until midday." – „Boss, you can`t really mean that!" With a damning gaze, Zazo left the room. Demian was rattled. Had he made a mistake? Raja had reported that hypnotizing Johan had been amazingly easy, because he suspected that Johan had already been hypnotized once before. Had the GU pushed him into a hypnosis that didn't go along with the new one? He called Raja, who explained to him, that it would be possible to over-ride an older hypnosis with a newer one by which the effect of the older one is possibly impaired. It was strange indeed that Johan had departed directly after the hypnosis. After all, he had intended to become a Looni and spy. The longer he analyzed the matter, the likelihood became greater that he had committed a major mistake with the hypnosis-action. He, of all people, who officially would certify the Looni`s righteousness, had been hypnotized at the Looni. How could it be possible to straighten things out again? With an apology, as Zazo said? Should he fly to Toronto and say: >I´m sorry, it will not happen again<? Something a lot better has to come up. Finally, the only possible solution was clear

to him: he had to sacrifice himself. He was personally the guilty one and not the Looni organisation. Exactly that had to be explained to the GU. Of course with that, his career at the Looni would stop for the time being. The Looni couldn`t afford someone like him any longer as a representative. Suddenly Demian realized that perhaps not only his career was at stake. Sometimes Zazo could be rigorous. This damned Ronda! Hardly had he appeared, and already almost ruined him.

At noon, a penitent Demian stood in front of Zazo. „Boss, concerning that apology, you`re looking at that seriously, aren´ t you?" – „Do you have a better solution?" – „No." – „So, how do you want to do it?" – „I`ll fly to Toronto and confess having acted out of jealousy. I`ll sacrifice myself ". – „And doing so, make logically clear, that we knew about Ronda and have an informant within the GU." –„I hadn`t thought of that, up until now." Demian became hot. „You haven`t thought of many things, my friend." – „Boss, what should I do?" – „You are right, things don't work out without victims, but it will have to be two." – „Sir, I`ll make it good again, really, it`s a promise. Would I be allowed to come back again, someday?" – „We`ll see." Demian breathed a sigh of relief. He knew Zazo sufficiently well to know that the answer could have been much worse. Gratefully, he shook hands with Zazo and bowed. Then, still in Zazo`s presence he phoned up the GU. He asked for the supervisor of the meaning-creator, Ronda, and saw, a few seconds later, Mrs. Dreyer standing in front of him.

IV. Chapter   -Ronda between GU and Looni-

After his arrival in Toronto, Johan, alias Ronda, immediately drove to the GU headquarters, where he had, that very same evening, a date with Gil, the doctor, who had given him the alias identity two weeks before. It hadn`t lasted ten minutes, when it was clear, that Johan had been hypnotized by the Looni. Mrs. Dreyer`s decision came promptly: „Ronda immediately has to become completely dehypnozised." So, I became myself again, and the key word >Bengal-sheet< that Gil had discovered within me, lost its magic.

The next morning, Mrs. Dreyer and I made up our minds on how to react to the Looni hypnosis. Was it already certain that the Looni used forbidden methods, and therefore had to be classified as a sect? „In principle, it is like that, so that you would have taken care of your task in record time", Mrs. Dreyer said. We were just in the middle of this discussion, when Demian called. The man seemed familiar to me, I just didn`t know anymore, when and where I had seen him last. He introduced himself as Zazos' assistant and asked for a meeting. Mrs. Dreyer gave him the date already for the end of the current week. Until then, we postponed any further discussion. On recommendation from Mrs. Dreyer I visited a conference, that was just organized in Toronto by Gideon, a meaning-creator colleague.

Gideon had the particular task of taking care of the Catholic Church. I guess, no meaning-creator had a harder job. Constantly, demonstrators waved posters in front of his private house. >Church instead of communism< and >freedom of religion instead of GU dictatorship< was painted there.

At the conference Gideon reported about an organization with the name >Opus Dei<. In comparison to this Catholic fight-troop, the Looni seemed to be harmless. Gideon reported, in which way the Opus Dei had tried to put influence on his son Daniel. In Oxford, where sciences were still recited live in the auditorium by professors, Daniel had studied law. The >Oxford-Law-Circle<, a classical supplier of refresher courses, stood under the influence of the Opus Dei. Each student, and also Daniel, visited these refresher courses. After it had become known that Daniel was the son of the >GU communist< Gideon, the leaders of the circle had put pressure on him. He should renounce publicly the GU and his father. Daniel did the exact opposite. He published the reprisals and by that helped the GU to get even more publicity. Shortly there after, a bomb destroyed his apartment and only missed him because he had gone to a pub for a beer. Daniel transfered to one of the usual Internet universities. Gideon was glad, nothing worse had happened.

Once more, the risks of our job were demonstrated to me. However, Gideon had also demonstrated very impressively the capabilities of a meaning-creator. His team had increased to a remarkable 350 co-workers. Among them highly qualified detectives helped him to determine the fortune of the Catholic Church, being payed when successful. The Catholic Church on the other hand, had organized more than the double amount of people, to repulse that >GU attack<. Whenever Gideon asked the Catholic Church for resolution, he was misled. Gideon had proceeded to document his work by three camera teams live on the Internet. Now everybody, even in the most remote village on the earth, could follow very closely, via net-TV, how the Catholic Church handled the idea of the Global Justice. This disclosure did not do so good for the Catholic Church. Their most loyal supporters were mainly located in the poor, out of the way places on the earth. However, these people knew exactly, that the GU fought for them. Sometimes there was only one single com-TV, in the village's pub. There, they watched live, how the Catholic Church hindered the GU. Many quit the church. Gideon`s TV-action became a full success. At the conference, Gideon reported of particular tricks he had invented to expose the hide-and-seek games of the Catholic Church. Although he was almost 60, he was more alive than some youngsters. We all know the result of his fight: at a cardinal conference in 2030, the power of the pope and his crusted way of thinking was broken. One year later GU and Catholic Church signed the first contract about the assignment of real estates and other assets. In 2032, the Catholic Church abolished the popehood. Many people don`t know it anymore, but until then, the pope, a chosen supreme priest, was supposed to be nearly as infallible as God.

From the beginning, despite our 17 year age difference, spontaneous sympathy connected Gideon and me. We had the same job with similar tasks, however that was not it. As we saw ourselves for the first time, we automatically smiled at each other. I think, we recognized our congeniality. In the evening, when a calm fell over the GU, we strolled through the Toronto night. Gideon lived separated from his wife and adult son. He thought more radically than me. Where I was looking for ideals, he had found realities. As clearly as I saw the conditions of the streets, he saw life. He was closer to life, and exactly because of that, he was more quick-witted and freer. Nothing, not even the GU, could impress him. I admired him. He became a good friend. Up until his death, three years ago, I learned much from him and his cool actions.

Demian arrived on Friday. He appeared in a gray suit, serious and fashionable. His address was heart warming: „Honourable Mrs. Dreyer, dear Ronda, I am here to apologize." As he said that, I saw what was coming. „I have not only broken the rules of the Looni but also general human rights. I let you get hypnotized, Ronda, without your approval. I did this, because of jealousy; of being afraid, your friendship with Zazo could have been revived again and could weaken my influence. I honestly regret it and would like to do everything, within my power to correct the mistake. Mrs. Dreyer ignored the apology and asked, how Demian had known about Johan, alias Ronda. Of course, Demian had prepared himself for this question: „We succeeded in cracking your communication code..", which was not sufficiently plausible to Mrs. Dreyer. „..and monitored all conversations of the GU? Then you had much to do.." – „No, not all of them, just those, that refered to meaning-creators.." Demian had agreed with Zazo about all answers. Therefore he was not shocked when Mrs. Dreyer let a GU technician come, who confirmed, that the code was yet not 100% cracked. Otherwise, certain alterations automatically would have happened. Demian played the penitent: „in order for you to see that I´m truly serious: we have an informant in your organisation." – „Who?" – „I´m sorry, but I cannot say that, otherwise I would turn into a traitor and would never be able to go back to the Looni. Mrs. Dreyer remained adamant: „I`m afraid, you`ll have to make this sacrifice." Demian requested time for reflection. In reality, he had agreed with Zazo upon which GU informant they would unveil. We went up to the canteen, and over coffee, Demian coughed up the name: Professor Willems. Immediately Mrs. Dreyer sent the security guard to Mr. Willems, who logically had already been missing for some time.

Demians appearance caused exactly, what it was supposed to, namely the exculpation of the Looni. It was the action of an individual and not of the organization. Concerning the Looni, I found myself at the beginning again. That`s what you thought! Complete the job in record time, just the opposite was the outcome. The maneuver of sneaking in had failed. I had to think about something new. Also on this occasion, Gideon inspired me. „Look at me, he said, „if I put in 350 people for my task, you at least can afford the half. You only have to appoint them meaningfully. Mrs. Dreyer recommended to first start my new office. „Arrange your office and collect your strengths", she said. She didn't suspect how perfectly I would miss these targets. „Furthermore your family and the new home are waiting." She knew that there was a lot to renovate in the old villa.

Julia had furnished the house amazingly quick, and invited the neighbours to a house warming party. She showed me the sights of the city and we planted vegetables in the garden. Paul hated the kindergarten and little Lilo kept us awake for nights. We were fine.

The office was decorated with flowers. Corinna had brought them as a welcome greeting. With a bottle of champagne, she stood in front of me and looked lovely. We emptied the bottle, and she told me that she already had collected all data about the meaning-givers. Interesting people are among them. Together we looked at the records, and her body heat beside me cried out pure eroticism. As she showed me the printed biographies, our arms touched. We both let it happen and it electrified us for some minutes. Until now, apart from the slip in Toronto, I had been loyal to Julia. And I actually had the intent of staying so. But I was hardly a match for Corinna`s juicy femininity. She played cat and mouse with me. If I became factual, she became seductive, if I became excited, she played the goody too shoes. The game was not new to me, I had always loved playing it. But this time my head wanted control. It granted the foreplay for me, but not the finish. By that, we played with growing enthusiasm the >who-is-excited< game during the following days. Slowly but surely my joys and desires were transfered from home to office. With a steady climb in mood I went to work, and more and more I became a nag at home. When I had sex with Julia, Corinna came to my mind. Corinna gave me glowing compliments, she said she was happy she could work for a boss like me. Julia criticized me, my bad mood annoyed her, and with two small children, life was not simple, anyway. All that increased. Especially, my desire for Corinna. When I started having sex in my dreams with Corinna, my brain had lost. Corinna knew that she had made it. She invited me for a meal at her appartment. The little bitch explained to me, that she wanted to show me how she lived, and how fine she could cook. We arranged this for the next weekend. I told Julia, I wanted to visit a meaning-giver that weekend. That night with Corinna was a unique ecstasy. What came after it, was less intoxicating. Although I made it clear to Corinna, that I would stick with my family, and even though Corinna assured me laughingly, she was cool enough to handle things, consequences were hard. Less and less I was at home and more and more frequently with Corinna. That honey was so sweet. Finally, Julia gave me an ultimatum: „either you change your attitude, concerning me, or I`ll go!“ I decided in favor of the family and asked Mrs. Dreyer for Corinna`s transfer. I didn't suspect that with this Zazo`s plan became reality little by little.

Zazo called me shortly after the inauguration of my office and invited me to a private dinner. „As a pay-back, old fellow, you know, I can`t stand misunderstandings, and besides that, it is high time that we meet again.“ I was looking forward to the reunion. Speaking with him on the phone, I immediately sensed the old familiarity, without a bit of mistrust or enmity. In his typical way he said: „Next Monday, 18 o'clock, Waterside avenue 17, you`ll probably find it by luck old guy, won`t you?“ and laughed mockingly with it. He was still the same.

Waterside Avenue, that was the finest address in San Francisco. Here lived those, whose ultimate principle in life was material pleasure. They usually worked more than they lived. The district was protected with intelligent fences and army flocks of rent-a-cops. As >Insiders< we quite often had visited such enclaves and carried off some nice things. The rich people, that lived here today, I granted their affluence, they themselves had worked for it. The heirs of the mega-rich could not afford such houses any longer. They had to handle their 1,5 million dollars more economically. Whoever lived here, was either brilliant or had worked hard. Both were to be admired. There was no reason for envy. The people, that burglarized such vilas today, were from other stock, mainly they were drug-addicted with their endless greed for more. At the steely entrance I was welcomed by name and transported with a minivan to Zazo`s house. There, two model athletes stood at the skillfully forged iron-gate in blue shirts with a golden sun on the breast. An avenue of old chestnut trees led between meadows, ponds and brooks to Zazo`s fairy-tale palace. As it is usual in state receptions, Zazo expected me on the gallery stairway. We embraced each other. I still knew his obligatory back tapping from earlier times. In this way he demonstrated full of goodwill his superiority. This time I didn`t want to be inferior to him, and so we tapped each other in gracious contest on the shoulder. Of course we had become older, but the old bond immediately was there again. We looked into each others eyes and knew that we, in the core, had stayed the same: fighters and rioters. He showed me his palace: „I really prefer living here, in this beautiful educational centre. Here, the 2^{nds}. are trained to be 1^{st}_ chiefs." In the cellar was an unbelievable water-palace of white marble. Different steambaths, saunas, whirlpools and a gigantic caved swimming pool left room for no more wishes. „If I remember correctly, you prefer eucalyptus steambaths." He was right and once again I admired his elephant`s memory. In our youth, we had been in the sauna together, at most three times. „Here everything exists", he said, „and after tea, we`ll steam ourselves mentolly." He laughed about his pun.

An oversized world map hung in his study. Per Looni-location, a mini laser-projector was installed. As we entered the area, he said: „Members", and immediately the lasers projected constantly changing numerical figures into the air. „As you see, in fact, numbers are climbing, everywhere." There were approximately two hundred mini-projectors, therefore just as many Looni-centres. „Eight years ago, you would have only seen five centres and these even with sinking numbers. A classical example for glaring mismanagement ". He grinned: „Even good religions need capable managers. Can you imagine what I would have done with the Catholic Church? The GU wouldn`t have had as little trouble with me." –„Don`t be so sure of that", I thought of Gideon. – „I know, you have established that club from the beginning. Big congratulations for that. So, finally we both did something well with our lifes. And as coincidence has it –which, as you know, in fact doesn't exist· we in the end are up against each other. –„Why against? Do you think that I want any bad for you? Zazo laughed heartily: „You any bad for me? No, quite definitely not. But I think, the GU has no understanding of my poor little Looni."

At this moment, Zazo reminded me of Mouräne. Who sometimes had a similar style of sly behaviour. Zazo, of course was better by class. He promptly brought up more agreeable things: „Do you know, what has become of Michel?" –„No! Do you?" The topic >Michel< still had a particular attraction for me, because he was Zazo`s mild opponent. „That nutcase lives from you, from the GU. Now and then he paints a picture and sells it, without telling the tax office, that evil jack. –„And where does he live?" – „If it was up to him, he would still be living in Ronse, today. But he was happy to catch an active woman, who has shipped him to Northern Italy, in the proximity of San Remo, Bussana, the nest is called, I believe. –„Where do you know that from?" – „Old friends just interest me." Zazo asked me to talk about myself, and I told him about the Parisian street fighting times, about Julia and the two children. About the Insiders, I said nothing. He listened very alertly and analyzed every last detail of my facial expressions and wording. I figured that he could size me up just as well again, as in our youth. Then, we went into the sauna.

The swimming pool was a subterranean natural lake with rock caves. Zazo had had a deep bore drilled, from which hot water bubbled constantly. So, the lake remained steadily well-tempered and the brooks in front of the house were fed with fresh water. There was everything, which hearts could covet: water cases for back massages, discreetly illuminated rock caves with stalagtits, heated massage benches from marble, nozzles in the lake`s bottom for sole massages as well as steambaths and saunas in different variations of temperatures and smells. After the eucalyptus steambath we had a massage. The masseur, a Roman gladiator, made clear to me, how tense I was. For that evening Zazo had dished up a divine buffet. I shoveled pounds of mayonnaise covered shrimp salad into me, prepared unspeakably delicious. „You are the most important guest, we have ever had here", Zazo declared, and reacting on my skeptical grin he confirmed: „Yes, that`s for sure! You decide on the fate of the Looni. Who could be more important for us?" Obviously, he set great store by giving more weight to the moment. We drank excellent red wine and philosophized about genetically manipulated generations. We agreed that people should in any case release our own genetical codes to cloning, brilliant, as we were. Everything was simply the best on this evening.

For the following week, we arranged a three day sightseeing-tour through the Looni imperium. Zazo was to pick me up at home. „Sea-Side 45", he knew our new address without me having given it to him.

„Corinna has not accepted her transfer", Mrs. Dreyer said. „She has left us." A strange feeling crept over me. And actually, one day before my Looni roundtrip, she stood with shiny eyes in the office corridor: „I had a longing for you." I knew exactly, that it was wrong, but I took her into my arms. I had no chance. She had bewitched me. Her solid gentleness, her eyes, her youthful body, all that stirred up in me a state of unrestrained desire. This woman had completely beaten me into her spell. She embodied Eve, the original woman. „The neighbours moved, I have the key", she smiled, and not even five minutes later I enjoyed each of her movements. For hours, she played with me, almost drove me mad with ferocity and ecstasy, hardly felt touches and lagging. Sweaty we stuck together and stated how perfectly our bodies fitted each other. Late in the evening, I drove home, badly tempered because of all this bad conscience.

Zazo drove up with an ultramodern nuclear fusion glider. As a child I had always dreamed of such a vehicle. The thing was the same at home in the air, on the water and on the earth. „If one wants to fly, one normally must start at airports, but I have a heli-permit", Zazo declared. Therefore he could start and land on free places with approval of the owners and the air-traffic controllers, and exactly that he demonstrated. Ten miles outside of San Francisco we reached an unused agrarian road. He exchanged some words with the air-control and then pushed forward the energy lever. Vertically we shot into the heavens making me sick. „Sorry, I should have warned you. If one knows, what will come, things are not quite so bad", Zazo amused himself. Already a few minutes later, we flew quintuple at the speed of sound. Two hours later, we landed in some kind of natural park, close to Tokyo. Isolated, some pagoda temples stood between the trees. „I also like this educational centre very much", Zazo said. „Here you can see a Japanese garden of the finest." Softly the glider landed between two pagoda temples. At a closer view the buildings had gigantic dimensions. Everywhere, blue shirts swarmed around. They mowed lawns, rowed in small wooden boats on dark lakes between waterlilies and raked leaves unendingly between borders of flowers. Zazo was greeted kindly, but there was not a bit of personality cult. As I addressed him about that, he explained: „Am I so stupid, as the pope, at that time? I am one of the chiefs. Furthermore, for the Looni mental values are more important than people." He had scored one more point.

In a Japanese tea ceremony, we enjoyed, under an impressively carved wooden roof, some green tea. „Gyokuru Hikari tea", Zazo said. It must probably have been something special. The rite was full of bows and slowness. Time lost its meaning. A gong from the neighbouring pagoda temple stopped the tranquillity. We went over, „to the meditation", as Zazo said. Thousands of Looni sat in a foyer, as big as the ice stadium of the Parisians STEELSHARKS. „How big is your terrain?" I asked and Zazo answered barely: „3000 acres", we had to be silent then and to sit quietly. Because I was not accustomed to the way of sitting during meditation, I received as an act of grace a stool. Most sat on small pillows, some experts directly on the ground. Nobody spoke a word, no head guru, nothing, only silence. Finally, I had almost fallen asleep,when someone hit me with a stick on the back. It came so unexpectedly that I was suddenly awake. Being on edge about what could still happen, I waited, but nothing happened at all. Then, I saw that another guy, in front of me, also received a powerful hit on the back. He also didn`t flinch. At the end of this strange session, somebody beat some pieces of wood together, becoming more and more quick.

Outdoors in the park, I asked Zazo about the meaning of the blows on the back. „That`s just a small support for sleepyheads", he explained and laughed once more at my stupid face. He had to take care of some business and offered for me to join him. I wasn`t under the impression that they, because of my presence, staged any special show. Everything passed off with a cool matter of course. Zazo let report the 1st– chief, the leader of the centre. First the pleasant, then the unpleasant news, so he used to practice things in principle. The increasing numbers were the pleasant part, an unpleasant one the dispute with local authorities about constructing permissions and additional purchases of land. The 1st– chief explained: „There would be a very particular possibility: 100 acres of neighbouring land, at the time cultivated with rice, belong to the GU. Although we have offered them the double surface in another place, they are not willing to talk with us about a sale. Maybe, your friend, the meaning-creator can arrange things? Zazo looked grinningly at me and didn`t wait for my answer, at all. „We`ll see." he said. So, they knew who I was. The cooler I looked, in retrospect, at the hit on my back. On the phone Zazo spoke in Japanese with an „old friend and local politician." Zazo had already in schooldays been a genius at languages. I remembered that in those days, he had learned Arabic in his free time. After the telephone call, he said that it would probably work out now with the additional buys and the building permissions. The both of them discussed an additional plantation for vegetables and after Zazo had seen the planning figures, he decided, first to buy land and then to raise bigger buildings. I asked them, whether they, like GUGLOBE, would have a planning-computer, whereupon Zazo disdainfully responded: „We don`t like the idea of such planning shit. Free market economy is required, much more effective and above all much freer. Since when are you actually such a regulation freak?", with what he had opened our first discussion about principles. We agreed on the necessity of a world-wide inheritance regulation. „So that the deck could be shuffled anew once again, he said. After this action however, he wanted to have back the old system again. The old structures of power were broken, it would last centuries until such mighty mega-rich would have grown again. „Every hundred years such an inheritance action, would be enough. The colossus of GU administration means thousands of controls and non-freedom, completely like in totalitarianism. I want to live freely, without big brother. And I know you, old buddy, being just the same freedom loving, at least from the old days." He was right, I had always loved freedom more than anything else, and I had always hated administrations. But concerning the GU, I disagreed with him. He no longer wanted to keep away his 1st–chief from work and led me into the park. There, we sat down in a wooden boat, rowed around indiscriminately and struggled. I defended the GU: „50 percent unemployed means 50 percent people without chances. Those are the ones, who need us." · „That`s not correct! Now, that the deck is shuffled anew, everyone has a chance. All people, being too lazy to organize themselves or to cultivate a piece of land should starve. Take us as an example. We`ll soon be independent from your subsidies. And what is the reward? You come along and take away everything from us again. Is that just?" – „If we take away something from you, nothing is said, at all. Furthermore, your craftspeople fit better into the Middle Ages, than into the present day market economy. For things computers and robots take one hour, you need one day for. Do you want to turn back time?" – „Why not? Less robots and more nature! If the world works better then?" – „That doesn`t have much to do with reality. Market economy wants to offer things as cheap as possible, it wants to rationalize." Our discussion went back and forth like this and we couldn`t agree. Finally, from me, this sentence slipped out: „You`re just the right one to talk about freedom, you, the one, who keeps his Looni like sheep on the grass. Zazo became grim: „Sheep on the grass? What put this idea into your head?" Diplomacy and tactic didn't matter to me. I was, for sure, not the official meaning-creator speaking worthy words. I was like in the old times, I provoked him: „your group pressure is so strong that people have no chance of ever getting away from you again. Whoever steps out of line, is disciplined with brain-machines or vanishes, never to be seen again." Inwardly Zazo amused himself. „This Ronda hadn`t learned anything more since the school days. He had remained the same hot-head", he thought and grinned to himself. Outwardly, he complained: „My dear friend, now don't be impertinent. You know exactly how I hate violence. Brutality isn`t my style. Maybe one can reproach one Looni or the other for a certain overeagerness, but the matter itself is not bad, at all. There are black sheep everywhere, also with you. You can be sure that anybody who comes to us, can also leave, whenever they want. You, yourself have experienced it." - „My dear Zazo, you probably don`t want to deny, training people and making them dependent on your ideas with everything at your disposal?" – „And what would be so wrong about it, if our ideas were good?" – „That you steal freedom, chances to become independent, killing individuality." Zazo smiled compassionately: „Okay, if you were speaking to me as an official meaning-creator, then you would speak differently. And if you wouldn`t be my friend, I would answer you differently. Therefore let`s leave things as they are, let`s speak clearly. You won't be so stupid to claim, that the flock of sheep, honoring us, perceive a strong inner wish to be mentally free and independent! These, oh so freedom-loving brothers and sisters have only one thing on their minds, namely to finally find someone, that tells them, where to go." – „And because it`s like that, you should just encourage them to become independant, and not put them on the sheep`s grass." Zazo smiled tormented: „Didn`t you try to practice exactly that as a meaning-giver in your Parisian time? And didn`t you yourself in the end become the boss of a flock of sheep? Tell me, did they promote you from a realist to a dreamer?"

Dostoevsky`s >(Grand Inquisitor)< came into my mind. At seventeen, Zazo and I had emptied several bottles of red wine with the >Grand Inquisitor<. At that time, we had agreed: The devil was closer to reality than Jesus. And today? Had I actually turned into an idealist? Yes, it was like that! Mrs. Dreyer had converted me. Instead of accepting things, as they were, I wanted to turn them towards the good. I had landed on the complicated side of life. And how complicated my situation was, Zazo demonstrated in a masterly manner to me.

I argued, that we were not given spirit and mind to surrender, confronted with the stupidity of the masses, which Zazo helped himself to a vehement fit of laughter. His arguments were unmerciful: „How many clever spirits have considered that humans admittedly are able to speak morally, but not to live morally? From Plato to Nietsche, to Sabrò and finally to the miserable attempt, to remove evil genes from our genetic blueprint. Can you remember the German gene-technician, that invented the anti-agression bomb and wanted to persuade the Chinese, to drop such bombs over the whole world? In the end, all had agreed: if they would throw the bomb and would genetically manipulate humans to the good, they would die. Therefore, only a few idealists remained, who voluntarily manipulated their reproductive genes to the good. And what became of their children? Nobody has heard anything about them, except that they had become vegetarians! I`m quite sure their genes died again long ago, swept away from the strong and selfish ones. Whoever has sufficiant money today lets the reproductive-genes be manipulated for prettier, more intelligent, healthier and stronger children, in other words: for better prerequisites in everyday life struggles. And the few, that have seriously lived for love and morals, have been murdered without exception. Boy, what kind of fairy-tales are you talking about?“

I argued that a new era would approach mankind. The GU would make redundant the struggle of life. People would finally have the necessary rest to find themselves, without brutal fights about shares of life. „Fight and self-interest are only necessary in the market economy. There, all those who want to struggle, can let off steam. The other half of mankind has enough time and space for idealistic values. But it is exactly them, who you want to make dumb like lambs.“

Zazo answered: „What do people do if they have time? They`ll think like the devil about sitting down and becoming idealists. They`ll sit the whole day on the commu-sofa and devote time to the newest 3-D games, interactive films, shows and the Internet. A few hyperactive ones may jump around, playing 3-D cyber-games with their MOSTs (moving-sense-trampolines) or play tennis once a week. Your idealists are passive up to the point of neglect, and their uselessness doesn't in the least disturb them. At best, such people are looking for a hero, who they can run after. Emancipation and responsibility you`ll find in only one among thousands. You GU idealists with your wishi-washi GU philosophy, without contours and without a solid opinion. The only reason why you have success with the people, is your idea of the basic-care. Admittedly a nice idea. Could have almost been born from me. But your philosophy of freedom is bullshit. People want to know, where to go. With that we`ve reached the start again. And believe me, our Looni are well.

I had no chance. And Zazo just lay one more on it: „Your GU abandons people. If it were up to you, everbody could become an idiot on the commu-sofa. At least we take care of our people. And if you want to criticize us, you`ll first have to offer a better solution. Criticizing alone, that`s easy. We just know it by the the theory of contradiction. Each advantage has its disadvantage. Criticism without a suggestion for a solution is like piss in space. And if you should actually develop better ideas, please sell them first to your own club. After all, they pay you for creating meanings, you meaning-creator." With laughter Zazo tapped me on the shoulder. I was boiling with rage, rage towards myself. I had come too early, to badly prepared.

Zazo was merciful. In former times he would have enjoyed his victory to the fullest, now he covered it up by continuing his tour through his empire. Just as in Copenhagen there were also in Japan all categories of model businesses. We viewed an organic gardening business centre, where the finest vegetables were planted on 800 acres. They looked even more tempting than the GU-fields where only basic sorts were grown. Hundreds of Looni worked on the fields. „We use no chemicals. We give vent to nature, except weeds. They are pulled out traditionally as you can see. Statistically, organic nutrition lets us live five years longer", Zazo proudly declared.

In the evening, I wanted a hotel. A Looni closet in the pagoda temple didn`t appeal to me so much. I thought it possible of being awakened in the morning with a tap on the back to join the meditation. In the hotel bar Zazo let two enchanting geishas come. „As you already know, they are lady companions, like it`s customary here." The two were actually traditional geishas and very agreeable companions. We drank hot sakki, and were informed by the girls on the latest political information of the city. Just before midnight I was in bed and brooding. I lacked a strategy for the job. I could not fall asleep. It became light again, when I finally got an idea. Only the mind-machines could be a starting point. The indicator, they had inoculated me with in Amsterdam as a protection against destructive mind-machines, could prove that mind-machines are used. I had to find out, how long after a manipulation this proof was possible, and snatch, as evidence some Looni. Voluntarily no one would admittedly come along, and also there were no apostates, but I still had my Insiders. Did I have any other choice but to kidnap with their help some Looni? The act was illegal, true, but I didn't see any other way. If it worked out, the illegality would be excused by the success. If it didn`t work out, the kidnapped had never been treated badly, and nobody would ever find out who were the kidnappers. I could blindly trust my Insiders. I had no worry of pulling this off with them.

After breakfast, Zazo showed me a Looni clinic at the edge of the pagoda town. More than a thousand beds and the most modern medical technology, free access to everyone, that could pay. „Just recently we had two bigwigs from the GU as patients", he said with a complacent grin. That astonished me, high functionaries from the GU got themselves treated at the Loonis' and not in GU hospitals? Zazo delivered a plausible explanation: „Our doctors are at work with their heart and soul. They don't think of money or closing times. And if we need, as an exception, a specialist from the outside, we pay better than the others. Therefore, our clinics are the best. And you know, if it is about one`s own health, the best is just good enough. We are always three months booked full in advance.

Then he demonstrated how far away the Looni were from the Middle Ages. In one of their pagoda temples they had built a gene factory for organic computer memories. „We are constructing bio-computers of absolutely first rate. Have a look! In front of us was laying in a glass with a nutritional solution, a pulsating cell-mass. Zazo pushed the thing into a metal casing, as big as a shoebox. A „spectrotomograph", he explained. He asked me to talk to the >homunculus<. „It is already programmed", he said. I asked the shoebox who brings more justice to the earth, the GU or the Looni? The box needed a few seconds and then answered: „The question of justice is relative. The GU is just for 44% of the earth`s population with its basic-care, the Looni for less than 1%." Zazo found the answer mediocre, and I had no desire to revive the discussion of the day before. „We also have a small robotics factory", Zazo told me and showed an adjoining assembly room. „Here you can see robots, which are so delicate, that their movements are hard to be distinguished from humans. Incidentally, the GU is one of our customers." A young man appeared with a tray on which stood two glasses of fruit juice: „May I offer a refreshment ? Freshly squeezed mango juice." - „Thanks a lot, Ben ". I was surprised that Zazo knew the name of the guy. He explained: „Ben, that`s an eccentricity of mine, I call every robot like this." With a closer look, it struck me, that Ben`s features were somewhat stiff. But besides that, there was no difference from a human being. Zazo enjoyed my astonishment: „He is a prototype study constructed from bio-brain and filigree robot, both of these things you`ve just seen in the raw state. He said to the robot: „Ben! Old game! Tenfold speed!" I could hardly

98

believe my eyes. The robot ran away at an unbelievable speed. I could barely perceive his legs. No human could move so quickly.

Zazo wanted to show me many more things, but I abstained. I didn't want to grant him even more triumphs. Although, in Toronto, they had prepared me about the magnificence of the Looni imperium, reality, however, pulled me down. I confirmed Zazo, having put the performances of his organization impressively under proof. Essentially I only wanted to relax with some glasses of beer and fly back the next morning. Zazo compassionately tapped me on the shoulder, for which normally I would have given him one. At night in the hotel, I dreamed of a Japanese street gang. First I got by really well with the boys, however, more and more they turned out to be fractious and as tenacious as chewing gum. Finally it was clear that they were Looni. They tried to convert me, and weren`t willing, by no means, to let themselves be discouraged. Finally I yelled at them, to leave me alone. I could not like their organization. However, they continuously spoke to me unflustered. I tried to go away, to run away, to beat them, nothing succeeded. They remained and I didn't hit them. They avoided this too skillfully. They persuaded me on and on and on. Bathed in sweat I woke up.

Zazo said in parting: „Call me, whenever you feel like it.“ Mutely I nodded and embraced him amicably.

Back in San Francisco I welcomed my new secretary, Miss Wandercast, fifty years old, big heart, kind and hard-working. With her, nothing could go wrong. She was at the moment organizing my first meaning-giver meeting. „Things have to be done", she said. In Corinna`s notes, she had found >meeting of meaning-givers/ Canadian mountains< and suspected, I would have meant the mountains, in which I myself had learned skiing. She was well informed. She had reserved the camp for the middle of February. Leaving the office, I thought of my last meeting with Corinna in the neighbour-apartment. I could not hold it back and looked at the door sign of the neighbour-apartment. I got goose-bumps, when I read: >Corinna Vand<. The next day, my flight went to Toronto. There, I met Mrs. Dreyer and Gil, the GU-doctor.

My report made Mrs. Dreyer thoughtful. She asked, if it would be possible to convert Zazo to the good. The man would be of incalculable value on the right side. „A devout wish !", was my commentary. I assured her however, that something fitting would come to my mind. After that I had a date for a control examination with Gil. I wanted to ask him inconspicuously for the indicator, in particular, I wanted to know whether a destructive mind-machine manipulation could be proven with the Looni, I thought of kidnapping. If I asked too directly, he would certainly have gotten stupid ideas. Therefore, I asked him, for how long my indicator would still be effective. He answered: „The hard one, that you`ve received, brings the two day powerlessness only in the first three or four weeks. Then, the effect becomes more and more weak. After two months, we already need technology for the proof." – „And who has the technology for such a proof ?" – „Each moderately equiped physician. Are you worried, of having been manipulated with your last visit at the Looni? – „With these people nobody knows .. ." – „Your last vaccination is one month old. You would therefore have been powerless one day long. Do you have memory gaps? Do you lack a day?" I negated, and asked incidentally, how long after a destructive mind-machine treatment one still could work with indicators. „With the normal proof technology for up to two years ". That was enough for me.

Then, the festive days came. Paul and Lilo were amazed at Christmas trees and New Year's Eve fireworks. On the 10.01.2030, I flew to Paris in order to visit my Insiders, Paris had snow once more. The boys were actually happy to see me again. For two days we celebrated and enjoyed from Paris, whatever could be enjoyed. I don't want to enter here more intensively about my boys, because the Parisian police would still today put down money for their names. Much had not changed since my parting as a meaning-giver, anyway. Joe, my successor, had a knack for it. For the Insiders, he was too quiet, much too quiet. The plan to kidnap a few Looni, however, didn't fill them with enthusiasm either. It was known that the Looni secured themselves better, than some politicians. And really, if I would have suspected, how good their system was, I would have immediately said farewell to the plan. But at that time, I needed all my persuasive power to bring them around. Like so often, my thoughts became clear with the narrative: „We don't nab them in their own territory. There, we have no chance. We must catch them on neutral ground. Sometimes some Looni visit special congresses or similar things."

Demian was stubbornly solicitous to collect points. He was quite certain of having done no mistake this time. Against Zazo´s instruction, he had stuck to shadowing Ronda, and, what happened here in Paris, justified everything. Ronda wanted to kidnap Looni with five petty criminals ! Demian documented the plot with forgery proven analogous technology. Nobody should be able to accuse him of having played tricks. As Ronda explained, he soon would ask Zazo about fairs and congresses, in which Looni are represented, Demian had heard enough. He packed up his things and called Zazo.

Zazo felt like he was in a trivial criminal film. Demian had, against explicit instructions, shadowed Ronda, and that guy wanted –even more stupidly- to kidnap some Looni. Where should so much idiocy lead to? Demian and Ronda, in a contest about overeagerness. They seemed to have sought and found each other. Perhaps it would be the best, to let them act and wait quite calmly for the result of all that chaos. On the other hand he was annoyed by Ronda`s boldness more than by Demian`s disobedience. He had treated this twit, in a sentimental memory, as a friend. Should the thanks for that be a vicious attack? Zazo decided, to teach Ronda a first lesson.

Back in San Francisco I was in a high mood. The Insiders stood prepared for any action. At home my return was celebrated with big joy, and in the office everything ran perfectly. With Zazo, I had made an appointment for the coming weekend „for a chat" in the sauna paradise. Miss Wandercast urged me to work: „You must care about your meaning-givers. It looks, as if two of them have worries." She had sorted out the e-mail and had found a message from Anja/Los Angeles and from Edmond/Philadelphia/Pennsylvania. Anja had trouble with a >magician circle<, and Edmond wanted to get out. I didn't know either of them, the first meeting of my meaning-givers would take place in one month`s time.

Spontaneously, I flew to L.A. . Anja picked me up at the airport. With her long, reddish brown hair, I would recognize her. She was that, what people commonly call a >power-woman< : watchful eyes, small and alive like a mouse, always ready for a roguish smile, she was full of strength and energy. She was just like me in former times and took care of her frustrated with heart and soul. It had displeased her that more and more youngsters were taken in by the Voodo hocuspocus of a Brazilian magic troop. The three kingpins of the magic troop were a man and two women, that had built up a more and more growing >magic circle< with stung Voodo dolls, magic rituals and skillfully staged accidents. Anja had printed her investigation with all proof of manipulated accidents on fliers and distributed in the thousands. Superscript: >The anti-magic<. That had called up the concentrated hate of the magic circle. A bloody chicken at her front door and a threatening letter to her daughter, gave her trouble. „We should give the Voodo artists a magical lesson, that takes away their desire for hocuspocus once and for all.", I said. Anja asked: „But how could we do that?" Suddenly, I got an idea: „With good technology." With my communicator, I contacted the GU personnel data base. There, I found under: >specialists< and >special effects and technical support< an Englishman: George Wright. I called him and described our problem. „Sir, if I understand you properly, real magic is needed against wrong wizards." The man pleased me. He mentioned that he would have a few nice tricks in storage. Just with reference to his favored British style I asked George, if it would be in the area of his possibilities to let us come into the pleasure of these technical marvels. „For a meaning-creator I´ll do almost everything", he answered. We arranged a meeting two days later, at his house in Brighton.

I used the following day in the office, to contact Edmond, the second case problem. Edmond portrayed heart rendingly how he had taken more and more a fancy to the life of the Amish. Without technology, strictly according to Calvin's teaching, a Swiss evangelist from the 16th century, he lived for some weeks on a farm in Morgantown, close to Philadelphia. He couldn`t fulfill his job as a meaning-giver anymore. His bad conscience had already become unbearable, not taking sufficient care of his youngsters. I indeed had already heard once the name >Amish< , but I didn`t know, what kind of people were behind it, so I asked him for an explanation. Looking dreamily, he explained that God and nature are close together. Immediately, the Looni came into my mind – the same aphorism ·. With the Amish, however, things had a tradition for centuries. Since the Middle Ages, they lived without any technology, which means also without mind-machines. Edmond explained that simplicity of life is a guarantee for not frittering one`s life with consumption and other useless things. „We only live for God," he said, „and if you have found a substitute for me, I`ll never touch a telephone again. As he said that, I knew that he was serious and promised to find a substitute as soon as possible. In the GU data bank, I looked up the Amish: >anabaptists, refusing child-baptism. Old Order Amish, against any kind of secular deflection, for example jewelry, art, culture, technology. No use of electricity (no technical vehicles). Today circa 2 million members, mainly in Pennsylvania, Montano, Idaho/USA, climbing tendency. Protestant Christians, strictly seperating church and state, in the 11th Conference not present from conviction, nevertheless acknowledged as a religious community< . In other words: Edmond was in serious hands, I didn`t need to worry about him. For the substitutional meaning-giver I sought in the GU personnel data bank, category: >meaning-giver candidates<. There, I found, after putting in our location, over a hundred applicants, sorted after their qualifications, different test-results and self-portrayals. It took me the whole day to finally take two people on the short list: a woman and a man. Most applicants were graduates of social pedagogic universities. University degrees didn't matter to me, probably because I myself have never studied. For my selection, other things were more important: loyalty to the GU, in other words: real ideals, outgoingness, ability to prevail and cleverness (test analyses). I don't want to deny that also the video self-portrayals had caused sympathies and took influence on my decision. Gabriela from Italy and Svenna from Lapland were in the final selection. I called them and asked, whether they were prepared, to become a meaning-giver in the USA. Both were surprised and highly pleased, however Svenna told me, that he`d just fallen in love with a fisherwoman, having her own boat. It seemed like he wanted to become a fisherman. So Gabriela became a meaning-giver in the growing Amish country.

Late in the evening, Miss Wandercast had left for some time, I closed the office. Magnetically, I felt drawn to Corinna`s door. I knocked –no reaction-. I rang. She opened and immediately stunned me. As if I rang at her door every day about this time, she kissed me and said quite naturally:

„Nice, you`re here. Come sit down, I`ve just opened a bottle of wine." I sat down at her table. We drank wine. All furniture from her old apartment was here. She read my thoughts and said: „I just need your proximity ". Then she smiled making me feel dizzy. The wine tasted good, earthy, she sat beside me and let me fly to heaven with her well-trained hands.

Next morning, I flew to George Wright. I had never seen such a chaotic conglomeration of computer components, minirobots, lasers and other technology. George proposed an interesting solution for me: „I have two apparatuses, with which you can confuse your magicians: a mini-positron - disintegrator and a voice-transformer. For the disintegrator however, you will need a gun license, class C-1." I radioed the GU administration in Toronto and received on the communicator the application form for the C-1 gun license. Five minutes later, the form was sent back and a further 10 minutes later I printed out the C-1 license, validity: four weeks. I was amazed, even the original GU hologram was lasered by the communicator on the document. George explained the disintegrator to me. The thing looked like an antique telescope: „Whatever kind of subject -up to two kilograms of weight- appearing in the cross wires, will be disintegrated exactly at that point. Zooosh! And it`s gone!" He demonstrated the effect on a vase. It vanished within a second. „The magicians will be surprised if their Voodo dolls dissolve into thin air. By the way: irretrievable. Therefore, be careful. And now to the voice transformer. The new thing about it is the directional modulator. The soundwaves can be manipulated so precisely that you can turn any person into the mouthpiece of your own texts. The modulator perfectly simulates the frequencies of the speaker. If somebody says: >I want to go swimming today<, you can let him say: >On Sunday we eat pizza<. George aimed with a strange pistol at me and I asked: „Has it already started?" Better said, I wanted to ask it. Instead of that I heard myself asking: „Is tea ready?" George explained that a certain practice had to go along with it, so that the wished text was no longer than the actual one. „Otherwise it might become too magical," he said. He lent me both apparatus for four weeks.

On Saturday I drove to Zazo. He was somewhat cooler than the last time. I questioned him on the topic >education<, and quite soon we were talking about congresses. Zazo told me, that within a short time, a medical congress, where the Looni would put half of the advisers, would take place in New York. „Everybody wants our technical knowledge. We are simply too good for this world." Zazo said. I had the piece of information, that I wanted.

On Sunday I had time for the family. Finally I was back at home again. I had >free time<. I noticed myself, living from a desk diary like a manager of the market economy.

At the beginning of the week, I demonstrated to the wild Anja the anti-Voodo-technique. She was enthusiastic: „With this, we can disgrace them publicly. Because next Tuesday, the magic circle will give a show in the cityhall, probably as a reaction on my anti-magic fliers. Throughout the city, posters are hanging with the superscript: >Magician Circle Los Angeles invites: Great magic show<. The idea, of giving the Voodo artists a public lesson, immensely excited the both of us. We had another couple of days to practice.

Four days later, things started. I could perfectly handle both apparatus and sat on the lighter`s seat above the stage. Anja had placed herself, with a blond wig, in the first row. We had placed a gigantic poster with the writing >MAGICAL CIRCLE - UNIQUE< in the stage background. The Voodo artists suspected a small token from the hall leaser and didn't suspect that I, in short would add, by a remote control, one single word to that beautiful saying: >MENDATIOUS<. However, first their show started. I let things happen slowly, just as the illusionist on the stage. With those tricks, that had

106

to do with the disappearance of things, I was involved a bit. First I vanished the magic hat, then the magic stick. The public liked it madly. The illusionist approached a crisis. When I vanished two of his four iron tires, he disguised his lack of composure. He abandoned everything, wiped the sweat from his forehead and hastily left the stage. The public was confused. The Brazilian Voodo triumvirate entered the stage. Vain, as they were, they wanted to greet the public one on one. Anjas part began. She got up and called: „There they are, the three Brazilian Voodo priests. Their business is fear and scares." One of the women went in front of the stage and called down to Anja, the text came from me: „we are honorable people, our flag, there above us, is waving for our honesty." She seized her throat and seeking help she turned back to her companions. The other two didn't understand her anxiety. Before the three could speak together, I added to the poster the little word >MENDACIOUS<. The public whispered. The irritation of all participants increased. The three were stunned. The man stepped out to the front in order to make a comment. I let him say: „We are really swindlers." – The guy hesitated and wanted to begin anew, he repeated: „Yes swindlers!" His hand at the throat he tumbled back. The three ran from the stage. In the next five minutes, nothing happened at all. The perplexed public began to complain. Finally, another illusionist entered the stage. He put a small box on the table. Just before he could begin with any magic pieces, I vanished the box. Seeking help the man looked around and left the stage. Again, nothing happened for five minutes. The public became refractorious. Then, out of the Brazilian triumvirate, the woman appeared, which until now had still said nothing. I let her say: „We are poor pigs." Hastily she left the stage. With it, the show was finished. The curtain fell. On this evening nobody entered the stage anymore. Angrily, the public left the cityhall. They had admittedly paid nothing, but had also never seen a more stupid show. The next day the headlines read: „Magic circle organizes bungler show." The Brazilian Voodo artists left Los Angeles a short time later.

In the middle of February, I led my first ski camp. All my meaning-givers had come. More than two meters of newly fallen snow made things difficult and turned the trip with the ski-doo into a spectacular show. The thing overturned constantely and let us vanish into the powdery snow. Jeff didn`t loose his serenity and his humor for a second. He made a big effort, to teach us, the rigid children of the city, skiing in deep snow: „Weight to the back, relax the knees, use your poles and hop, jump into the curve!" Unremittingly, he tried motivating us. But soon the legs were too heavy. Although I could already fairly ski, fine powdery snow was an insurmountable obstacle, at least if it was about changing directions. For two days, we looked like snowmen. Then we transferred our activities to cross-country skiing which caused Jeff to take his laser-pistol, because of the Grizzlis. We explored the Canadian wild forest and the borders of our physical fitness. We didn`t see any Grizzlis, presumably we were too loud. I got to know my meaning-givers well. Except Jack, a know-it-all of first class, I liked them all very much. Out there in Canada`s clean air, the thought ripened, to finish that affair with Corinna. My brain should be capable of mastering the lowest instincts. Doing cross-country skiing through the snow glittering crystal forest, I also doubted if the kidnapping of some Looni would be the right method. However, I couldn`t think of a better idea, either. Things went very quickly. The three weeks were suddenly gone. The clean air in the mornings, the daily skiing, common cooking and discussing had cleaned our souls. I was sure that my meaning-givers had found a good line to me, except maybe this know-it-all Jack.

We returned to everyday life.

The congress hall in New York was loaded with security systems. In the fair's catalog was written: >19th March 2030: medical specialists fair: The benefit of the spectrotomography in health precaution<. In order to be able to inspect the hall, I introduced myself as a meaning-creator, pretending to plan the organisation of my own congress. Logically, they explained everything up to the last detail to me. After this demonstration it was clear to me: we could only snatch the Looni in front of the congress hall. Indoors, it was too risky.

From New York I flew to Paris. I informed the Insiders, and we concretised our plans. Following ancient methods, we wanted to carry away the Looni in a stolen vehicle. „The best would be to find a police car and disguise ourselves as cops, in New York that's still the best method." –„It just costs a little bit." One guy from our troop should negotiate with the local gangs in New York.

I flew back to San Francisco. The children became ever cuter, Julia also. Miss Wandercast had worked out a folder with reports about the Looni for me, arranged alphabetically by topics. She said, it might be useful, to have a quick look inside.

The first evening, leaving off work, I passed by Corinna's door. At home it occurred to me that I had planned to finish things with her, as soon as I was back in San Francisco. The second office evening, I went to her, to finish the story. When she stood in front of me, she kissed me casually and said: „please excuse me, but today it isn't a good day for me, at all. I have much to do, and I'm expecting a guest, you know." – „A guest?" – „Yes....., a nice young man." – „A nice young man? What kind of nice young man?" –„Oh, I have probablly fallen a little bit in love, you know." – „You've fallen in love with a nice young man?" – „Yes. Are you angry?" – „Me, angry? How could you think that?" –„Well, then it's fine. He is staying for one week. Just come on Wednesday of next week, in the evening then I`ll tell you everything." I said goodbye and stood in the corridor, like a bucket of cold water had fallen on me. I had been gone for four weeks and the little bitch had fallen in love with another guy. I went home and put on a fire. I was cold. Although Julia was especially nice to me that evening, I couldn`t get Corinna and her lover out of my mind. I saw the two in front of me. Corinna straddling her legs, and I added a piece of wood. Julia and I had a tender night. I thought about the two the whole week. What sort was he? Likely, much younger than me, after all I was sixteen years older than Corinna.

On Wednesday evening I stood in front of her door with a bottle of good red wine. She looked delightfully as always. Curiously, I inquired about the new one. „Whether it is love, I don't know," she said, „Jo is just so young, twenty-two years old, and so shy." – „Shy?" – „Yes....., not just like you..." I took her hand and caressed it softly. She put her head on my shoulder and I kissed her hair. „Yes, you are so direct..." I kissed her mouth. She put her hand on my dick and my brain in paralysis once again.

Leaving her I reflected upon my situation. What had I planned and into what had things turned? Again, I had enjoyed the fruit. But wouldn`t I be an idiot scorning such joys? >mastering the lowest instincts< so I had thought in Canada. Coming now out of her love cave I was sure: it wasn`t the lowest instincts, that we devoted ourselves to, no, it was the highest. Maybe she would soon be completely monopolized by this Jo, but even then I didn`t want to miss her. I was sure: as unrestrained as we whirled together, she couldn`t drift away with this shy Jo. I was indispensable to her, too.

At home, it was strangly quiet. Nobody was there. „Shopping at this time?", I wondered, but then I found the paper on the kitchen table:

110

„We are back in Paris. I cannot live with you any longer. Good luck with the other one. Please, leave us alone. You can see the children when they are older, and understand everything better.
Julia.
Ps.: You can admire yourself on TV, channel C-78.

So, it was written in July`s manuscript. I didn't want to believe it. Being giddy I went to the TV and watched C-78. There Demian appeared. He held one of his colourful speeches:

„Dear Julia, a thousand thanks, having chosen this channel after our telephone call. The program is copy protected and can be retrieved twice. If you want your spouse to watch it too, please watch it only once. However, I´m quite sure that one presentation is enough. What you will see, happens in a neighbouring apartment of your spouse`s office, at the same time. With the lady, your spouse has cultivated this very special type of relationship, for some time. We saw ourselves being bound to this disclosure, after your spouse started, together with a gang of Parisian terrorists, the attempt to abduct some of our physicians. Become now a witness of a live transmission of a special type. Maybe, you should take your children into the nursery.“

The 3-D picture dissolved itself and after a short waiting period, I saw, I became hot and cold, myself, undressing Corinna, full of greed, just, as I had actually done it, six hours before. I observed myself stunned in the intoxication of the senses. After some time the picture faded, and Demian reappeared: „Hello Ronda, I am sure, you can understand me. We could have done worse with the pictures. We could have played cat and mouse with you and the Insiders, but your friend, my boss, considered the present action sufficient. Only so much still: whoever plays unfairly sinks unfairly, at least if he deals with us. In this sense, improve yourself !" The picture faded.

Never before and never after in my life, was I stirred like this. Within minutes everything had turned. The family was gone. I knew Julia. I would not succeed in winning her back in any foreseeable time. The original trust, she had in me, was destroyed. She was conservatively monogamous, in excess, as she often enough had emphasized. In addition, the anonymity of my Insiders was broken. With our last meeting, we had delighted ourselves loudly in memories. If all that had been recorded..., for what purpose would Demian use such proof? Give it to the cops? In the same way, I had, a long time ago kicked Mouräne out, I`ve now been caught myself. I had to warn the Insiders. In all abundance, the Looni were now also able, to prove my illegality in the job. They could drop the bomb on me, whenever they wanted. Aside from that, my last plausible plan to come up to the Looni, failed miserably. Where had my perspectives remained? What was to be done first? I had to go to Paris. By telephone I could not warn the Insiders, there were maniacs, who saw it as sport to constantely decode communication data. On the way to the airport, I drove by the office. Could Corinna have possibly been conspiring together with the Looni? I considered everything to be possible.

Nobody answered. I cracked the lock and: look at this: no personal things were in the apartment any more. The good furniture and pieces of decoration were cleared, only junk stood around. My bird of paradise had flown out. I took the next free plane to Paris.

Trying, to find Julia in this city, would be just as hopeless as the idea of becoming rich through the lottery. Only coincidence could help. Besides that, my intuition told me that she lived with the children outside the city. But even if I would find her, nothing was to be expected, except for dramatical scenes.

My Insiders, them I found immediately. First of all, we made sure that our vicinity was safe from interception. Then, I told the boys the complete drama. They were a hundred times cooler than me. We recapitulated our last meetings and agreed: „Much we had not talked about. We hadn`t mentioned „Mistral". We had just talked in outlines about some ambiguous things, but not enough, to give somebody ammunition against us. I already felt better again. Fifty hours, I had not slept, so, after a few glasses of red wine, I fell into a comatosed sleep in the Parisian spare bed. When I woke up, three of my boys sat in the next room to cheer me up. We talked about the Looni. Our kidnapping plan was dead, that was clear. Also clear was, that Demian was only a whipper-snapper and Zazo played the actual game. I called Zazo. „Hey, Ronda", he said, „the sun isn`t shining so much, at the moment, is it? What goes up, must come down, right?" I nodded mutely. „Two women ran away? Take comfort, there are more of them. Your sneaky behaviour, however, was just too perfidious. Your enthusiasm had to be damped a bit. Be glad that I was in a good mood at that time. Incidentally, if you, in future, will hold your criminal streak under control, I would, under certain circumstances be willing to dispense with informing your boss." He laughed powerfully and supplemented sarcastically: „One should give everyone a second chance, shouldn`t one? May I help you in anyway? Mutely I shook my head. „Well then, take care of yourself. Call me, if you`re better off." – „so cool!" was the comment of my boys. „You can`t reach that guy with normal methods." – „How could I catch him at all?" –„This boy flies so high that you can only shoot him like a clay pigeon." –„It`s just the same, as it was with the fascists, who raped Susann; these idiots have also become humble only through our special treatment." – „But in a similar way you won´t be able to carry him off. For that the Looni are much too careful. A hundred percent that they are still observing us." One of my boys still had an old P3-paralyser, „stolen three years ago from the cops, things like that don`t exist anymore, today. In any case, this thing sheds modesty." I knew what kind of apparatus he meant. The French police had put into use in 2027, shock paralysers like this on a trial basis. The purely physical effect was rather harmless, just a shock paralyser. Psychically seen however, the P3-paralyser was something special. The shock affected particular parts of the brain so in many cases personality changes occured: the concerned became unequivocally more modest, in police-jargon >more moderate in behaviour<. Finally, the highest French court had prohibited the use of P3-paralysers, because of injury to human dignity. „Of course they can`t catch you with the thing, otherwise you will loose your job immediately." – „Better, we do it for you." It was clear to me that the GU would never tolerate a meaning-creator, who put into use such a weapon. On the other hand Zazo could, if he wanted, let the bomb drop on me, already now: a meaning-creator, that wanted to kidnap Looni with Parisian two bit criminals, called >Insiders<. Zazo himself acted illegally. I admittedly couldn`t prove it, but I was sure of it. I knew him well enough. Within our discussion, concerning mental freedom, his contempt of humans had been quite clear. „Useless parasites ", he had called the majority of the human race and added with a gloating grin that the Looni „take intensive care about such fools." With all his actions, he protected himself and his organization so perfectly, that nobody had a chance to prove him of illegalities. My Insiders were right, just a few months ago, I didn`t have the smallest scruples, in punishing with illegal methods, in a similar case, the religious fascists who had raped the girl of one of our boys. The constellation was the same: we were sure that legal methods had no chance. Did I have to think differently now, merely because I had become a meaning-creator? Concerning Zazo, there were only two alternatives: either he remained undisturbed in his actions, or he was given a lesson, in which the paralyser

114

would be optimally suitable. My Insiders expressed it more drastically: „With the walking on eggshells method of the GU you can`t catch that guy." There it was, the foreseeable conflict between morals and reality. The high ethics, that Mrs. Dreyer wanted to bring closer to me, stood on the one side and on the other, the good old familiar mercilessness of the life struggle. I knew just too well, that noble morals couldn`t do anything in the fight against smoothe crooks. I thought of Gideon. Would he have come up with something more clever? Something legal? Maybe a TV-action, a better masked investigation? The more I thought, the surer I was that Zazo would sovereignly repulse all attacks. To leave him unshorn, however, was out of the question. The sword of the archangel Michael was closer to me, than Jesus' mercy. I was a fighter and beat those on the head that acted arrogantly evil. Zazo was dangerous to the public, and he had destroyed my family. The paralyser was exactly the right thing for him. The boys knew about the conflict in my conscience: „We`ll do it for you, you can count on us." –„That`s out of the question, it`s my part."

With the paralyser in the bag, I left my friends. I remained two more days in Paris. Two days with time for sneaking thoughts in the city of familiar ways. I suspected, things would work themselves out, as always. One had to only give them their time. My life had reached a fork, at least in one direction it offered no possibility of return and by that would decide over everything that should follow. If I were to choose force, I would have left the way of respectability once and for all. I would loose the meaning-creator job. The mind, that usually led me, said „no !" and recommended the power of the long way. However, my heart won. I boarded the plane to San Francisco with the paralyser in the GU executive case.

The house was incredibly empty without the family. Deep sorrow crept up my throat and proved that I had turned from the bone-strong street-wolf into a vulnerable romantic. Alone in this big house, far away from the laughter and tears of my children, the end of my civil career was established. Furniture and small junk, that Julia and I had picked out full of enthusiasm, lost their meaning. Mrs. Dreyer, calling me, presumably on the basis of her phenomenal intuition, nothing mattered anymore. I regressed, became a wolf again. And exactly that I had to be, if I wanted to catch Zazo with the P3-paralyser. Such an action was only to be realized with the coolnes of ice. I became cold and calculating.

A few weeks later, I invited myself to Zazo`s. I wanted to find out, when and where he would appear in public. I could catch him only outside the Looni terrain, because even as a special friend, I was each time stripped searched from top to bottom by his security people.

Zazo was not as open minded as before, or did I imagine that? To my wish, we sat in the luxurious steambath again. I tried to loosen up the atmosphere with a few jokes, however he remained closed. I explained to him that for the completion of my GU report, I wanted to do a portrait of him on a public relation tour. „Or don`t you appear publicly anymore? –„Rarely. I`m already too old for such knick-knacks." – „Probably too lazy." – „What about your family? Is your wife already back ?" – „No." – „Insulted?" –„Seems like that." – „Quite unforgiving that baby, isn`t she?" – „We`ll see." – „Don`t worry. Everything will sort itself out again." – „I think so." – „The idea, of kidnapping my people, however, was super bonkers." I was quiet. „You deserved the lesson. Better this than unemployed." – „Yes, now leave it. Now, what about accompanying you on a PR-tour?" – „If it has to be." I needed two more weeks before I forced him to tell me of a lecture date in London.

On the 28th May 2030 Zazo intended to give one of his rare appearances, outside of Looni centres, in the Creative London Theatre. Under the motto >time for the soul–Looni wisdom<

the advertisement was published on all commercial communication ways. Almost everybody, who telephoned, mailed or was somehow interactive in London without being charged, received Zazos advertisement and was told the date of his lecture. The Creative London Theatre was equipped with more than 50.000 seats. The lecture would be transmitted on six TV-channels. Zazo`s name was not mentioned, consequently following the Looni philosophy: Contents are decisive not people. Zazo revealed a secret to me: „the island apes, by which he meant the Englishmen, have until now developed just a small sense for our religion. They have been simply too cranky for generations. This nation is predestined to the isolation of the gene-code for stubbornness." He looked upon the London lecture as a historical task. It was about cracking the British stubbornness. Only because of this, he for once placed himself on the stage. He thought life was actually too short „for such banalities". I was sure he would experience no banalities in London.

Of course there were difficulties to overcome. The Creative Theater was well secured. Furthermore, Demian was still on my heels. I suspected him, of having spied on me in Paris with the Insiders and planting Corinna in my being. For my own security, I put him on the wrong track: At the same time as Zazo`s lecture date, I organized a meeting with my Insiders in San Francisco. I presupposed, that Demian controlled my communication, therefore we spoke in code. The code was so that Demian –even if with some efforts, but in the end- could crack it. We feigned a break-in into Zazo`s splendid villa, precisely at the time of Zazo`s lecture in London. Two days before the lecture, I made an appointment with the Insiders in Paris. In the home like bushes and short cuts of Belgium, I shook Demian off. Nobody could shadow me against my will in my native country. Historically valuable and incriminating health I set over the English Channel in a speedboat. Promptly to Richard Einhorns concert on the 26th

May 2030, 20 o'clock GMT, I was in the Creative London Theatre. The Netherlands Philharmonic Orchestra played brilliantly as usual, and I inspected very calmly, with some sheets of music under one arm the access to the stage and the possibilities, to hide in proximity to it. A gigantic wardrobe stood in the next room of the prompter`s cabin. Having been ideally suited for a partition wall. I rigged it up during the following two nights. When the security people of the Looni came, they had no chance of finding me.

Then, Zazos lecture day came. He had given me a card for the first row and was presumably not at all surprised that I had not come. Demian had told him about our break-in-plans, and consequently Zazo saw me in the custody of the San Francisco police. In fact I was closer to him than anybody else. I had reckoned with at least one of his security people in the prompter`s cabin and therefore taken with me my blowpipe. The blowpipe still remained from the Insiders' time. A special manufacture from aluminum: telescopic, interior-lying lamellas from carbon, ideal for projectiles from long steel tops with silicon bottoms. Silently and absolutely accurate within ten meters. I had taken with me some narcotization tops, that I could have nicely dealt with in that narrow cabin. But nobody was there. Through a narrow slit in the curtain, I saw Zazo standing on the podium, less than two meters in front of me. The paralyser in hand, I listened to him. The way he was speaking, and how he had treated me in our last personal conversations, one could not get the idea, he could inflict sorrow on anybody. On the contrary, he radiated warmth and sympathy. Once more, his charisma took hold of me. I began to doubt. Was Zazo really to be condemned? O.K., he had a rough sense of humor and made others his play things, but was he evil, because of this? The longer I saw him in front of me, the bigger my doubts became. I had to really force myself to switch on my mind. Why had I come here? Why had I been so sure that he did evil? Of course, it was his charisma, with which he bamboozled everyone, not only me. And he bothered the devil about the millions of people, he had crowded together in his organization. For his personal advantage he let croak people and morals. And this fascinating radiation really made him dangerous. Not just all the Looni, but my own family had become his victims. Zazo just said: „All humans strive in their hearts after peace. Peace between nature, God and themselves", when a glaring flash of lightning from my prompter`s box put an end to his sanctimony.

Within a thousandth of a second, Zazos brain was the arena of confused reactions: All stations of his previous life raged through the brain. His body wounded, tortured by the loss of each control. The consciousness was outside the body. Lying down there, on the stage, he saw himself, the convulsing jerking body. Then, it became dark. Around him it whispered and muttered, hollowly and becoming more and more loud. What was that? Suddenly, he knew: they were spirits and demons, who wanted to move him into their middle. They whizzed around him and quacked, cooed, gargled. They knew that they would get him, that he would soon belong to them. He wanted to escape, away from this darkness, the eternally restless. Going back! He wanted to go back into his body and screamed: „No! No "! However nobody heard him. It was the small death, that he lived through, an experience, that he would never forget. His bodyguards held him fast.

„That hit it on the spot." I was sure to have done the right thing, when, seconds after the shot, Zazo`s security people hunted me down. The hoopla in the foyer was perfect. The spectators rushed to the exits and the press was virtually just as quick with me, as Zazo`s bodyguards. „Why have you done this?" – „Who are you?" They screamed through the room. Camera lights blinded me. „The scum deserved a smack in the face, I only said, and then the London cops carried me away to the central police station. From the juridical point of view there was not too much to be read into it: even easy bodily harm was contested, because the body was not injured, and there were enough experts, who had investigated in favour of the Parisian police, that even pain in a true sense wasn`t caused. They even were of the opinion that the exceptional experience, being procured to the afflicted, was rather more a value than a damage, but as said before, the highest court had prohibited the thing for reasons of human dignity and self-determination. Of course I was condemned because of forbidden arms possession and one or two other counts, in a summary trial. I had no police record, was a meaning-creator, and had received some mitigating causes, therefore they took into consideration my three days in police custody in a London jail, and only fined me.

Mrs. Dreyer still visited me in the London prison. She was very sad. Sad, concerning my personal development. All that legal jargon didn't interest her. „Why didn`t you come to me?" she wanted to know. I thought: „Because your answer wouldn`t have helped me." I said: „Because I was too furious." I didn't want to hurt her. Under tears she handed me over my termination papers. „After your dismissal you can travel for another week on GU expenses to resolve your things. Cards and communicator please deposit with Miss Wandercast. To you personally, I wish all the best. I hugged her, for the first and the last time.

Even stranger was the meeting with Julia. Mrs. Dreyer had sponsored her trip to London. She sat close to me but yet was far away. No nice word, no dear gaze. „You have changed very much", she said and: „Don`t worry about us. We are fine. I asked about the children, and she made me understand that they were fortunately still young and would forget quickly. „They find some stability in the kindergarten", she said and unnecessarily added, that it would be better, if I would leave them alone for a time. It was the first time that I experienced how quickly great love can mutate to small gestures. I asked her whether she could imagine, ever coming back to me and listened to her pragmatism. She first had to take care of herself and the children, she said, and that it would be nice, if I would let her have, these and those household appliances, via her parents. She could not imagine developing „romantic feelings" for me, once again. With her parting, I wanted to hug her, too. But more than a warm handshake wasn`t possible.

V. Chapter   ·Rondas Odyssey·

My last free trip went from San Francisco, where I had given up house and household effects, to Paris, however not because of Julia and the children. Them, I had also given up. I just couldn`t think of any other place, that I could call home. However, the streets of Paris weren`t any longer my streets. My Insider friends admittedly did everything to keep me in a good mood, but I couldn`t see the city´s dirt any longer. My friends altogether covered GU care, and if they didn't sit on the commu-sofa, they earned themselves a few pennies on the side, moonlighting as rent a cops for shops and tennis clubs. It bored me stiff. We had become old, children dominated the gangs. Their fun wasn`t our fun anymore. I became a GU care recipient, got an apartment just near my buddies and soon we were together every second day. That really wasn`t imaginative. But what was the alternative? Where could it be better? I thought of Canada. There, in the nature, I had always felt good. But I couldn`t reach Canada anymore, I lacked the money. „Europe also has nature," I thought. Yes, in the countryside, there I would live healthier: better air, no dirt, no noise. I could work on a farm, even if the merit would be only negligibly better than the GU basic care. An activity in nature would be good for me. The idleness was unbearable for me. From my last money, I bought some awfully expensive outdoor equipment: thermo-suit, thermo-jacket and thermo-shoes for temperatures between plus 30 and minus 40 degrees Celsius, a round thermo-tent, a thermo-sleeping bag, air mattress and a mini-cooking set. Everything together surged less than 4 kilograms and fited into a backpack, that was not bigger than a soccer ball. Absolute high-tech equipment, breatheable and a 100 % waterproof, my most valuable posession for the next years.

On foot, I hiked through the summer landscape, towards the south. With the feelings of my childhood, I smelled grass and flowers. For a long time, I hadn`t kept an ear on bird chirppings. Amazing, how quick smells, ambiences and sounds could turn back the decades within seconds. At night I lay between crawling bugs on the meadow and looked at the sky, the infinite universe. Millions of suns, that nourish thousands of planets. So far away, but despite all technology they remained unattainable. Because I had properly checked out with the GU, I could pick up in any city, by finger- and iris- identification my basic care coupons. Now and then one had to work a few days. At the care offices, I met like minded, or better said, the other „houseless" (according to the official GU jargon). I was astonished, how many men, but also women, had chosen this way of living. For every five men, there was approximately one woman; so the most curious pairs existed. I learned the sign language and the honorary code of the tramps. A semi-circle with a line to the right, doodled discreetly on a wall, for example meant, that in the next street on the right side was to be found a bunk with a roof. Helpful info for rainy days in a city.

My equipment rendered first class services. I noticed soon that many tramp colleagues were keen on it. They constantly had wet clothes. My stuff was always dry. They froze or sweat, I was fine. Their tents shredded, mine was resilient. What should I do? It was obvious that someone would try to snatch my treasures away from me. Therefore, I organized teflon color, better said, I swiped it in a specialist`s store, because its' price was exorbitant. It had to be teflon color because the physical qualities of my equipment couldn`t get lost. With a brown/grey color, I smeared things so nastily that nobody wanted to have it anymore. Otherwise, there was little crime among the tramps. They didn't steal to their capabilities. Finally, tramps received a higher GU care than people with a home. Furthermore, tramps didn`t want a bad image. Everybody was fussy in disposing one`s garbage properly. In any case, that`s how it was in Northern European countries. The Southern Europeans, leading the way, the

Portuguese, surrounded themselves with rubbish in their forests, that any disposing of garbage lost its sense. Yes, within nine months I came down to Portugal. Nine months, which went by like nine weeks. I learned about edible herbs, fungi and berries and bathed in the crystal clear water of springs. Time lost its meaning. The only annoying things were the care offices in Portugal. It was generally known that Portuguese authorities worked miserably, but just how bad, I had no idea. Coming, one day, once again unsuccessfully from a Portuguese office, the computer installation was defected –supposedly, they were just unable to serve it-, I remembered the old idea of working on a farm. I was really up to my head in Portuguese dilettantism, and I didn`t feel like working in the Spanish heat. Therefore, I started on my way back to France.

After one year of wandering, I crossed the border Spain/France at Bayonne. Indeed, I had home feelings. From Bayonne, I first tramped up the Atlantic coast. With brown tanned tourist girls, I amused myself in the waves and now and then also in the dunes. Work only came as GU work. Finally, I reached Creon, an idyllic little town, east of Bordeaux. At the local market, I met a wine grower, who was looking for helpers for the vintage. Because he fiscally wanted to put down the expenses, I had to check out with the GU care. The farm was centuries old, completely in contrast to his wife. With the face of an angel, she moved in the truest sense of the word, extra-ordinarily. Although married women actually are not my thing, I didn't have a chance against these attractions. As it had been with Corinna, the matter was elementary. She looked at me and I knew: our union was only a question of expectant, glad filled hours. The farmer controlled his jewel without a fault. A hard attempt and during the vintage simply hopeless. In the second week of the vintage, I sank my scepter in her sweet apple. We created the empire of the senses when we suddenly heard him puffing up the hillside. That was the end of my rural working time. I

124

escaped down the hillside, and he followed me crying for two long hours. Somehow I felt sorry for him, on the other hand I was glad, not to have such worries.

In Bergerac, I found work with the vintage again. Monsieur Pellier had specialized in noble, heavy wines. Everything surrounding him was clean, that I finally was sitting in a bathtub again. We slaved away around the clock. In the evening, nourishing cuisine was served. So things could be endured even though the payment here was also barely higher than the GU standard. At the end of October the harvest was brought in. I tramped further on.

The Dordogne valley became more and more beautiful towards the east, but nevertheless discontent came over me. In the meantime, I had had enough pleasure of nature. Slowly, but surely the wandering life started to bore me stiff. I lacked a goal! Something, that made sense. I had to laugh. I, the meaning-giver, yes even meaning-creator, sat by the river and was looking for a meaning. As long as I had arranged meanings for others, it was not necessary, to think about one for myself. And now? I had become a tramp because I had lost my home. For one year I had lived like this and had learned a lot. Not much new could arise from this way of living, anymore. Furthermore, nature slowly became uncomfortably autumnal. What should I do? My steps began to become hesitant, my thoughts stubborn. Strangely lacking orientation, almost crippled, I roamed around for days, in the area of Puybrun.

Zazo had, after the >outrage<, as Ronda´s action was called in Looni circles, to fight with Demian very soon. He wanted to „unburden" him wherever it was possible. He knew a mental weakened „boss" in front of him. But Zazo was clever enough, to assess his own situation realistically. Through Rondas attack, he had lost the old self-consciousness. He had become doubting, especially, if it was about big contents: life itself had become more ambiguous to him, and human beings themselves more complicated. Nevertheless and perhaps exactly because of that, he didn't want to abandon the Looni to Demian. Doctors and friends had advised him to retreat, to recover and delegate the daily business to a competent successor. He knew however, which power Demian would get into his hands, and what he would do with it. There was no successor, there could not be one, at all. The system >Looni< was tailor-made for him personally, and the secrets of the system were too highly explosive. No one must know, what happened behind the scenes. Thanks to his razor-sharp mind, he still easily controlled Demian`s ambition. He let him take care of tiresome work, hinting about old sins, and holding out the prospect of returning to the top, at the earliest in seven years time. In one respect however, Zazo still underestimated his pupil, and that concerned Ronda. As if led by a magical hand Demian could not stay away from Ronda. During Ronda`s entire hobo time Demian had shadowed him. Zazo knew nothing about it.

I sat in Camps at the bank of the Cére and thought about the symbolism of my career. I had failed especially because of that man, who had been the reason for my promotion, Zazo. Already in our youth, he had brought me little luck. Stress and anger were mine, ·and only mine, not Zazo`s – permanent companions, when I was together with him. Teachers, department store owners and freaks made me – and only me· into the scapegoat for our common actions. Now I was offside again, and Zazo`s image was better than ever before. Once more, I had made myself the loser and him the winner. Being with him had its attraction in comparing strength. However, it only took strength and didn`t give it to me. With Michel, the third in the alliance of our youth friendship, the principle worked exactly the opposite. Michel was too soft to measure strengths and had always given it to me with his soft style. Being together with Michel was strengthening, because our actions were useful, admittedly,

126

also a little bit boring. Maybe, there were such fateful fixations between people? Was that the solution? Was life about finding those, that bring benefit and luck? Was it about looking for fertile alliances? If yes, would being together with Michel still today be advantageous for my life? Even if it was not like that, it interested me what had become of the old friend. So it came that he, who had already given me strength in youth, should give it to me, now again. The idea to visit Michel inspired me immensely. I remembered Zazo`s words: „He has caught an active woman, who has shipped him to Northern Italy, in the proximity of San Remo..." The nest began with „Bu ", more I couldn`t remember anymore. Well tempered I trudged the direction: Italien/San Remo/Michel.

Autumn turned uncomfortably over into winter when I came on the Via Romana to San Remo. Powerful winds shook the palms and my first way led me to the care office. There were much less tramps here than in France, so that I didn`t have to wait a long time for my coupons. One thing however, was a disadvantage: the few >houseless< that existed, had to do, according to GU rules, strictly social work, which meant clearly more work than in France. Presumably because of this, tramps in this area were so rare. For me that stood for: hardly having arrived in San Remo, already being conducted to the beach, collecting seaweed. By barrels, we brought the gluey stuff for drying on meager fields. Food and fertilizer were made from it. With every method, they tried to free the Mediterranean from the nuisance of seaweed. In the meantime even the Balearens were threatened by the alga carpet. Alga-fishery was regarded as an innovative, promising business.

The small village with >Bu<, near San Remo, could only be Bussana. More exactly said, it was about two villages: >Bussana Nova< and >Bussana Vecchia<. The history of this village was also very symbolical. Three hundred years ago, the community of the Catholic priest of Bussan Vecchia had been killed by the roof of the church in the middle of the sermon. An earthquake raged precisely at the moment as the priest spoke the words: „may God give protection against earthquakes to the the holy father, (who they called the pope), the sacred Roman, Catholic Church and their believers ......" For a long time the half destroyed village stood empty. They built Bussana Nova. Bussana Vecchia later became an artists- and tourists- village.

The baker, that I asked in Bussana Nova for a painter, called Michel, gave me for >Michel-Pintore< in Bussana Vecchia, a small cake, „because he likes this so much." One of Michel`s paintings hung over the sale bar. „A gift, already today already worth thousands of dollars", the baker told me, full of pride. Obviously, Michel had lost nothing of his old charm.

On the way up to the old Bussana, the clouds cleared up. The sun shone on olive groves and greenhouses full of carnations. One tourist carrier after the other passed me by. From Monacco, Nice, Antibes, yes even from Milano art tourists came to Bussana. I found Michel between two olive trees, lying in a hammock. He read a book: >The secret doctrin of the Knight Templar< from Allan Oslo. Me, standing in front of him, twenty years after our last meeting, he saw as being quite normal. He was happy: „What belongs together, will always find each other again", he said and didn't suspect, how very much he hit my symbolism nerve with it. He was heavily enthusiastic about his reading matter, and with some glasses of red wine he talked about his newest perceptions. „Imagine", he said, „what is equally important for Jews, Christians and Moslems, is the old testament. Despite all differences, Moses` laws are the components of these religions. And with that the big deceit already starts." He told me that these religions have only become so influential, because the old testament is based on fear and power. „Humans were pounded into their heads that bad would happen if they didn't live according to the laws of the church.

128

On the other hand Jesus, Mohammed and many others have proven, that it is a loving, benign God, whom you can meet in your higher self, and that the furious, ranting God of the old testament has nothing to do with God, the Creator and All-Embracing. God is above revengeful feelings and rewards. The threatening, brutal God of the old testament sprang up from the brains of power conscious spirits. Their material thinking, transfered on God within the old testament, is possibly the expression of the fallen angel, Satan, or how ever you´d like to name the material shadow of God. Whenever it is about materialism, money and power, whenever fears and scares prevail, God, wanting to touch free souls, is far away. In other words: the God of the old testament is in reality the devil. Imagine: whoever adores this God in fact adores the devil. Which explains why many, who do so, are materialistically so successful." The problem was according to Michel`s opinion that humans were made from flesh and blood and therefore „lose themselves again and again to the materialistic world."

I felt, like being in a church. Admittedly Michel seemed to give out some truths, but I wasn`t in the mood for his pompous thoughts. I wanted earthly things, was curious, wanted to see his pictures, wanted to know, how he lived, meet his family, observe the tourist`s bustle in Bussana, cook a good meal. I felt well, and that was because of Michel. He left no doubt that I was highly welcome.

His wife Celia really had power. She ran a gallery in Bussana and sold Michel`s pictures for exuberant prices. She forced him to come up at least with two sketches a day, for the daily business. „We admittedly don't sell every day two big pictures, like others do, but with the sketches and two big pictures a month, we`re still better off, than all the others." Michel twisted his face, and explained: „She only thinks of money and because of that, she is of course the devil's fat prey. But if I were to sell my pictures myself, I probably would be a customer of the GU." Celia countered drily: „If I understood your last theory correctly, we women are devoted to the devil anyway, so it doesn't really matter with that small money at all." Michel slyly smiled at me: „You know, I told her that until now, no woman has managed to be a philosopher or a founder of a religion, which probably has its reason in being closer to materialistics, than to big thoughts." – „After all it's us, taking care with our beautiful material body, that human life originates. So it's a small wonder that we are closer to life than you, high calibre aviators of thoughts." – „No chance!" Michel closed the discussion, and I proposed reconciling, to cook in the evening one of my special meals. I didn't suspect that, with this idea, I would advance to the permanent chief cook of a five head extended family.

Michels house was a three story ancient Moorish building. It had natural stone bows as fundamental elements and two rooms, on each floor. So there was not so much space. Kitchen and bath, on the first floor, on the second a room with a fireplace and dormitory and above that two more dormitories. At the very top, on the flat roof, was a small masoned chamber with sea view, that I freed from all possible junk, and filled with my air mattress. In the house lived Michel and Celia, their children Joel and Danni and furthermore Eve, a 27-year old beauty, a friend of Celia's. Joel, 13 years old, took after his father. He painted amazing lifelike portraits. Danni was two years older and mainly had boys on her mind. Of Eve, I couldn't make head or tail. Mainly she slept in the fireplace room, but I suspected her, of having a special relationship with Celia.

In the first evening, I prepared a fondue. The ingredients Michel and I got from the supermarket. Finally, I could buy, what my heart desired, regardless of GU coupons. Michel paid cash. He refused, to order things over the Internet and to get them delivered. The Internet he didn't like at all. At

130

most two or three times a year, he sat in front of his ancient flat screen and watched TV. So, we went shopping: awfully expensive real beef fillet, pork fillet and turkey fillet. As sauce ingredients: Mayonnaise, cream, cream fraiche, garlic, horseradish, mustard, tomatoes, onions, pickles, capers, chili and green pepper. As further ingredients: Baguettes, butter, parsley, dill, cheese and grapes as well as fruit juices and exquisite red wine. In view of the horrendeous bill, I could not hold back from saying: „That materialistic, diabolical soul of your wife`s has its damned good sides." With that I elicited a happy grin from Michel: „Luckily they are her sins, not mine." The fondue evening was a great success and the decision of the household was certain: from now on I was offered the cooking in the evening. I assumed the task, because I wanted to do useful things. Furthermore, I liked cooking, anyway. From Spaghetti Al Pesto to Wiener Schnitzel I let ramble the taste buds of my new extended family through European cuisine. Life in Michel`s house was grand. It seemed as if I had always belonged to it. My past was of only small interest to Michel. The travelling through Europe he liked, but with the meaning-giver and the meaning-creator job, he didn`t have any interest. Zazo also didn't matter to him. „He was always bad news. You know, but nevertheless, I`m too stupid for the modern world", he said coquettishly. Actually, he devoted time exclusively to his art and philosophical books. Celia was the whole day in the gallery. She looked after her customers by photographing Michel`s new works and offering them via the Internet to known customers and art investors. In the Internet galeries and on the web-sites of banks, she offered Michel`s works for somewhat higher prices. With her management, she had worked for him some small fame, still in life. She was sure that some tourists came to Bussana only because of Michel. Eve was a surfing instructor at the beach of Bussana Nova. In the summer, she taught tourists and beginners, in the winter advanced pupils.

Michel declared after a few weeks, that I could stay, as long as I wanted. He had spoken with the others, all agreed. I would suit well for them. He was touching.

The relationship between him, Celia and Eve interested me, having just miserably failed myself in this respect. „How are you handling this, your three?", I asked him and harvested his smile: „It looks more difficult, than it is, in fact", he said. „Yes, but are you doing as three?" – „Not so much. Celia and Eve like each other and sometimes we play together. That they want me to join them, quite rarely happens." – „And you? Aren`t you jealous?" – „The same, more rarely. I really like Eve very much." – „And your relationship to Celia? Is it tarnished by it?" – „Not at all ! Just the opposite." – „What? Is it so simple?" – „Yes." I was amazed. Where it concerned matrimonial relationships, I got completely used to different opinions.

Bussana, with its hundreds of day tourists was a hectic place which is why Michel for painting either disappeared to the roof, (in front of my cottage), or into the fields, between the olive trees. I soon noticed, that he needed quieteness, like hardly anyone else. I had much time, because my culinarious skills were always required only from 17 o'clock. I explored the surroundings, went surfing and fishing. Michel gave me his books. Remarkably however, with everything I did, I had, just after a short time, the feeling of being bored. I became downright melancholy. Celia recommended that I paint, sculpture, make pottery or write. I tried all possible things, however nothing exempted me from this sneaking boredom. Weeks and months passed. I had a lover, Ines from San Remo. There, in San Remo at the harbor we met, admiring the sailing boats. She wanted to marry and have children, which spoiled my fun of the liaison quite soon.

In the summer of 2032, Michel and I lay once more in the olive grove in our hammocks. He recited from a Buddhist`s book, and I drank red wine. Michel got annoyed that Buddhists didn't believe in God. For me it was O.K. . I was not faithful anyway. Michel thought, a religion without God stopped half way. „So the Dalai Lama can still be as spiritual as he wants, if he doesn't derive wisdom and love from the Creator, he just knows half the truth." I couldn`t divide Michel`s enthusiasm for such topics. In fact, I was enthusiastic about nothing at all at the moment. I thought about my future. Not that I felt unwell in Bussana. Our flat-sharing community harmonized in a miraculous manner. Ines, an attractive sculptor from Bussana had fallen in love with me, and now and then I visited her. My culinarian skills were in the meantime village known, so that the local restaurant >Osteria< engaged me for occasional speciality dinners. I was actually fine. Why then, did life, nevertheless, seem to me like a cage? Didn't I bare the sweet life? Michel thought that I might have to take a vacation from harmony. But that wasn´t the point. Admittedly, until then my life was shaped by fights. With my parents, I had fought for self-sufficiency, in the Parisian streets about power, with the frustrated about confidence and finally with Zazo about freedom. But it was not the fight, that I lacked. The harmony didn't annoy me, just the opposite, I enjoyed it. Michel rummaged in his philosophical fund of thoughts and finally said: „Maybe you need a spiritual teacher?" Me and a spiritual teacher! That idea spontaneously seemed to me as completely off the point. Teachers! Such things couldn`t be of use for me, at all. I was an anarchist! Nobody could tell me, and really, not even a single human being, something about truth or importance. I carried the truth in me. I didn't belong to the hord of sissies, that cling to the thoughts of others. „I don`t need forecasters!", I said. „Not forecaster! Just the opposite! Catalyst." Catalyst! Good gracious! The last time, I had heard this word was at school in chemistry class. I could just remember that catalysts had something to do with acceleration. „What in heaven do you want to accelerate with me? I am already speedy enough." – „Spiritual teachers, or gurus accelerate processes of individuation, that`s what I mean.“

Individuation or in other words becoming oneself, that was the topic, we had also studied as meaning-givers and meaning-creators with the GU concerning our frustrated and protégées. In other words: Michel recommended to me a meaning-creator in order to find myself. The idea offended me. Finally I was a pro, I was a meaning-creator. I had been it. There was nothing higher if it was about the questions of meanings and becoming oneself. I, the teacher, should turn into a student? I didn`t need that.

„I have learned everything, which has to do with individuation. Nobody will be able to teach me anything about it.“ - „I´m sorry, if I have offended you, that wasn`t my intent. Wait a second, I`ll give you a riddle: He leafed through his book and quoted: „A cow wants to go through a fence. Carefully she puts her head through the rods, then the neck, then follows the massive body. She has nearly passed through it, but the last tip of her tail doesn't fit through the fence. Why? How can that be possible?“ I had never heard a more stupid riddle. „Why such baloney?“ I asked and received as an answer: „The riddle is more than a thousand years old. You can only solve it if you are close to enlightenment. >Koans< such riddles are called. I didn't want to believe it and looked in his book. That strange riddle was actually written there. Michel said: „We Europeans are much too caught up in logic and reason. The gurus, that I mean, can crack this stiff western thinking and for that we need them, definitely not as intelligent forecasters.“

Since this conversation the idea of knowing without reason ghosted through my head, confusing and attractive, with the outlook on a fat reward: The enlghtenment. I wanted to be enlightened, therefore I read Michel`s books. Buddhism, was the lived tolerance. The only religion, giving other religions the same status, as themselves. Buddhism assumes that life is a sorrow as long as one is greedily hunting after things. Each desire must end miserably, at the latest with the death. So far, so good, and in general logical. But how could I lose logic? By sitting like Buddha under a tree and trying to lose any desires? Wasn`t I already desirous at that moment again? Michel tried to give good advice to me: „Meditate, sit and concentrate on the >here and now<", he said. I sat down under an olive tree and meditated. Besides thick calves and thirst on red wine, much didn't come along with it. Michel brought forward his best philosophies. He talked about the trees, surrounding us. About their growing and going, just like we do (eating their olives). About being all the same, whether I look in Italy at an olive tree, or in California at a redwood. Both things would make the same sense or nonsense. I listened to his outpours devoutly, however the feeling didn't occur to me that within short, I would lose my mind. So, it couldn`t go on. „How could I find a guru?", I finally ask him. „I think, you just have to go there", was his heart-warming mystical answer. „Okay", I said, „next week I´ll start." He had not reckoned with that, anyway he seemed to become abruptly awake: „What? You will start? Do you want to go to India or Tibet?" –„No notion, something like that is meant to be." On that same evening Michel fished out some books about Tibet. In his opinion, Tibet was better, because Tibet was one of the 24 sacred places on earth. „There, guaranteed you`ll find a guru", he said. He leafed through an illustrated book and actually found a photographed guru. „Look at this! There is such a guy." On the photo, a man was shown, in his fifties, bald headed, in bay wool coat.. Under the photo was written:

Tibetan mountainous country near Zo thang. Hermit-monks, as portrayed, are still today by the native population supposed to be sacred. Parapsychological abilities are attributed to them.

I was impressed, >Zo thang< was the name of my goal. I was even more impressed, however, when I read in the imprint of the book: >Zürich 1989<. The man had been dead for decades. But all this would not frighten me. I was determined to pursue that crazy idea. I could only win, and I could always come back. Michel told me that such gurus sometimes became stone old. I think, he wanted to give me hope that the man on the photo was still alive. An incompetent attempt for a realist like myself.

VI. Chapter   ·Ronda and Tibet·

So it should move on, direction Tibet. My extended family was honestly sad. I had to promise each of them, also Eve, that after the „trip to the enlightenment" I would come back. Celia, Ines and the restaurant >Osteria< sponsored a return flight to Calcutta within 3 years. Michel put $ 100 U.S. in my hand: „So that now and then you can cook something nice."

Demian had endurance, concerning Zazo as well as Ronda. After Ronda had become one of the bohemians in Italy, he stopped seeing him as an acute danger. Nevertheless, Ronda remained a factor of insecurity. He was Zazo`s only friend and had proven that he was good at all possible surprises. Even if he momentarily had nothing in mind with Zazo and the Looni, it was possible however, that he would reappear someday, in order to look for contact with Zazo. The supervision cost a mere $ 50.000 U.S. annually, therefore nothing in the comparison to the risk of a noncalculable youth friendship. Ronda remained shadowed. Zazo showed less and less verve. In the last year, he had only brought up the foundation of a Looni symphony orchestra. Numbers of membership were stagnating, and new projects were hardly ever started. The reached seemed enough for him. If things continued like this, the descent would be inevitable. Then, at the latest, Demian saw his chance coming. He organized the regular meetings of the 1st– and 2nd– chiefs and by doing so, he little by little took over the management of the organization. Zazo knew about Demian`s activities and let him have his way, ·not because of weakness, he had the calming certainty of having the upper hand·. He didn`t know exactly, where the Looni society would steer to. The limits of growth would soon be reached, furthermore, it appeared too trivial to him, just to augment quantitatively power and influence. To save and refine the reached would be a more worthwhile goal. Mind-machines had to be programmed agressively only occasionally. Things ran smoothly as they were. The Looni symphony orchestra gave him great joy. Thanks to the quality of the ensemble, it already belonged to the absolute world top, after a short time. The future of the eager Demian was to him just as uncertain. On the one hand he saw the ambitious guy as too unscrupulous as a successor, on the other hand such a gigantic organization needed a strong hand. However, on one point, Demian was actually still ahead of Zazo, and that involved Ronda. Zazo still had no idea of Ronda`s shadowing.

After arriving in Calcutta, I went to the care office. I knew that the offices were sowed thinly in the mountains so that one has to receive the coupons for several months in advance. They told me that in my goal region there were also offices in Bhagalpur and Darjeeling. If I wanted coupons immediately, I first had to clean the hospital for two weeks. That didn`t provoke me much, finally enlightenment called. Therefore, I moved on to Bhagalpur. The train to there cost $ 15 U.S., fritter bread with cheese $ 1 U.S. a piece, and the historical train to Darjeeling $ 5 U.S.. Michel`s money melted like snow in the sun. Of course I would have been able to live more cheaply. So, for example, also a GU-bus, that would have cost me nothing, went to Darjeeling, but the historic train really was something special. Built in 1881, the >toy-train< surmounted 2100 meters of height difference between Silliguri and Darjeeling in 24 hours. With at most 6 m/ph, it took care of time losing its meaning again. In Darjeeling, I could get coupons for six months in advance, because I wanted to go into the mountains. Prerequisite for the stack coupons was four months of work in the GU tea plantations. „Mon Dieu", I thought, „the way to enlightenment is stony." As a tramp in Europe, I had gone to the authorities weekly. There, two or three days of work were of no consequence. But now? Four months non-stop of tea picking? That was a tall order. I did it. I didn`t have any choice. Michel`s money should cut it for more than one month. The tea picking was a science in itself. With the first cut, we only took the brightly green sprouting tops of the shrubs. >Orange Pekoe< was the name of this best, most powerful quality. Then came the second cut, the middle leaves, called >Pekoe<, and finally the rest, >Broken<. Depending on, if the leaves were shortly steamed or intensively dried, green or black tea originated. Many Europeans worked on the plantations. The guests were accommodated in the usual GU tents. I preferred my own special tent, it had become a real home. Discreetly, I questioned a few people about those „alleged gurus in this area " and harvested nothing but mockery and stupid remarks, more or less to the motto: „you mean those, that were extinct a few hundred years ago? Four months of picking tea went by quickly. The search for a guru had proceeded until then only little encouraging.

Following a spontaneous intuition, Zazo had engaged his best high-tech man with Demian`s stalking. Of course Demian reckoned with such actions and was more than careful, but Zazo´s man was perfect. Despite all precautions, even Demian had no chance. Zazo`s motives for Demian`s stalking were long term ones. With current surprises, he didn't reckon with Demian. The more astonished he was, when his man just after one month presented the following record: „Well, what about our Ronda?" – „Boss, I´m sorry, but I need more money." – „Why is that?" –„Your Ronda has just flown to India. Under such exotic conditions control is a bit more expensive." – „What does the fool want in India? Where did he get the money for the flight?" – „Sponsored by his artists. He wants to look for a guru." – „For what?" – „A guru. A holy man, a pre-prayer." –„Good gracious. Things become more and more ludicrous." Zazo had the same feeling. Why did Demian have Ronda shadowed?

From Darjeeling I hiked up the mountains northward bound. White snow summits glittered in the distance. There behind the Himalaya mountains I wanted to go. On the gravel way through the hilly, green mountains, I felt pretty silly. How on earth could I have become addicted to such a crazy idea, looking in the Tibetan wilderness for a guru? That must have been the Italian red wine. Why, I nevertheless always continued, I didn't know until today. Every day, I did thirty kilometers. In Gangpa, a village with five hundred inhabitants, I visited the only restaurant. There, natives sat in front of the Internet TV and drank infernally hot, self-burned fruit schnaps. They spoke English and were accustomed to tourists. I became acquainted with Yanman, a man in his late fifties, who with his stature, reminded me of a gorilla. Yanman invited me to schnaps drinking, he had brought from home a one litre bottle. Curiously, as Yanman was, he wanted to know everything about me: grown up where? Work? Children? Family? Ambitions? I had no problems telling him my story. Only my one ambition, the guru, · with that I had my difficulties; that thing finally seemed really too naive to me. I didn't want, having just arrived, to become at once the village idiot. Yanman laughed a lot. He told me, he was a Samadrog, half nomad and half farmer. He and his family possessed a solid house in the village. From dried mud-bricks, he had built it with his own hands. In the late hours, Yanman invited me there. I explained to him, that I was well accommodated in my tent, but he stuck to his gun, I had to meet his family. Shortly before midnight, we staggered a bit tipsy into his house. There was still a lot of action. Between twelve and twenty were the five children, they had, he and his wife. More exactly said: his wife, because Yanman told me that people in Tibet were not so fussy about fidelity. Not that they openly two-timed. They enjoyed passions discreetly. An ancient Tibetan saying goes: >The houses of my friends swarm with my children, my house swarms with the children of my friends.< Therefore in Yanman`s house lived besides the children, mother and official father also grandmother and official grandfather. The shack was fantastically loud. Five children! In Europe, things like this hardly existed any more. More than two children were also in Africa and Asia the exception. The GU namely had drastically shortened the basic

140

care for those, born after the first child. From the view of finances therefore, already the second child was a burden for the recipients of GU care. World wide, people were irritated because of this >injustice<. They spoke of a privilege of those who were better-off, namely those, who worked in the market economy.

Yanman didn´t know such problems. He had seventy-six goats, who gave him twenty litres of milk daily. He made from it three wheels of cheese, each one kilogram. Per wheel, he got $ 6 U.S. . Furthermore, he produced fruit schnaps and liqueur-wine, that he exchanged with the beekeeper for honey, with the shoemaker for shoes, actually for everything, he needed. GU, authorities and laws weren´t of interest to him, at all. Once, someone from the tax office visited him. „A nice fellow ", Yanman said, „he liked my liqueur-wine so much that he slept a whole day in front of the fire place. In his family, nobody was idle. Grandmother manufactured jackets and sweaters from leather and wool, grandfather grew tobacco, the children helped with the goats and in the vegetable garden. Yanman`s wife backed fritter bread by the stacking. Yanman`s family was well-off.

The house was clearly smaller than Michel`s. Half of the inhabitants slept in the big room with the fire place, in sleeping niches, that were built into the walls. The other half distributed itself upward, into small chambers. I slept on my air mattress, in a respectful distance from the fire place, because of the sparks of the glowing coal. For breakfast was served the usual salty butter-tea, that the Tibetians pound from black tea, butter and salt in wooden vats. Additionally Tsampa was given, barley grains, that Yanman`s wife toasted in a pan over the fire place. Carefully, I asked, whether there still existed something like „gurus " in the area. Yanman said, that this would be something for the elderly, and actually, ten years ago, grandfather had heard about a quack. He would have been living near Mount Everest. That was in my direction. With the parting, Yanman gave me a goatskin bag with fruit schnaps and some dried Dri meat. „There, where the wise live, it`s said to be cold, he said.

Three weeks later, I was in Golam, a town with a bus connection to the rest of the world. There was even a hotel, where I booked a bed and a bathroom for $ 10 US. The English magazines in the foyer were one year old. A stylish, western lady sat at the hotel bar. She nodded at me in solidarity, we were the only palefaces. I joined her over a beer. She told me that she had visited her father and now wanted to go back to England. No exciting story up to now. On my question, about how she had liked it in Tibet, I had to listen to the story of her horrible lodgings. „Try to imagine, three nights, where I had to sleep on straw in a pigsty." I was aghast and thought: „If you knew, where I had already slept. With her silk- and Cashmere- outfit the mouse really didn`t fit into a pigsty, at all. Discreetly I asked her why her father had offered her nothing better than a pigsty with straw, whereupon she resigningly considered: „He loves such things. He stepped out of civil life, although he was so successful. She told me the tragic history of her father: „He was a successful chemist. One of the best, nearly a Nobel contender, yes indeed. Then, he met this Eckehard in his club. A charlatan. He followed him all the way to Tibet. He simply left everything standing as it was. My mother and I, we didn`t understand the world any more." – „What kind of a charlatan is that guy?" – „A guru, a nutcase, someone, who believes, in being able to improve the world, by constantly sitting on some pillows." – „A guru?" – „So he is called, but in reality, he makes fun of everything." – „Oh yes ?" – „Yes, no matter, what I told him, he didn`t take me seriously, at all." – „And your father?" – „He is enslaved to him. He hasn`t got his own opinion anymore and he is always talking of louuuuuve." She sobbed heart-wrenchingly and I really felt sorry for her. To comfort her, I took her hand. There the whole frustration broke out of her, and I had the girl in my arms. She was

142

attractive and felt good. If I had known the course of the evening previously, I would have been able to save the 10 dollars for my room. Tanja Berninger was her name. At breakfast, she told me, where the charlatan had his cottage: „Twenty kilometers by taxi to the northwest, at the fork take a right, direction Tatschpur. At the entrance of the village, on the right side, goes up a small path into the mountains. There, you only can proceed on foot. Five kilometers on foot, can you imagine that! You need at least half a day for that. Then you`ll see two small stone houses on the left mountainside, and before that a few tents." – „Tents ?" – „Yes, some of his disciples live in tents. A dreadful gang. Are you really going to try to get my father out of there?" – „I`ll see, what I can do." She gave me her telephone number in London.

Two days later, I stood in front of the charlatan`s cottage. The house was the same as she had described it. House and stall built from natural stones, the heavy wooden door skillfully carved. Three pup tents stood in front of the house. No human being was to be seen. At the door, a brass bell hung with a long rope. I pulled at it and was surprised about the powerful sound, that echoed through the valley. A young woman with short shorn hair opened the door. „May I help you?" she asked in perfect English. „Is Mr. Eckehard at home?" – „A moment please."

Waiting in front of the door, the feeling of perfect absurdity came over me again. Now, here, in the Tibetean wilderness I rang at a stone cottage and asked for a man, whom I had never seen. What should I ask him? Then, Eckehard stood in front of me. The first impression is crucial, one says. This man seemed to me extremely harmless, anyway. His age was hard to tell. Anywhere between sixty and eighty could be possible. With his brilliant blue eyes he smiled at me well tempered: „What brings you here, stranger?" –„I met Mr. Berninger`s daughter in Golam." – „Ah, you want to meet Mr.

Berninger." – „No, actually I was curious about you." – „Well, then come in."

I came into a dark room where four people sat behind a curtain on small pillows and stared quietly in front of themselves at the ground. A few candles burned. Eckehard gave me a pillow and pointed to the floor. I tried, sitting like the others in the tailor seat. Eckehard whispered to me: „Breathe quietly and deeply. Nothing else. No thinking, only sitting." Then, he sat down on his pillow. I thought of the meditation with Zazo in Tokyo. Would somebody here also hit me from behind? I also thought of Michel and Celia. I was sure they were thinking at this moment of me. Suddenly, Eckehard spoke to us: „We permanently notice thoughts in us. Thoughts about us and others. Thoughts about yesterday and tomorrow. We are surprised at how difficult it is to be without such thoughts. In fact, things are so simple. We are sitting here at this moment and thinking only of our sitting and breathing." Then, it was quiet again. Why was I sitting here? Why should I think of nothing? Why were they not allowed to think about themselves or others? The Looni also meditated. Was meditation a method, to untrain autonomous thinkings? Something similar could not happen to me. Not at all with this Eckehard. In comparison to Zazo, this old male was harmless. Six supporters! Six! Ridiculous! Zazo had six million... . My knees and feet ached infernally. Why this inhuman seating position? The others didn't move. I unfolded my legs. The tailor-seat was not only uncomfortable, it was unbearable, in the end I wasn`t a tailor. Somebody banged a gong. All got up, bowed and left the room. I would not be able to run so quickly for the next ten minutes. I massaged my poor feet and Eckehard sat next to me. „So you are curious about me? How is it that I come to this honor?" –„I cannot say it exactly. It`s rather by intuition." – „Rather by intuition? What do you want from me intuitively?" I thought. Now to ramble about enlightenment would be embarrassing. Essentially I already had enough and toyed with the idea of taking a plane

144

quite soon back to Milano/Italy. My answer therefore was a bit snotty: „Honestly said, I don't know it either. –„Maybe not a bad position for a start", was his astonishing answer. „Starting position, for what?" –„For that, which one truely wants, or that, which one is truely, who knows?" His twaddel annoyed me. I tried to lead him away from his reserve: „Something one truely is? What truely is a person?" His answer was at least as snotty, as mine: „Nothing!" – „Nothing? What`s that supposed to mean?" – „Nothing, it means exactly that, namely nothing. There is nothing, you truely are or what separates you from others." · „Then I`m finally nothing more, than the chair there in the corner ?" –„If you really know that in the end, my friend, then it is like that." It was clear to me, that the old coot was a poor madman. I was nothing but a chair, in the end. I wanted to know, how far his mental derrangement went and asked: „and if we sit there in the dark, mute and quiet on small pillows, are we then trying to be chairs?" The attack was fresh. However, Eckehard was not to be moved from his serenity. With a friendly smile and a small bow, he praised me: „Nice, you certainly have been very attentive. We do exactly that. If we sit quietly, we can recognize ourselves in the chair." The old man slapped himself on the legs with laughter. I fluctuated between pity and the feeling of being ridiculed. Anyway, this man was not after recruiting new members. Was he really crazy? Would an „almost Nobel Contender" waste his time with a maniac? Had Mr. Berninger himself become crazy? There was something, about Eckehard, that awakened unpleasant memories in me. What was it? As he tapped me on the shoulder, cheeringly, I knew it: Zazo! Zazo tapped me on the shoulder the same way. And Zazo ridiculed me the same. Yes, that was it. I felt ridiculed. „We can play such mind games for hours", he said, „not, that it isn`t fun for me, but I wanted to go into the vegetable garden. Therefore, let me make a friendly suggestion: From a thousand questions, you can immediately ask five, then we`ll pause, okay?" – „That`s like in a fairy-tale", I joked, „five free questions." –„Well, come on, no inhibitions!"

I spontanuously decided in favor of the long-standing Sensity Test of the GU: „What do you believe, are the most important things in life ?" Again, he laughed. „How many important things would you like to hear about then? If I list five of them, your right to question is exhausted for today." – „If it`s like this, let's see: for the first: the two most important things." He poured salty butter tea into earthern tea bowls and handed one over to me. „You make things easy, dear ....." – „Ronda" · „O.K., Ronda, you make things easy for me. The most important >thing<, as you called it, is momentarily this wonderful tea for me. Isn`t it quite excellent?" I felt deceived about one answer and asked: „And the second most important thing?" – „I think, that`s the song of life, that this extremely gifted bird is singing outside momentarily." Now, as he said it, I also heard the bird. I hardly had time to get annoyed over this stupid answers, because he asked me: „What, do you believe, Ronda, surpasses the tea and the chant of the bird?" –„Now the idiot even turns the tables", I thought, however, the situation was altogether so absurd that it didn`t matter anymore. I had only the choice, of continuing the conversation on his conditions, or leaving the guy. I had come from Italy to meet a guru, and here I was joking around with one, at least with someone, that pretended to be one. I decided to become more serious: „More important than drinking tea and listening to birds could be having a harmonic relationship to one`s surroundings. To nature, to people, to oneself, to time, to death, to all of the elements." – „That may be", he said, „but, where does this harmony come from?" – „I thought, you could solve that riddle for me", I returned the ball to his court. „Oh, so you are looking for the solution of a riddle. A secret recipe for a harmonic life, so to speak. And the solution of the riddle consists of some kind of enlightenment, to find in the mountains, with a guru. You are, if one wants to say so, a romantic. A lovable quality, that has given us an enormous amount of wonderful music and enchanting poetry. I was amazed. So completely mad, this man didn`t seem to be, after all. „Believe me," Eckehard said,

„Enlightenment doesn`t exist. It doesn`t exist in the same way, as the deliverance through a harmonic life. If you ask me: The best you can do, is, to let go of any hope on such a glorious future. Life is as it is. There is no better life, not through enlightenment, not through a guru, not through meditation, nor a beautiful house, an ideal partner or a lot of money." What Eckehard gave out there, didn`t sound crazy at all. Just the opposite. He played down himself, and his importance as a guru. Zazo would do the opposite. But, if there didn`t exist any enlightenment and no deliverance through a guru, why were his followers sitting with him on small pillows and living in tents in front of his house? Eckehard observed me. He suspected what I thought. „Why do some friends sit here with me, you want to know? These people came for the same reasons as you, hoping to find a teacher or a spiritual leader in me. In fact I cannot be that, and I told them this again and again. But they don't believe me. He laughed severely. „No, seriously. I can be a companion only in the beginning. Maybe someone, who learned, how refreshing it is, to live exactly this life, and not the dream of a better, future life. However, that`s perhaps enough for today. If you want, we can talk tomorrow a bit more. You are anyway welcomed as a guest from the heart." He stood up and got me a wool blanket and a bowl with walnut fruits. „You can sleep on one of the sitting mats", he said. I explained to him that I was more at home in my tent. So, my tent became the fourth in front of his door.

I got to know the others: Ivonne, that had opened the door for me, came from Rome/Italy, Desire, a seventy year old woman from Switzerland, Jacques, a thirty-one year old Frenchman, and Mr. Berninger, Tanja`s nice father.

Zazo had made up his mind for some days, before he had Demian`s spy come to him. Of course, the man would not have come voluntarily, respectively, not without warning Demian. Therefore, Zazo had sent two of his bodyguards to

India, to collect the man smoothly and well packaged. The boys had flown with a glider to Calcutta and from there, camouflaged as tourists in the Himalayas, went with a rented cab to Golam. Not even three days later they collected Spencer, which was the man`s name. Shortly after, they delivered him to Zazo. Before Zazo spoke with him, he put him under a specially prepared mind-machine. After that, Spencer was convinced that Zazo embodied the good and Demian the bad. Willingly, he reported: „Ronda has pitched his tent at an old man`s, who in Tatschpur is called „the wizard". Four other people also live there". –„And what are they doing there?" – „Most of the time meditating. Otherwise collecting wood, planting vegetables and philosophizing about life." – „And what are they philosophizing about?" – „I could show you some records if you want." – „Do it. But take notice!Only for me! For Demian, you have only the usual information ". –„Go your way." One day later Spencer was already back in his hiding place on the opposite hillside.

It was still dark, five o'clock in the morning, when Jacques got me out of my sleeping bag. „Bon Jour, mon amis. If you want to meditate with us, you must get up now." I got up. There, we sat, without breakfast, with painful knees and feet, in the tailor seat. The session seemed to bring no end. Carefully, I unfolded my perished feet. The tailor seat was a torture seat. The gong came like a deliverance. The others bowed and exited. How could they just do that? Even Desire seemed, despite her seventy years, to have no problem with her joints. After the sitting came breakfast. In the building, that Tanja had called a „pigsty" , thick wooden planks were piled up against the wall, being put together on demand as seat benches and as a big table. At the front of the room was an oven, emitting a pleasant warmth. Desire baked fritter bread, that we ate warmly with Ghee, Nepalesean butter, and marmalade. A delicacy! Salty butter tea was served with it. Mr. Berninger wanted to know how I had met his daughter. I told him how very much she had looked forward to the civilized England. I told him nothing about her sorrow and our more intimate encounter.

In Eckehard`s group, everyone had his task. In the Shang, the community administration of Golam, there even existed a GU branch office, that was busy twice a month. There it was possible, to receive in return for a fortnightly cooperation at a dam project, coupons for one month. With the coupons, we could receive flour, sugar, rice and a few other elementary things. Ivonne, Eckehard, Jacques and Mr. Berninger went every second month to the dam. Eckehard said, if it would be up to him, Milarepa`s food would be completely sufficient, but he supposed, he could not expect the same thing from the others. Milarepa, an ascetic, who died centuries ago, had nourished himself exclusively on stinging nettles. In Eckehard`s opinion the GU was one of the best inventions of mankind for some thousand years. I didn`t mention the fact that I hadn`t been slightly involved in the formation of the GU. In Tibet, at that time, barley, wheat, corn, millet and potatoes, which meant the five treasures of the Tibeteans, belonged to the basic care of the GU. The God of pity, Chenresi, should have given the Tibeteans these five treasures, millennias ago. Eckehard actually now and then cut stinging nettles and Desire cooked >Milarepa`s soup< from them. She took care of the kitchen wholly, and didn`t want to divide this task with anyone else. The others looked after the vegetable garden. Ivonne wrote a book: „Over the interactions between man and woman" –she meant the mental interactions.

After breakfast, Eckehard joined me. „Hard-working, hard-working, having sat already so very early", he joked. The topic was an irritating one for me, because my feet still ached. I asked him whether Zazen is a practice for masochists. He was silent for a while and then said: „Maybe you sat too long at the beginning. It is not about feeling pain. Important is the Now of thoughts. If you want, I`ll give you a short lesson on sitting, later." Hesitantly, I stated in agreement. Cheering me up, Eckehard tapped me on the shoulder and went into the house. Desi, sitting nearby, was enthusiastic: „He likes you. So voluntarily, Eckehard usually doesn't offer help." – „Why? Is he normally such a grouch?" –„Grouch definitely not, but concerning support, he is stingy. He receives us only once a week for single conversations. Dokusan it`s called." – „Dokusan. What do you talk about at these Dokusans?" – „About oneself, about life, about everything. The best is, to ask him yourself. He just invited you to a Dokusan." She told me that Eckehard had a very regular routine. „After meditation and breakfast he goes into his room for two hours for the daily composing. With the spinet, he writes songs, that twice a year are picked up by a musical manager. People say that hits were among them, which have brought much money. Eckehard puts this money into the restoration of an old cloister, that was destroyed by the Chinese Communists a hundred years ago. Nobody knows, if he is ever going to settle in this cloister.

In the afternoon, I went to the Dokusan, meaning, I visited Eckehard in his room. The room was small. Just a bed, a chair, stools, a table, and the spinet fitted in there. It was cleaned up and bald, like in a monk`s cell. „Come in, young friend. Sit down there on the stool. I have made a nice cup of tea. We sat at the table and Eckehard was amazingly talkative: „You must not think that Zazen, which means our meditative sitting, has anything to do with torture. Some zen masters admittedly believe, that the overcomming of pain strengthens their zen, but I see things differently. Concerning our sitting, only the attention counts, nothing else, only attention. Artificial difficulties, pain during sitting and special incentives we don't need. Therefore, if you want to practice Zazen, begin slowly, don't strain yourself. Ten minutes are enough in the beginning. But we don't want to be hasty. You`ll probably first have to decide, if you want to follow the Zazen way at all." – „Exactly! What should the sitting be good for?

150

What does attention mean?" – „With the sitting you have the most stable, awake position, that a human being can have. Because stable and awake you have to be, if you want to be attentive for the moment, which means during breathing and sitting. If your thoughts digress, and that happens again and again, just watch this digressing and get back with your thoughts to breathing and sitting, unremittingly, again and again. That is the whole practice." So much babbling about sitting appeared a bit strange to me. I asked: „why so much jibbering about such a simple matter? Sitting is supposed to be the most passive and boring thing." · „It`s not about sitting", he said, „it`s about attention. You should learn, to concentrate on the Now. If I were to explain all the advantages to you, you would think while sitting all the time of my words, and that would deflect you even more." – „Too much to consider" – „Truly. We have no motive during our sitting. Zazen knows no motives, no dreams, no ideals, no goals." He showed me the odious tailor seat. „Three solid points you have on the earth: the two knees and the fanny. (Beginners extend the fanny over a pillow.) You cross your feet over your thighs, for beginners, one foot suffices on one thigh. Do you notice how solidly you`re sitting?" I noticed how uncomfortably I sat. Eckehard had the opinion, that I had enough declarations for the beginning, and wanted to finish the Dokusan, however I wanted to know what the attention was all about. Finally, he let himself mollify: „Attention influences all your activities. The contemplation of things, people, animals, plants, stones, and so on essentially only need one thing: Attention, or in other words: absolute awakeness. Only if you are awake, you have a chance, to see things, how they really are. Only then can you recognize your real self and see your soul mirrored in all existences. But now we have philosophized enough." With that, my first Dokusan was finished.

It was certain for me that Eckehard was no charlatan. Perhaps he really was a guru, I would work it out.

From then on, I always sat for only ten minutes, and was surprised, how frequently my thoughts could digress in such a short time. I was annoyed about my lack of concentration. In the evening it became quickly cool so we crawled early into our warm sleeping bags. The early sleeping also had its sense, because we got up again at five o`clock in the morning. Desire, Ivonne, Jacques and I slept in the tents. Mr. Berninger was accommodated in the „pigsty".

After some days, I wanted to know, which helpful task I could take care of, whereupon Eckehard said, he knew something nice for me. After composing, he wanted to show it to me. About lunchtime, it started then. „Take with you some fritter bread", he said, „we have to walk a bit." We went up the gravel-way, towards the summits. In neck breaking speed, the old man climbed over stony slopes and gargling mountain brooks. I could hardly keep up. Finally, we reached a tree-nursery. „Here you can help me plant pines and firs", he said. I was able to breathe again only five minutes later. „Where did you get such a condition from?" I asked him. He ignored the question and showed me, how I could bring from a nearby brook, water into the tree-nursery. „Later the roots will pull the water alone", he said, which led me to the comparison: „You help trees in the same way, as people." His answer was stunning: „Exactly the opposite. I have to endanger your livelihood." – „What? Why that?" – „You have too much of it. One must dry you, like little babies." He laughed loudly, and made me curious once again: „What do you mean by that?" – „What the water is for the trees, is the mind to you", he said. And because I looked at him half pityingly, half blankly, he complied by adding: „The mind makes you strong. You arrange the world with it and pack everything in boxes. One day then you notice, that you have packed yourself in the box. Then you come to me and ask me about the meaning of your cages. What remains for me, than draining the sources of your complaint, your superior mind?"

· „And are we better off without our minds?" · „With the mind your ego controls the world, better said, your small ego, completely following the motto,: >sure is sure< and: >better no surprises<. You admittedly become in fact even bigger material by that, but mentally smaller." – „And when we`ve lost the mind, do we land in the nut house?" Eckehard received a fit of laughter. „You won`t find here far and wide a nut house. We are here not in New York or Paris." – „But a life without a mind? What remains then? This time, Eckehard seemed to have to die of a far more vehement fit of laughter: „Nothing at all !", he finally came out with, „absolutely nothing at all ". At this moment it was clear to me that this man already had lost a little bit too much of his mind. I asked him, how he wanted to attempt the stealing of our minds, and he said: „The mind is the slave of the will. At the moment, you have learned to look at life without wishes, the mind is unemployed." His thoughts were not quite off the mark. Maybe, they even met a deeper sense, but honestly said, I still considered him an unworldly nutcase. From pure politeness, I continued talking to him: „To look at life without wishes what does that mean?" – „O.K.", Eckehard said, „you are already trying again, to question me, while words cannot really help you. Nevertheless, I`ll try to explain: „With Zazen you`re training the Now. Within the Now there exist no wishes. The Now can only be now. If you are now, you see people and things as they are without your wishes. If you see people and things without your wishes, you see their true self. As long, however, as you stumble around with your small ego in the dead end street of your wishes, you cannot be Now, cannot see people and things as they really are. The mind, that is steered by wishes, dissolves in the Now to nothing. This nothingness is the truth, that you might call enlightenment. And what I´ve told you now, my dear friend, are words, from which you can know nothing about. For such knowledge you have no other choice but sitting. He laughed and tapped me on the shoulder again. I had understood a lot. The sitting, would turn off the wishes, the wishes, that manifested themselves during sitting in a thousand distractions. Eckehard supplemented: „the bad thing about words is that they are born from wishes, and bear wishes. If you were to try, on the basis of my words to be especially weak willed, particularly mind killing, you would already have fallen into the trap of wishes again. There is really no other solution, than the pure Now, the unintentional sitting."

Zazo listened to these words several times and was surprised about himself. He had never taken hermits and starry-eyed idealists seriously. In this case he knew, however, that Eckehard owned a knowledge, that had until now been hidden from him. His obligatory mockery got stuck in his throat. Instead of that, he became curious. As a precaution, he checked, just as he did every day, his own mood: had he turned into a softie through Ronda`s paralyser shock? No! He knew himself to be powerful and critical. There was nothing soft, at all. He was curious about how Ronda`s experiment would continue. Spontaneously, he decided to accompany it parallelly, and to practise sitting by himself.

Some evenings later, I was sitting despite all pains already for twenty minutes, when Eckehard held one of his short addresses: „You would like to know, where to go. You want the good things, and you want to make them repeatable. Both however, knowing, what is good, and making the good repeatable, you can only realize, if you have order and control over things. And because this is like that, you are even during the sitting far away from the truth. You sit fat and slumped in the middle of your wishes, in the middle of your small ego. Like this, you`ll never make it! You must kill your small ego! No wishes! No goals! Also not concerning sitting. The small ego is worse than a chameleon. It camouflages itself perfectly, and should you nevertheless catch it, it changes itself in the moment of its death into a proud horse on which you, erectedly sitting, gallop through the prairie of your own high-handedness. There is nothing about which you can be

154

proud of. Not at all of the death of the small ego. Nothing remains besides the sitting."

Although I understood the sense of the words, they however, remained strange to me and not very realistic. Zazo felt the same.

Then, the ten-day working time came to the dam. From Golam, we drove with approximately twenty other people per bus to the neighbouring valley. Dam and hydraulic power works were built there. On a hanging scaffold we plastered with pails and spades the dam's walls. We worked from 8 o'clock in the morning to 13 o'clock. Then, the usual GU-lunch was served: vegetarian meat with potatoes, soy-sauce and rice. Out of big mugs, salty butter-tea was poured. Work continued from 15 to 18 o'clock. Eckehard insisted on sitting every morning, also during that working period from 6 to 7 o'clock and in the evening from 20 to 21 o'clock. He was also of the opinion that it would not harm us to work more than only these two weeks. I was glad to move, after these fourteen days, ditches in my tree-nursery again. To see the little trees growing brought me more joy, than plastering for days.

One evening, I was passing Eckehard's windows when a furious shouting took place. As it turned out, Eckehard yelled at the poor Jacques during the Dokusan. I was shocked. I wouldn´t have believed Eckehard capable of such brutality. I asked Desire, and she declared to me, that some Zen masters even beat their students with the stick. She said: „It's been told about students, who became suddenly awake through a powerful blow, which means having become enlightened by that. He also scared me once, without palpitation of course, but it hasn´t helped me." When Jacques came from the Dokusan, I asked him whether the screaming had been of use to him. He just indicated no.

One day, I suggested holding two goats to produce goat cheese. I told them about Yanman. Everybody, of course wanted delicious goat cheese. From branches, I built a stable woodshed. For two goats and rennin, I spent forty dollars. After that, I had on my back, two more hours of work each day: seeking feed, milking, pressing cheese and drying. I mixed herbs into the cheese and became a recognized cheese specialist.

The death of the small ego dominated Eckehard`s philosophy. He was content with nothing. I was not sure, if I was making a big mistake following him. Didn`t the Looni follow the same principle? >death to the individual, asocial ego<? Wasn`t that the same, as >death to the small ego<? Why should it be good to mutilate oneself? What was so bad about individual wishes and ideas?

With the next Dokusan, I asked Eckehard very directly: „Why should I kill my wishes? What is actually so bad about individuality?" – „Oh, I don`t think you understood me correctly", he said, „with the death of the small ego, it is not about giving up oneself. Just the opposite. What remains after the death of the small ego, corresponds absolutely to you, it is you, absolutely individually. We also call it the >true self< that you`ll find there. Nobody, that practices Zen, prescribes himself to somebody else or a foreign matter. We always are within ourselves, strong individuals. But it has to be said that not everybody is suitable for the Zen way. To whom pleasure, power or money are the most important things in life, he is neither capable nor willing to follow the Zen way."

The days passed, and their course became ever more monotonous. That basic melancholy mood widened itself again in me. I lacked concrete life contents. I had always been an activist, anarchist and street-fighter, family father, GU idealist and now? Goat shepherd and gardener? Sitting on the shelf? More monotonous, things couldn`t get. Doggedly I tried to kill the small ego. I sat and sat, day after day and tried to kill thoughts and wishes of the future and the past. Finally, I asked Eckehard in the Dokusan: „doesn't it go against nature, if I always just sit and kill senses?" I was amazed at my own words: „Kill senses...." Good Heavens, I had turned from a meaning creator to a meaning killer. Yes. I tried to kill meanings. And lost by doing so, all happiness and enthusiasm for the beauty of life. „Isn`t that against nature?", I asked Eckehard. –„Dear Ronda, it is not about destroying the value of things. Just the opposite. At the moment, when things aren`t pressured by your wishes any more, they come to validity in their true value. We don't try with the Zazen to take content out of things but, to free them from our small mental goals and one-sided interests." – „Do you want to say, that things lose their value, as soon as we give them a value?" –„You can say it like that. We search continuously for benefits and stain our surroundings in this way of seeing things. We classify people and things by their usefulness, and therefore haven`t got the slightest notion, of how they really are. Take death for example. We fear it because it brings us no benefit. It finishes our search for benefits, therefore we fear it. The fact is, that death is highly useful for mankind and the whole globe. But such advantages don't interest the small ego. Only the personal benefits interest the small ego. Because of this primitive way of seeing things, our world turns into a puppet`s theater."

Thoughtfully, Zazo listened to these words.

One day, I discussed with Jacques about that miserable small ego. He had his own idea on the matter: „The opposite of the small ego is the big ego. Do you know, what the big ego is?" I didn't know it. His answer was plausible: " If you watch yourself from above, you are in the big ego. The human being is the only creature, who can reflect upon itself. We can see ourselves amid our actions from above, we can laugh about ourselves. No animal can do that. And at the moment, we are doing so, we are standing above all things, and the small ego has lost. I laugh about myself quite often. It`s refreshing and defeats the small ego vehemently. When I`m back in France, I`ll open my own Zen Order. There, we`ll practice the view from above." I asked Jacques, what Eckehard thinks of his idea, but Jaques just indicated no: „He has his own ideas." I was dealing with the idea of the big ego for days. Actually, I succeeded in looking at myself from above, regularly during my actions. One day, I asked Eckehard about this matter. „The idea of self-reflection is quite nice", he said. „There are people that reflect themselves even into their dreams and in doing so, catapult themselves onto higher spheres. We, practicing Zazen pursue something else. Our goal for centuries has been called >true self<, we`ve already talked about it. The true self has a more complete meaning than the >big ego<. We see ourselves not only from above but also after the death of our small ego, our true self sees things and people as they really are. With the big ego you delight yourself with great feelings, seeing yourself from above. I would say, exactly at the moment, when you`re enjoying this great performance, you`re sitting with your big ass right in the middle of the small ego. Therefore forget about the big ego. Kill it in the same way, as the small ego." I was disappointed. Once again I was left hanging. This Eckehard ruined everything. I was completely bitter. „Nothing remains", I grumbled, and Eckehard nodded: „There is no hope."

Zazo smiled hearing these words.

After more than seven months (seven long months), my sitting took another quality. Pain lost its dominance. Instead of that something grew like contentment. It had turned into casualness to sit twice daily, and when I sat, my thoughts calmed down. Quietness and some nice vibrations originated. Distractions became ever rarer. In everyday life, my actions became more serene and concentrated. I had a feeling of increasing clarity. In the Dokusan, Eckehard admonished me, not to hold on to these great feelings. „Beat them dead ", he said. Sometimes, I hated him.

One day, he asked me, if I felt like working with a Koan. I told him about Michel's Koan >Why, couldn't the cow's tail pass through the fence?<. He knew it and laughed: „Well, all right, if you already know that, what about this one: >What is Mu?<" I was puzzled: „What? That was it? >What is Mu?< That was even more stupid, than the story with the cow." Eckehard told me that this Koan had already, a thousand years ago brought Zen students to desperation. But thousands of Zen students also would have found through >Mu< the truth. „Concentrate on >Mu< as strongly as you can. Whenever your mind wants to think about something else but >Mu<, lead it back to >Mu<. >Mu< and once again >Mu< should be your life. If you have become one with >Mu<, you will know the answer."

The time, that followed, was brutal. I took the goats up the hillside and thought: „Mu! Mu makes the cow." I made cheese and thought: „Mu, in all things? In the cheese? Mu, only a saying? Mu, Mu !" I worked on the dam and thought: „Mu, a word without meaning? What is Mu ?" I sat at the Zazen and concentrated on Mu. To be one with Mu! How could it be possible, to become one with Mu? Was Mu a symbol? Was it the same as >nothingness<? If it was like that, I could think with the same emphasis: „Nothingness, nothingness, nothingness." Should my mind finally be killed with Mu? The deathblow for arranging thoughts through the concentration on a stupid word?

Weeks and months passed, and I could not solve the Mu riddle. In the Dokusans Eckehard encouraged me again and again: „Think Mu! Be Mu! Find Mu! Don't give up! Several times I wanted to fling down the idiocy, he didn't admit it.

I tried to satisfy Eckehard with many various attempts at an explanation: „Mu is a symbol. For the insignificance of words and human values, for the size of the cosmos and the minuteness of the human being. Eckehard characterized some attempts at an explanation as interesting, others he qualified as flat. Nevertheless, with this answer or that answer I still hadn't found Mu, at all. He said: „You must eat and drink Mu, Mu should come into your stomach and your stomach should be Mu. Everything is Mu. Concentrate on Mu !"

One day, I was completely fed up. „Shit Mu", I complained in the Dokusan. Eckehard responded surprisingly: „I think, too, you have quarreled around enough with this glowing iron. No rallying calls, no encouragement anymore. „Maybe it would be good, if you make a pause for some time. Go back to Europe or hike a bit through the mountains." His indifferent reaction didn't please me, at all. Had I failed in his eyes? Had he given up on me? I said, I would think about it and frustrated left his room. As a result, the more intensively I plunged into >Mu<. In this time, I had dreams of extensive love affairs with beautiful women. Not only the mind, but also instincts and urges had a voice.

Zazo accompanied Ronda during the Mu experiment. Just like Ronda, he tried for months, to find Mu and to think Mu. Of course he didn't have as much time as Ronda, but he knew Ronda's frustration. This Mu was extremely unpleasant, especially, if it was taken seriously.

After the last frustrating Dokusan, I decided, to keep away from Dokusans for the following weeks. With Mu, the whole talking didn't make any sense, anyway. With Mu I stayed. There were only two possibilities: either I gave up and drove back to Europe, or I continued with this crazy Mu. I didn't give up, and Eckehard once again had successfully goaded my ambitions with his suggestion of leaving Mu.

160

Unconditionally, I plunged into Mu. Everything became Mu, for long weeks. In this most vehement Mu phase, Eckehard asked me one day to pick up the coupons in Golam and to bring some bags of flour and rice. For such transportation purposes, we used Desire`s trolley, strong Swiss high-class workmanship. So I stood, with the trolley in hand, in Golam`s streets and tried to think Mu. I noticed all these bustling people. They hastened through the streets as if time ran away from them. Time, it was Mu for me. Being amazed I observed how seriously people regarded their doings. I could remember having been the same in earlier times, now all the rushing was completely strange to me. Like ants, they seemed to me, ants, in a short ant life. We humans were tiny, in comparison to the universe and God's timeless existence.

I reported my experience to Eckehard, and he complained severely: „Don't merely think, that you are better or more clever than any fruit salesclerk in Golam. Only because you lazily sit on your rear, twice a day and hunt Mu, it doesn`t make you a better human being. Consider, Ronda, the urge for recognition is a typical chain of the small ego. Don't stray from the way, remain with Mu.

Zazo listened to the wording of this Dokusan three times.

In the following weeks, I saw Mu in each idea, each feeling and each action. I thought Mu and I dreamed Mu. I sensed as if I was shortly about to lose my mind. It didn`t frighten me because the loss was also only Mu. With this bewildered spirit, Eckehard sent me, a few weeks later, to Golam again, to get food. There, I stood, confused like never before, in this buzzing city and thought: „Mu", as I suddenly understood. An unruly laughter came over me. A laughter, in which everything was contained, the important and unimportant, the contrasts and contradictions, the big and the small, the nothingness, the everything, the Mu. The laughter freed me from my search for truth, the search for enlightenment and the search for myself. There, I stood by a white-washed wall and laughed out of the deepest depth. Some passers-by bowed, one never knows whether a nut or a wiseman is standing in front of oneself. Most people didn`t take any notice of me. My mood became easy, because there was nothing to lose and nothing to gain any more. I recognized: „Actually, all is one! Contradictions and contrasts exist only at the surface. Importances come and go, as the circles of atoms in the endless universe. What holds everything together, is boundless love. For me, it was the Creator`s love. Each planet, each creature, each plant, each stone was a child of his soul, his love. I went through the streets and knew all the people, knew the animals, the plants and myself. I was very grateful, to be able to live this life.

As I went back, Eckehard came towards me. He looked at me and embraced me: „Congratulation from the heart, you have done it. I knew that the city would help you. Personally, he made a mug of tea. Desiree was astonished, and Eckehard explained to her: „Our friend Ronda has overstepped the threshold to truth. Desi was enthusiastic. She embraced and kissed me. Outdoors in the garden we sat on wood pieces and enjoyed our tea. Eckehard advised me to continue the regular sitting, because „also the enlightenment evaporates, if you don't care for it. But from now on you can go your way alone. You don`t need me anymore. That sounded like a farewell, and it was also meant like that. „Not that I want to throw you out, but you`ll find your place somewhere else. Stay here as long as you want. Someday you`ll sense that the time has come to leave. We both did not suspect that this would happen very soon.

The others were excited. They bombarded me with questions: „How did you manage that? What did you do? How did you feel?" I could essentially give no answers, because my experiences, were beyond all words. I told them that presumably the work with the Koan had brought the breakthrough. Jacques started the very same day to think about Mu.

During the next days, I showed Ivonne how to handle the goats and make cheese. She thought, she would stay there the longest of all, furthermore she loved goat cheese more than anything else. After the cheese production was transfered into Ivonne`s hands, I had two hours more time, a day. I used this time for walking in the nearby surroundings. With spring came dreamy beautiful fields of flowers on the hills. Crystal clear streams came from the melting snow, and over me a pair of bald-eagles screwed themelves higher and higher. Amid the idyll suddenly something flashed on the opposite mountainside. It was immediately clear to me that the flash had no natural origin. It came from metal or a mirror. There was no way but nevertheless somebody was there. I didn't betray the observation and strolled back to the house. In the protection of darkness, I wanted to check what this reflection was all about. I didn`t mention the incident to the others, they weren`t created for such actions. As they went to the sitting, I sneaked up the mountain. From above I approached the position, and only five meters before it, I heard a man muttering. I was totally astonished when Eckehard`s voice quacked from a headphone. The man monitored us! Step by step I went nearer and finally stood one meter behind the man. He hid there, behind a perfect camouflaged network, sleeping tent and high-tech devices. Offhandly I grasped him. The perfect stranglehold from my youth`s days, I still had not forgotten. The poor fellow was so scared, that he pissed in his pants. I asked him, what he was doing there, but he gave no answer. I grabbed him more solidly and asked once again. He was silent. I strangled him and let him wriggle like a fish in the air. „Last chance ", I said, „if you don't speak now, you`ll never speak again. He was silent. I dragged him down the hillside to the others. The crashing stones were so loud that the others interrupted their sitting and waited for us in front of the house. I explained to them that the guy was monitoring us. They asked him: „Why?" He was silent. Eckehard led us into the house. There, he placed himself in front of the guy and looked him into the eyes: „We know that you are a good man. Therefore, don't make things more difficult, than it is necessary. Who sent you?" Eckehard's presence was more unpleasant to the guy than my stranglehold. He swallowed, sweat and finally collapsed within himself. „Demian ", he uttered. „Who is Demian ?", Eckehard wanted to know, I explained it to them. „And now ?" Desire asked, „this Demian will expect his report. If it doesn't come, he'll worry about his man." We agreed to let the man run unconditionally, everything else would lead to even more complications.

Spencer had been cool despite the awkward situation. He was a pro, and Zazo's mind-machine had worked well. He purposely had given Demian's name and not Zazo's. Back in his shelter, first of all he radioed Zazo: „Sir, they have discovered me. I told them that I'm working for Demian." – „Another name didn't occurre to you? –„Everything seemed little believable to me. The guys are clever." – „All right. Then inform Demian now and after that, give a copy of this conversation to me. Spencer radioed Demian: „Boss, they have discovered me. We've been made." – „Do they know, that I sent you? –„I had no chance, boss, they would have bumped me off." – „You idiot, you stupid idiot, drive immediately to Calcutta, near the airport is the Firna Hotel. We'll pick you up there." Demian hung up and Spencer, gave a copy of the conversation to Zazo. „You are not going to drive to the Firna Hotel. Take the next plane to Bombay. There, we'll meet in the Looni guest-house", was Zazo's order.

Demian feverishly thought: Now Ronda knew that he had shadowed him. Of course he would suspect that Zazo was behind the supervision. Sooner or later he would complain to Zazo. Maybe, he would even get a new paralyser. Nobody knows about that ! Anyway, there was a high degree of possibility, that Zazo would find out about the matter through Ronda. If that were to happen, his succession as a Looni boss would definitely fail. He could really imagine Zazo`s reaction. He forever and ever would get into Zazo`s bad books. There was only one solution. Everyone, that knew about the whole incident, had to vanish, for good, all of them: Ronda, his prayer brothers and sisters and Spencer. All that had to happen immediately and silently. He called his special commando for ultimate cases.

Zazo thought. Demian ordered his special commando into the cellar, safe from interception, for which his plan was clear. He wanted to get rid of Spencer and Ronda, maybe also the remaining Zen followers. Should he prevent the action? As long as Demian sat in the cellar, he could not reach him by radio. For a counter-action, he had to activate a glider and at least two of his specialists. The expenses would be enormous, and would possibly cause a battle between two Looni gliders. If something like that were to become known, a loss of image would be inevitable. Furthermore he had not forgotten that Ronda, this idiot, had shot him with the paralyser. All that went against an intervention. On the other hand, he had grown fond of Ronda in the last months. The common Zen practices, he had, despite all distance, created a certain mental connection. Above all, Demian`s brutality nauseated him. He adjudicated, against all reason to send forward, a protection commando.

Demian made available his private glider to the two killers. He, himself sat down in the cellar and didn´t foresee that Zazo`s protection troop had started half an hour later. He didn`t foresee either that Zazo, thousands of kilometers away from him, tried to reach him with all methods.

VII. Chapter   ·Ronda`s Return ·

Eckehard called Ronda. „I don`t know, what you`ve done in your previous life, and I don't want to know either. But that you are shadowed in this wilderness, is of no good meaning. I also can feel that other things will follow, bad ones. You should take yourself to a safe place." –„Where to?" – „Go up to my cloister, a three day`s walk from here. Passing through Tatschpur, follow the direction north. After two kilometers, you`ll find a footpath, in a wide valley, going along the river on the right side. Follow this way for approximately eighty kilometers, then you`ll see the half completed cloister on the left side in the mountains. I thanked him for his help and packed up my things. Ten minutes later, I said goodbye to the others. They were confused. The infinite silence, that had characterized Eckehard`s valley for years, was gone from me within a few hours.

With the consciousness, of serenity within myself and within all other things, independently of what ever happened, I cheerfully went through Tatschpur. Although I didn`t know anybody there, some people greeted me. Suddenly the strange sounds of a glider were heard. I knew, they were comming to look for me. I also knew, they would fly to Eckehard`s and would question him. In the first moment, I had worries about my friends. However, the more I thought about the situation, the more I was sure that Eckehard would have a hold on the situation.

Demian`s people didn't land at the turn-off to Eckehard`s cottage, just before Tatschpur, as Spencer had proposed. They flew directly into the valley, in accordance with Demian`s instructions. First priority was for Ronda to be taken care of, as quickly as possibly. They landed ten meters in front of Eckehard`s cottage. Eckehard had sent the others to pick water up at the river. He approached the two killers

166

and called out: „Are you Ronda`s friends? Do you want to visit Ronda?" The two looked at each other and nodded kindly: „Yes, where is he?" – „He asked me to tell you, that he..." At that moment, Desire came up the hillside with a bucket. Eckehard hesitated and shouted to Desire: „Bring the water into the house, Desire." The two guys were pros. „I`ll ask the old bat, and you this winner, here", said one of them to the other and went after Desi into the house. Eckehard had no choice, but to report that Ronda had gone to the old cloister. He described how the cloister was to be found.

It was easier for Zazo`s people to find the cloister. They just needed to follow the induction tracks of the other glider. On their monitor, they saw the glider landing for a second time. „In two minutes we got them", they reported to Zazo. Precisely two minutes later they hovered over the other glider and asked Zazo: „We got them, Sir. Should we dismantle the crate? Zazo`s instruction was short: „One of you go out to protect Ronda. The other one remains over the glider and make sure that it makes no stupid moves.

Demian had made himself comfortable in the cellar. At the door of his cellar was shining: >Total Security<. That meant: Absolutely no disturbances! The servants, above in the house, knew that he was not to be spoken to, by anyone.Not even by Zazo, who had been calling constantly for one hour and who became ever more furious. He got the same answer, as all the other callers,: „Demian is out of the house, he`ll presumably be back quite soon. In fact they knew that Zazo was Demian`s boss. But Demian`s instructions were clear-cut: >Total Security< that means: Nobody, and absolutely nobody, was allowed to disturb him. In this respect, Demian was rigorous. Demian therefore sat, cut off in the cellar and wanted to delightfully grant himself, live, in 3-D, via satelite, Ronda`s showdown. He had just witnessed how his people had taken care of the hermit nutcase and a Zen old bat. He gave them the order, to let them both live. These people would inform nobody, and maybe later he might still need them. His glider took off, direction >old cloister<. In high spirits, he allowed a fruit salad to come. „With lots of pineapples", he said, and his housekeeper, annoyed from Zazo`s threats, dared the hint: „Sorry, Sir, but Zazo is sorely trying to reach you." –„What does he want?" – „No idea, Sir ." – „Let him call me later again." – „May I connect him with you next time?" – „Only by exception."

Zazo had permanent contact to the protection commando. They had the other glider under control. Ronda, was nowhere to be seen, neither infrared- nor induction- sensors could locate a third organic life form. „There are only these two people from Demian", they reported to Zazo. „Luckily, the whole show takes place in this solitary hilly country", he thought and tried for the last time, to reach Demian. The housekeeper said: „Just arrived. I`ll put you through." – The laser-projectors had not stabilized Demian`s picture yet, when Zazo was already yelling at him: „You call back your boys immediately from Tibet, my friend, otherwise I`ll make goulash out of you still today. Demian paled. He heard over Zazo`s line: „Demian`s gorillas are behaving quietly, Sir. Should we do them in? Simultaneously, his people called him: „Boss, a glider is above us. A Looni glider!" –„Stay quiet. No actions", he said. This way, Eckehard`s cloister was protected from becoming rubble and ashes again. The personnel of the two gliders received the order to fly back. Demian stood in front of Zazo three hours later.

I heard the glider starting again. It flew northbound, which meant to the old cloister. I continued in the direction of the cloister when a second glider flew over me. That made things even more strange. Two gliders because of me? A little bit exaggerated. There must be other things happening. When a short time later, both gliders, quickly gaining altitude, flew over me on their way back, I knew that the scare was over. I decided to go back to Eckehard. Because I was anxious about, what had happened with Eckehard, I made big steps. So, I only needed half the time for my way back. Round about midnight, I put up my tent just before Tatschpur. On the following day, at noon, I reached Eckehard`s. They told me that two musclemen had kindly asked about me. We couldn`t make any sense out of the strange events of the last days. What was so special about me, that they shadowed and sent gliders after me? Understandably, the others now wanted to hear the complete story. Shortly after, I explained everything to them, just as I have summarized it here, in this book. Eckehard finally hit the nail on the head: „Your fight with Zazo indeed was a long time ago, but these people think in long-terms. Maybe, they still have respect for you? Maybe they anticipate that you`ll become important to them, once again? Maybe, it`s your future? The second glider seemed to have called back the first one, maybe there was a dispute between Zazo and Demian? I think, it wouldn`t be the worst thing if you were to contact Zazo.“

„Boss, I only acted out of care. I was afraid, he might become dangerous to you once again.“ Demian fought despaired. „Only because of this I still had him shadowed. The expenses were modest." – „And why did you send the glider yesterday?“ – „Just a panic action, after Spencer was exposed.“ – „Panic with the possible result of death?" Demian was quiet. Because Zazo didn`t submit to say something, Demian finally continued: „Good heavens, boss, after all, this idiot has shot you down. Even if he had been wasted, it wouldn`t have destroyed the world.“ – „Exactly, Demian, now we come a bit closer to the truth. You are cold as artificial ice. My welfare doesn't touch your heart, because you haven`t got one. If it were up to you, you would prefer, becoming the boss of the Looni, better today than tomorrow, and putting me as a long term patient in the nut house. It´s just your bad luck, that I`m too strong for you.“ – „Boss, that is not true. I`ve always ..." – „Be quiet! Ronda was a risk for you because he was an old friend from my youth, one of the few people,

169

that could emotionally approach me. You wanted to control exactly this risk. And if you were seriously to deny that, I would still today put you under a brain-check machine." Demian knew that Zazo wasn't joking. He wanted to spare himself from the brain-check machine. „O.K., boss, you won. And now?" – „Now you pack your things and look for a new job." –„Boss, you cannot do that, because of this fool..." – „It is not because of this fool. It is because of your own foolishness; this, we Looni cannot afford any longer. At most for one month you can still live here in the guest-house, then you must find your own housing. You will not enter your old house ever again. I myself, will sort out, what belongs to you. With that, Demian was dismissed. He couldn`t believe it. He had reckoned with some things, but what happened exceeded his imagination. He wasn`t to be a Looni any more? Zazo actually was out of his mind. Such an affront he would never pocket.

The next day, I was in Tatschpur again, this time for telephoning. Even more people, than the day before, greeted me. I was already known. I spent twelve of my last $ 23 U.S. to receive Zazo over an ancient sound picture line. „Ronda, I`m sorry, because of all the hassle", he said, before I had time to speak myself. „What is all that nonsense about? Would you be so kind to explain it to me?" – „Well of course. Should I pick you up?" – „You can drop in, whenever you want." – „Okay, in two days, I am with you." When, in the evening, I told Eckehard about the telephone call, he said oracularly: „He said, he would pick you up? I suppose the new world burdens you a heavy responsibility." In retrospective it is clear to me, that Eckehard constantly carried inside of himself the spring of knowing, that I had seen lightening up briefly, laughing at the whitewash wall. Because of that, he saw future developments with clarity and intuition. At that moment I was kept from such an understanding. Too many new things confused me.

Zazo`s glider landed directly in front of Eckehard`s house. I was not badly amazed, when the great Zazo bowed to Eckehard and said: „I was very much looking forward to this meeting." It seemed as if Eckehard liked Zazo, he invited him to a „nice cup of tea". On the wooden planks in the pigsty Zazo explained over a salty butter-tea: „Demian shadowed you from jealousy. Our youth friendship was a thorn in his side. By luck, I found out about it, early enough. So, it happened that he shadowed you and I shadowed him. Because of this I had the pleasure of your Dokusans for some months. An inspiration of first quality. I am sorry, if I invaded your privacy by this. · „There is no privacy within the Dokusans", Eckehard said and he asked Zazo: „was all that listening of good use to you, in the end?" – „Yes, very much. It put my development further, of course not as far, as my friend Ronda." He told us that he had sat parallel to us for half a year. „Of course, in respect to the time difference I sat at other times, but I sat for one hour a day. To resolve that >Mu< Koan, I only tried half-heartedly, the daily business is just too busy for it.

Zazo refused Eckehard`s invitation for an overnight stay in the pigsty. He wanted to go back as quickly as possible. Urgent decisions were to be taken. Quite naturally he invited me to his house in San Francisco, and quite naturally I accepted his invitation. I sensed that my life led into this direction. So the farewell to Eckehard and the others came unexpectedly early. Eckehard looked into my eyes. „You`ll make it", he said and embraced me. I didn't know whether I would ever see him again. From the others, only Jacques visited me once, later on. As we climbed into the glider, Eckehard shouted: „Don't forget the sitting! It sounded as if he meant it for the both of us.

Flying back with me to San Francisco was for Zazo: „as symbolically matching, as always. There, where our discourse began, we can find a second cycle", he said.

San Francisco! The bad experiences of this city had lost their sting. I came back as someone, who rested within himself. Not being like in former times, full of enthusiasm and ambition, blind of energy. No. Instead of ambition and fame, had stepped in the certainty, never wanting to be anybody`s governor for nothing anymore. Instead of enthusiasm and activism flowed a deep understanding of life inside of me. Because of this, bad memories were of no importance anymore. The symbolism, that Zazo had talked about, had its positive aspects. In particular, I felt his willingness to a new personal approach. I didn't speculate over possible consequences of such a new start. The goals of the GU mastered me no longer. Nevertheless, I wanted to give Zazo and myself the chance for a new discussion of life. Just because of that, I travelled with him. During the three-hour flight across the beautiful Pacific world, I discovered that Zazo was actually trying to be more open. Cynicism and irony, his continuous companions from the past, had given way to the attempt of understanding the world as it really was. If he was looking for a meeting with me on this basis, I would be pleased to assist him. After all, he had practiced Zazen with us, even though from a distance. Apart from that, I didn`t have any other plans, concerning my future residence. I knew that, no matter, where I was, I would be one with the divine creation. Inescapablly, I would be at the right place at the right time.

Demian didn't enter the guest-house. In fact he knew, that Zazo had him shadowed, but Zazo should know that he wouldn´t accept such a humiliation. Zazo should be aware of a coming confrontation. But Zazo could not know, what it would look like and more importantly, at which bank and which account, he had embezzled some money. Of course, Demian had made provisions for bad times. $ 15 million U.S. he had deposited in all possible countries. Several identification papers he constantly carried around with him,

172

among them, two camouflage identities. In the following days, Demian did everything to shake off his tails. He spent half the day in the New York subway. Then he took the fast train to Chicago, like a schoolboy without a ticket. Having arrived there, he was sure that nobody was following him anymore.

First, Zazo steered me into his sauna-paradise. It was a great pleasure for me to enjoy the merits of this magnificent installation again. When the body got intoxicated on heat and water, the soul grew wings. But contrary to the last time, this feeling didn't control me. Nothing controlled me anymore. Carefully Zazo tried to size me up, just like children do it with foreign children in playgrounds. I suspected that he had chosen San Francisco, and especially the sauna paradise, as a first meeting place in order to analyze me more easily. In the exceptional situation of physical welfare, spirit could still be most easily lured out of its reserve. He wanted to see how my reactions had changed and to what degree the new found balance was established. I addressed him, regarding his expectations: „Would you prefer, to be sitting on the side of the old Ronda? The one, that was blinded by the luxury and the elation of corporality? Spontaneously, he repulsed: „I´m quite conscious about you, not being the old one any longer. We have both changed." I abandoned his statement to time. Shortly after, he admitted: „Maybe you`re right. One clings much too much to old patterns of behaviour. If you were the old one, it would be tempting to interact with you as usual. I confirmed his consideration: „And in doing so, the old patterns only provide one`s petrifaction." He laughed and said, we would probably have a nice time together. When I, a little bit provocatively, explained that I had learned in Tibet, to follow the voice of creation and divine harmony, just like a true Looni, he rolled his eyes towards heaven and sighed: „Oh, dear. Let`s speak about something else. Now, it was my turn, to cheer him up by tapping him on the shoulder. His obligatory back-slapping! Astonishedly he looked at me.

At the Cornfield Morgan Bank, Demian had deposited $ 1 million U.S. on his camouflage identity >Edmond Grover<.

This bank was, just like a few other banks, since its foundation careful, to keep completely out the GU. Stockholders and customers had bound themselves to the disclosure of all assets. Nobody was allowed to posses more than $ 1,5 million U.S. $ in total fortunes. Most banks didn't take the same narrow view. They were cooperative partners of the GU anyway, because they made use of their legal possibility, of adopting the commercialization of inheritance related enterprises, for the GU. Mostly concerning middle-class and big enterprises, banks and special banking organisations arranged the inheritance law allocations between the GU, the heirs, the employees and those, that wanted to acquire the enterprise. The GU was only allowed to commercialize in the market those companies, parts of companies or shares, which neither a qualified bank, nor a Trade Union, would like to take care of. Problems rarely emerged from shares and smaller companies. Here, the majority of the remaining possessors had the saying. It was more difficult, when complete companies were concerned. In such cases, normally banks organized the commercialization. In doing so, they sometimes provided new management or realized different ways of acquiring, from employee shares to new public companies. Normally, the commercialization had to be completed within one year, corresponding with the settlement of accounts of all expenses and paying off the surplus to the heirs and the GU. Of course, banks preferably tried selling parts of the enterprises or the enterprise as a whole. Please excuse my blabbering side stepping into political economies and industrial management, but this topic was of big importance with the formation of the GU. Of course the inventors of the Global Justice idea didn`t want to endanger jobs or smash current enterprises through the new inheritance regulations, favoring the GU. It was fixed, with validity for all GJP parties, that those banks involved in the companies' financing had the first right of an economically meaningful commercialization, concerning inheritance affected enterprises. Because of that, a completely new, lucrative business branch has been created for the banks. If the financing institutes waived their right of comercialization completely or partially, the Trade Unions, which means the absorbing organisations of the unions got their chance and in last priority other banks or organizations of owners. Only if none of the involved groups wanted to comercialize, the GU was allowed, to act in this field of market economy. On the acquiring side, preemptions were entitled to the heirs, with highest priority of course for the preservation of the enterprise. Neutral experts and employee representatives accompany the valuation and comercialization of inheritance concerned enterprises. This new field of operation has helped the banks incidentally very much, after having shrunk quite significantely through the new inheritance law and in some cases were still shrinking.

Anyway at the Cornfield Morgan bank, they didn`t want to have anything, and really nothing to do with the odious GU. Where Edmond Grover was concerned, they knew, that he had inherited not more than $ 1 million U.S. . Mr. Grover lived on the interest. The financing of the house and other miscellaneous purchases were paid off monthly. The neighbours envied Mr. Grover, who rarely came to his new home, back from one of his world trips. They had to work hard to be able to afford such a high standard of living.

We sat in the fireplace room when the message arrived: they had lost Demian. Zazo was troubled: „The fellow is a living bomb, I am sure, he`ll try to take revenge." He told me about how he had thrown Demian out. Zazo knew about the hidden $ 11 million dollars and one camouflage identity. He had posted his people in the concerning financial institutions. If Demian tried to withdraw the money, the trap would snap.

„That would be embezzlement of Looni money", Zazo declared. He knew nothing about Mr. Grover in Chicago. Zazo offered me to stay in his house for a while. In his usual way he joked: „You can renounce your GU basic-care for that time." I accepted his offer, because I was sure that fate had not brought me to Zazo for the third time merely by coincidence. What it might be good for, I could only guess, but I would never try, to force things in any direction.In the course of time things would emerge by themselves. I could only help with some support.

Demian changed his outer appearance little by little. He grew a beard and shaved his hair bald. He visited the neighbours in polite regularity so that they got used to his new look. After three months, Mr. Grover looked more similar to his passport photo than before, and Zazo would never have the idea that this man had anything to do with Demian.

Every morning and every evening Zazo and I meditated for half an hour. He asked me about the >Mu< Koan, and I opened his appetite for that „glowing iron", as Eckehard had called it. Actually, Zazo tried once again to deal with Mu. However, just like the first time, his distractions were too strong. Permanently, he had to make some decisions. Almost hourly, he was asked for urgent advice and help. Since Demian was gone, his workload had more than doubled.

One day, he actually asked me, whether I wanted to adopt Demian`s job, I would be paid like a prince for it. I thanked him for his trust and refused. Zazo proposed of putting me in the position of Looni boss: „ As you know, I don`t want to work much longer, anyway. In the end, I want to have time for myself, just like you. Maybe, I`ll also live with Eckehard for one or two years and solve the Mu riddle. I had the impression that he liked me." I explained to him that I was not created for such tasks. „What I´ll do in the future, I don't know, but I for sure will not become the manager of such a gigantic organization. That`s not suitable for me. Zazo asked me which answer I would have given him, four years ago. I suspected that I would also have refused, at that time, even if for other reasons. „At that time, I was a GU idealist." – „And today ?" – „Today I`m a realist." He misunderstood this remark and began to shoot the GU down, whereupon I explained to him that I still thought the GU a meaningful institution. „Would you work for that club again, if they offered it to you?" – „Who knows? Maybe?" Zazo wasn`t angry that I had refused his offer. Maybe, it was just the opposite. He now knew that I had no interest in all his material things.

Demian had completely become Edmond Grover. What kept him going, day after day, was his hate for Zazo. To punish him, was his mission. For this purpose, Mr. Grover looked for different materials from army stocks. The Americans still afforded an army, because they were convinced, of having to fight against aliens in the foreseeable future. Many Europeans looked at this attitude as >paranoia<, however, also in Europe voices grew, saying, that with the increasing intelligence of humankind, the probaility would increase, of meeting alien, intelligent life forms. Anyway, Mr. Grover bought for a lot of money from US-army stocks: a laser-pistol, plastic explosives and various fuses. His real problem was that Zazo was extremely difficult to catch. Zazo`s appearances in public became ever more rare and he had no chance, of entering Looni territory with his arms. Letters, packages, gifts, visitors, everything was checked many times before it came into Zazo`s proximity. Nevertheless, Mr. Grover knew, that his time would come. He had excellent connections to several Looni departments.

„Now I know the solution for the Demian problem !" Zazo triumphed: „Finally, I could learn a bit from your hate attack. For the first time, Zazo mentioned my paralyser action. I knew he hadn`t yet digested the incident. „You are still blaming me for the paralyser attack, right?" – „May be." –

„Forgive me. I was an injured animal." – „An injured animal? And I was the hunter?" – „Exactly." – „That might even be true. Well, anyway, this time the hunter will do his job more efficiently, of hunting Demian, and not be shot down again himself." – „What do you want to do?" – „I`ll set a trap for him. Just like you did, he`ll wait for me, to come into his line of fire, and that can only happen outside of Looni territories. Demian indeed had still good contacts to some chiefs, but within the Looni territorries he had no chance. Our new security system is perfect." Zazo made me a witness of his Demian trap. He engaged specialists from London. „In those areas the Brits are the most reliable", he said. We visited a London security company, that had absolutely nothing to do with the Looni. Zazo didn't trust the chiefs of the Looni security. Of course he gave the official order, to secure his lecture in a congress foyer, to the Looni security department. However, behind the scenes –invisibly-, the London company would be present. Zazo suspected that Demian would override the Looni security system with the help of his old contacts, but then would be stuck in the London company`s web. „What do you want to to do with him, once you`ve caught him?" – „That`s my business." He added, reacting on my concern: „Don`t worry, I won't harm him. I will hand him over to the police or something similar... ." I proposed choosing the same theater, in which I had shot him with the paralyser. Zazo laughed, the idea pleased him. He said, I had a sense for theatrics. By that, the Creative London Theatre became, nearly exactly on the same day, four years later, for the second time scene of a Looni meeting. Zazo refused to choose the same date because of superstitions.

Mr. Grover received a telephone call from a public telephone booth in San Francisco. „Our friend is holding a new lecture in London on May 29. We can meet two days before, at 22 o'clock in Paddington station, platform 2. In the following days, Mr. Grover was in an extraordinary good mood. „The second time, the same theater, what a fool. But this time, he`ll not come alive out of there.

The topic „GU " was not left to rest by Zazo. „You would really work for the GU again? Even though you have become a realist? He had not understood what I meant by realism. I tried to explain to him: „I´m a realist, concerning myself and my surroundings. I have escaped the tiny world of egoisms. I stood at the white-washed wall and saw, what it is about people and things. Never again, I`ll hurry into things, full of idealism and ambitions, like I did in former days. And that`s especially about shoes, that don't fit. Zazo nodded, he understood the words, but not their meaning. Completely convinced, that there is no way out of egoism, he pulled the most vehement registers in order to convict me of self-interest: „And if I handed over the entire Looni organization to you? It would enable you, to go back to the GU, and bring them 80 million Looni, 40 billion dollars and a self-sufficient working economic system. They would kiss your feet. An appealing idea, isn`t it? If you were a meaning creator would you accept being Looni boss, or not?“ I negated: „Not even then.“ Zazo got annoyed: „You only say that because you know that I won`t give the Looni to you.“ – „I`m not so sure, if you wouldn`t do it.“ – „Optimist !" – „Realist !" We laughed, and Zazo, a specialist in extreme things, made the stakes higher in the game: „Imagine, I would hand over my Looni to the GU only under the condition that you would become boss of the Looni what would happen then? Would you then become the Looni boss?“ The question was perfidious. I didn't want to spend time on formalities, therefore I tried a mediating answer: „If in this way, a hundred million Looni could be helped to mental freedom, I suppose, I would have no other choice.“ – „You think, you could absorb my poor Looni into the GU and after that, leave them alone, as soon as possible. That total act is >freedom< for you, even though you know, that people feel bad, when you leave them alone.“ With that, we came to the old topic again: freedom! Four years ago, Zazo had turned in his favor without any problems, our discussion about Dostoevsky`s Grand Inquisitor and people`s fear of freedom. This time I wasn`t prepared any better on that topic, nevertheless, I was able to expose the one- sidedness of Zazo`s arguments. I asked him whether it would not be more appealing, to teach others their way to self-sufficiency, instead of simply cultivating their weaknesses. Laconically, he determined, his name wouldn`t be Sysiphos. I agreed: „Sysiphos, tried solving his problem with physical strength. But you have been given so much more intelligence, than hardly anyone else. You could afford, to achieve interesting ways. You are not bound to the simple ones." Zazo looked amusedly at me: „you`re trying, to make an idealist out of me through my ambition, you clever devil." I said: „It`s not about ambition or idealism, it is about the possibility, to come close to oneself and one`s life. He laughed and said, he was absolutely sure, to being close to himself and his life. Exactly that, I didn't believe: „Don`t you think it possible, that your soul wants more, than only pleasure, power and security?" – „Do you think that my soul would prefer, to run behind the big Mu riddle?" – „Behind the big Mu riddle and your determination in life." Zazo smiled bored: „In this life I won`t run after anything anymore, but in the next life, maybe. In this life, I`ve run enough. Now, pleasure, power and security are enough for me." – „With which you degrade into the life of a rabbit ! Maybe in your next life, you`ll be directly born as a rabbit." He answered that rabbits also had their fun. With that, the topic of „lifestyle" was closed for him.

On the 27. 05. 2034, Demian and his confident arrived at the purveyor`s entrance of the London Creative Theatre. He was the 2nd–chief of the Looni Centre in Los Angeles and was determined, in shooting Demian to becoming the new Looni boss. Demian had given him the job, one year ago, and urgently warned him, never to use a mind-machine. His opinion, that Zazo was causing manipulations with help of the mind-machines, had turned into a certainty for him, although he had yet not found out, how that system worked. He was sure, of using Zazo`s tricks one day for himself, or more to the point, in a few days, when Zazo lay under the earth. Then, finally his hour would come. In searching the theater, Demian and his executor soon had a find. In the first parquet, there was a dusty broom closet, from which they could see the stage. The 2nd. chief lasered a hole into the wooden door of the broom closet. Through this hole, he would laser, exactly on the millimeter, a much smaller hole into Zazo`s head, his admission ticket for higher tasks in Demian`s empire.

The two didn't suspect that all their movements and words were sent live on Zazo`s special wish to San Francisco. There, he sat in front of the chimney and was surprised. The 2nd– chief was completely unknown to him and Demian looked quite strange with his beard and bald head. Far more strangly, however, to Zazo was the hate, in which Demian wanted to destroy him. The fact that Demian was bitter because of his dismissal, was clear. But that he wanted to kill him, really surprised him. Why should it surprise him? Not long ago, he would have reckoned in principle with other people`s wickedness. Had the Zen sitting softened him already, after such a short time? He could remember, quite well, how a few years ago, he had quite naturally repulsed with athletic ambition the most vicious attacks. Fights of life and death had even given him a certain pleasure. Today, he only regarded such things as necessary and tiresome. He would not kill Demian, but quite certainly he would guarantee him a very special treatment with a mind-machine. He was almost annoyed with himself, of having initiated Ronda into his confrontation with Demian. Not that he was afraid, Ronda would betray the trap. The only problem was, that Ronda would make the tiresome confrontation with the tiresome Demian through tiresome questions even more tiresome. At the moment, he had no idea, why he had taken this Ronda from Tibet. Could this naive saint be of any use to him? Was

181

he an opportunity for his personality development? The answer would emerge in the course of the next months. Time played no role for him anymore.

I noticed Zazo`s irritation. The confrontation with Demian affected him more than he ever would admit to himself. He didn`t want me to join him anymore, if it was about setting Demian`s trap. When I asked him, how far things had gone, he only muttered: „It will start soon." I didn't try to push him anymore. All things had their time, and that was the same with him.

While Zazo took care of his businesses, I took walks in the city. The house, where Julia and I had lived, was inhabited by a doctor`s family. I became aware that our children were five and eight years old, now. Paul was certainly already at school.Had Julia found a new partner? Following a sudden intuition, I got on the Internet Julia`s commu-number. I sent her a short 3-D message: „Just landed in San Francisco and thinking of you. Are you fine? Would be nice, to see you again. Report. Ciao."

Demian was just leaving the Creative Theatre with the 2nd-chief, when Zazo`s trap snapped. It was a special pleasure for Zazo to appear as a 3-D laser-projection beside the supplier`s entrance. Because the London company had installed camera sensors everywhere, he could look at Demian directly. Demian saw him and immediately began to run. He knew, there was only one chance, and that was running away. But the tractor beams of the London security company paralyzed his legs. „Finished, it`s over", he thought and was right. A few hours later, he sat in the Looni centre of Southampton under the helmet of a mind-machine. The 2nd- chief of the Looni-Centre of Los Angeles met the same fate. The two were lucky, Zazo really had become more gentle.

A few days later, Zazo invited me for tea. As the sovereign winner, he presented a submissive Demian. I asked Demian, whether he still felt jealous about me and believed him, when he assured me that he would never be able to feel jealous of anybody, that enjoyed Zazo`s sympathy. The whole thing had been a regrettable error, declared Zazo. Demian`s jealousy had in reality been nothing else, but an exaggerated worry about his welfare. „Imagine, Demian was afraid, you could shoot me with the paralyser, once again", Zazo laughed. He added with a serious expression: „probably the reason for it, were his nerves, being a bit raw because of overwork. Starting today I have granted him an extended vacation." Demian laughed as if he were looking forward to the vacation. I felt really sorry for that man. He wasn`t himself any longer. Would he ever get the chance to find himself again? Was it possible, to undo, what Zazo had done to him? Zazo read my thoughts, because he turned to Demian and said: „By the way, Ronda is a strong proponent of freedom. If it would be up to him, each human being would be educated as an anarchist. Imagine this chaos. Agreeingly, Demian laughed. I argued that a free world with free people would offer more chances for everyone, even for power greedy sovereigns." Zazo didn't like me, attacking him safeguardedly by clauses. Cynically he explained, that Tibet had made me into an itinerant preacher. One might be afraid, that I could open a rival organisation to the Looni one day.

The next day, a language message from Julia reached me: „You look well. Yes, we are also fine. Jean, my new husband, is a good father to the children. If you happen to be in Paris, give me a call. Maybe we can meet then." She was still the same.

Amazingly quickly, the weeks passed by in Zazo`s house. We usually spent the evenings together. In front of the chimney or in the sauna, we discussed God and the world. It was fun. While Zazo was working, I informed myself on the Internet about the development of the GU and meditated. Zazo`s workload was enormous. He raged around the world with his glider, solved very different problems of Looni headquarters, developed new ideas and consolidated personal contacts. Sometimes, he stayed away for several days. The educational centre in San Francisco was his favorite residence.

My presence seemed to give him something, because he offered for me to be his permanent guest. There wasn`t much to do at his house, because the household functioned fully automated. Now and then, the house computer asked me for instructions, concerning the purchase and preparing of food. The newest robots and the most intelligent machines did the rest. Occasionally, I cooked in the evening some nice specialties. Cooking was still a great pleasure for me.

After a few weeks, the discussions with Zazo began tapering off. More and more he was looking for a confrontation with me. However, I wasn`t willing to quarrel with him about words and expediencies. For him it was important to see his actions justified. Yes, he was looking for my acknowledgment. And with all that he wasn`t even honest, which means, not willing to talk about aggressive mind-machine programming. Not that I tried to steer the conversation onto this topic, for me any real matter wasn`t the point. I wanted to reach him in the depths of his soul, suspecting that I would be able, to pull him on a higher level. But his small ego fought like a lion. He changed his line of argument. „Do you really want to say, it would be better for me, to sit in a stone house like Eckehard and renounce all temporalities ? Isn`t it normal that people strive for prestige and profit? Just a thousand five hundred years ago, the wise Konfuze said: >To whom success and money is donated, he is lucky to be high in God's favor<. What is so bad about it, when I`m successful? Should I turn into an impoverished moralizer? How many fools have lost the joy of life and then bewailed the lost time, only because of being so very righteous? How many honorable bunglers have

184

noted all virtues and brought only bad luck to themselves, their families and their followers. For millions of years, life has been a fight. Best off, are the best."

I didn't disagree with him. His arguments were valid, however they were only part truth. His particular qualities: intelligence, charisma and organizational talent, I didn`t want to devalue them. Just the opposite, in my opinion, Zazo possessed all assumptions for the highest knowledge. What prevented him from it, was his one-sidedness, he reduced himself to the material. Cautiously, I tried to make him see that it was not about losing something, but winning. I admitted: „Of course, at the moment, when spirit increases, materialistics automatically decrease." – „That`s what I said, you want to make a spiritualized fool of me, and when I`ve lost all the money and the Looni in one or two years, we`ll sit together meditating in the stone house, it`s just a pitty, that we then cannot afford any good red wine or a sauna anymore.

Our banter could have continued indefinitely. To sum things up, I decided to go on a confrontation course: „Where money and power are the most important things, the bad is not so far," I said. „Good Gracious, the old song and dance about good and evil. The devil, that gives wealth and power in exchange for the soul. You really can`t get anywhere with anyone with this. We quarreled about >good< and >bad<, and it turned out that Zazo believed in a universe, where no >good< or >bad< exists. According to his opinion, stood above all humanly >good< or >bad< the unity of the universe free from all values.

For days we philosophized, and because the philosophy is an escalating guild, I would like to quote only the essential here. Zazo said: „Assuming, God has created everything, assuming, God is good, and assuming, the bad exists on earth, then logically God would have created it. How can God be good if he created the bad? The most accommodating explanation would be that within God`s work the bad is the answer of material existence to the divine spirit. You know, without light there is no shade. Material existence would be a separate part of the unity and cause within its own existence dualities. Expressed in some nicer words: Material existence, limited by time, offers resistance against timeless spirit. If this were true, there would be no dualism beyond material existence. No death, no life, no good and no bad, no light and no shade. For us, bearers of material existence, good and bad can only refer to something, which is material. Good is, what is of good use for material existence, what supports it. Bad is, what hurts it. Kant, the special philosopher in matters of morals, said, those act morally good, whose motives could become principles of general legislation. As you can see, crucial is only the material existence. Now, under this aspect, look at freedom. A positive concept of freedom cannot mean leaving creatures alone, letting them fall free into the varieties of life. Especially not, when existence is weak. What is weak, needs supports, a strong hand, someone who tells them where to go. Most people are weak. I support and lead them and therefore act, in a moral sense, good. Better anyway, than somebody, abandoning them to themselves and their lack of orientation. What Jacques told you, concerning the big ego, exists one level higher. You can watch from above, the whole material existence, the entire cosmos. Then, many things will relativize, especially the question of good and bad. Such trivial distinctions, such as good and bad, depending on material existence, don`t exist in the origins of the universe. The highest entity has no values and is beyond primitive human morals."

Zazo had put aside his mask. He revealed his meaning of existence. A meaning of existence, that knew no values in its heart. He was convinced that the world was ruled by the laws of strong and weak materiality. He thought his arguments to be undefeatable, immune against any attack. But he was wrong, I destroyed his meaning of existence.

186

Zazo was right as far as the unity of all things indeed existed. At the white-washed wall in Golam, I had seen it. But it looked different from what Zazo thought. Dualities, good and bad, light and shade, life and death actually dissolved. However, they don`t dissolve into a nothingness without values. The unity is rather filled with that all universal consciousness, that I had felt as pure love. Some call it God. Some like the Buddhists are content with the derivatives. For me it was the original power of the Creator. Material existence cannot bear: itself, or new material existences, or souls, or individualities. Such creating acts were reserved to that all imbuing universal consciousness. God is the breath of our souls the same as he is the origin of all material existence. I had understood that in Tibet.

I tried to explain to Zazo the way: „Maybe the bad has its origin, where material existence thinks of itself as the most important thing and refuses, to acknowledge the individuality of the timeless, universal consciousness. Such materiality, no matter whether it is manifested in a human being or in an inhabitant of a planet of the Orion Beteigeuze system, thinks that only themselves are to be taken seriously, because of embodying absolute individuality. Perhaps the essence of such material existences, devoted to its own importance, hates the universal consciousness out of the awarenes of its own temporal and material limitation. But even if the bad is a dualistic necessary answer of material existence on the divine spirit, it remains there, where no material existence is, the indivisible (Latin: in-dividens), the individuality of the universal consciousness. Just that is the unity. Your big watch from above, therefore probably could have values and contents. You just have to fly a little bit somewhat higher.

Zazo got annoyed: „We are material existences and we know, that we are limited by time, you are right! Maybe we even hate, as you said, the time wasting idea of timelessness.

Maybe we are bad only because we are material. If we fritter our scarce time with the supposedly universal consciousness, do we extend our time through it by doing so? Don't we remain material, at all? Why should I fly higher than I can think, I poor materia? I hope you don`t dish out this idiocy of heaven and hell?"

No, I really didn't want to bore him with such fairy-tales. But I reminded him of the so-called „self-fulfilling-prophecies", prophecies, that make themselves come true: „Thoughts mold the world. Your thoughts mold your world. As long as you are convinced, that beyond material existence there is nothing but emptiness without values, you will never realize that it is love, holding together all developments and passing-bys."

Zazo laughed about the word >love<. Good and bad were for him only varieties of material being and it was the same with love –yet agreeablly- a positive variety. He triumphed: „Despite all your babbeling, you have no objective explanation for what is good and what is bad. And your alleged love is supposed to be without any material being nothing more than ballony.

I knew, we had reached the turning-point. If I could convince him now, I would have won the race. Carefully, I sorted my thoughts: „Your concept stops half way. Behind the dualism of death and life, light and shade, spirit and materials, good and bad, you only see the nothingness. You won't admit more, only the nothingness. If you would open yourself, you could experience more. Even the human sciences, being just at their beginning, have already proven that material things and time are nothing more but dependents of the light. Where the atoms of your body stop and where the atoms of the remaining world start, is just an unimportant question of materiality and time. And both, materiality and time, are dependent on the light. Perhaps this light is just a part of the universal consciousness. In any case, it is more elementary than any materiality and any time. If you think about unity, that unity which is beyond the nothingness, such unimportant, dependent things like material existences and time completely lose their priorities. Unity has more to do with elementary things like light. The human being as a time dependent, material existence would realize the limitedness of its own importance, which would lead to reality. Even for you a way to God, to love, whatever you want to call it. To fight that love is bad, to be devoted to it is good. It`s so simple. It won't harm you or your body if you stay as you are. Your soul will suffer, because it will become a slave of material existences, unfree and without a chance, to live love. Strange, isn`t it? For material reasons, you limit the freedom of others and in doing so, you`re automatically building the prison of your own soul."

Zazo was evidently impressed and muttered: „the invariable light, that determines time and materiality, as Einstein said..." He turned to me and asked: „and behind all definitions, contradictions and dependencies is where this universal consciousness is supposed to be?" – „You can rely on that." – „And the meaning of all that training?" I told him about Mrs. Dreyer`s theory of vacation and supplemented it spontaneously: „maybe God regenerates his cells in our souls." Zazo quipped: „with so many rotten souls God will probably need a hospital quite soon. But people say that 21pure souls are enough to save the world. I saw the insecurity in his eyes and tapped him one more time on the shoulder: „It`s not necessary,to ridicule things, it`s not at all so bad."
That evening, Zazo went to bed thoughtfully.

At breakfast, Zazo talked about an alteration in his lifestyle: „Strictly speaking I have nothing to lose, at all. Even if I gave up the Looni, I could live until the end of my life on the fat of the land, revel and riot, not giving a hoot about stress and

189

disputs. You have actually opened my eyes.The time has come, to live, finally to live for myself and not for others, not anymore for power, for fame or honor. Finally, I don`t want to withhold anything from my poor soul, right?" Laughing he tapped me on the shoulder. Cheering him up, I tapped him back on his shoulder.

In the following days, Zazo trusted me with historical studies,which he had pursued for years. It was about 43 truths, he suspected were in the so-called Ark of the Covenant. 43 basic truths, that God should have revealed to humans ages ago. I was astonished. Zazo and God? At first sight that didn`t really add up: „You could imagine, God giving truths to humans?" – „Let`s say, I believe in certain magical forces . You can call them divinely, if you like. Anyway, the Ark of the Covenant probably harbors highly interesting cosmic strengths. Some historians claimed, the German dictator Adolf Hitler would have dug it up in the Egyptian desert. Actually, a hundred years ago, Hitler had driven an enormous expenditure with his Africa-Corps to come into possession of the Ark of the Covenant. But he didn`t find it. Zazo was sure that the Ark of the Covenant had been dug out of Salomo`s Temple long before Hitler. Salomo, David's son, had built the temple in Jerusalem, 935 BC.. . Presumably, the Ark of the Covenant was buried in the catacombs of the temple in 597 BC. . A few hundred years later the Romans destroyed the temple, burying the catacombs and with it the hidden Ark of the Covenant. In 1127 AD. the Knight Templar Ritter founded themselves, in Zazo`s opinion, especially because of the Ark of the Covenant. On the pretext of protecting pilgrims, they took possession of the destroyed Salomo Temple. In 1199, he supposed them of having found the Ark of the Covenant in the catacombs, layed open with lots of difficulties. Later, in 1338 AD., the Knight Templar split into several free-mason`s lodges, because they were pursued by the Catholic Church. Zazo was sure that still today freemasons were hiding the 43 truths from the power hungry people of the world.

I asked Zazo what he would do with the 43 truths and received a lecture about power in general and in particular. Zazo considered the biggest advantage of the Global Justice Movement was that nowadays hardly any political fights existed between states on earth. He found it astonishing that democracy limiting parties became stronger and stronger, however, the two strongest proponents of this political direction, the Market Oligarchy Party (MOGJP) and the Intelligence Party (Intelligence-GJP) defended unrestrictedly the Global Justice system. Zazo thought anyway, that time would be ripe for the 43 truths. The only problem was, that the guardians of these truths were ony „degenerate oldies, with nothing more in their brains but tradition." He trusted me with having found through investigations for years, that in the last millennium the >Arabic Lodge< had been the guardian of the truths. He had found their successors in London. „Shortly before I could surprise them, they had vanished without a trace. Their news system was much better than I had thought ". His investigations had continued, however. Now, he was certain about having located the guardians of the truths in Switzerland.

Zazo was irritated, when I assured him that those 43 truths admittedly interested me from a historical point of view, but not because of any supposed substance of truth. „I´m very sure, the 43 sayings won`t offer anything more than those things, we discussed a few days ago", I explained to him.

Zazo looked at me with big eyes: „You don`t know, what you`re saying! For thousands of years, humankind has been after the Ark of the Covenant. Hundreds and thousands have died for it. Magical forces are attributed to it. Imagine, the original wisdom of the earth...., and I succeed in bringing it to light. Even the origin of the Global Union fades in comparison to such principle power."

I corrected him: „I know quite well, what I`m talking about. And had you grasped the meaning of my thoughts, then you would know that there cannot be any higher truths, than those, we have talked about. It doesn`t matter, whether it is about spirits and magic, about aliens, the existence of the globe, the stars above or our souls, the origin of all things is the same. And exactly about that, about the origin of all things and the coherence of all strengths, we have talked.

Zazo came round: „I must admit, your argument about the light was not too bad. And it makes sense: we, existing out of our materiality shouldn`t take ourselves so seriously. Finally, science indeed has proven that material existences and time only are dependents on the light. Maybe, there, where light originates exists no time and no materiality." – „And nevertheless light originates." – „Yes, it`s astonishing. But only because of that, it`s proven by no means that any divine Creator created the light or anything else.By the same right of course, you would have to ask, who created the divine Creator." – „If you really try to give things a meaning with human logic, you should know that the question of >who created what?<stops exactly at the question of God. Here the conception of God begins. Apart from that, a definition of God anyway, is beyond simple human logic. And besides that I can assure you, the universal love, I had experienced, being more than a cosmic coincidence." Once more, Zazo indicated no. In that moment, he seemed to be overcome by a certain melancholy. I comforted him: „the 43 truths are probably interesting. Quite often God has helped humans out. Zazo`s nodding became more and more thoughtful.

When Zazo could arrange it, he practiced Zazen with me, twice a day. First, we sat, as usual, half an hour in the morning and a half hour in the evening. That „real world", as he called it, entailed too much work. In the course of time, we sat longer and longer. Finally, we reached two hours of daily sitting. Zazo worried about his connections to the Looni world: „If I continue like this, Demian might be right, and the Looni will wilt like a flower." – „You said, you could live with it." – „And you would enjoy, watching the Looni wilt, right?" – „If your Looni were a rosebush, the thought of next spring would comfort me." As I said this, it was clear to me, as it was clear to Zazo, that the Looni organisation would inretrievably perish, if Zazo didn`t give artificial respiration to it. He had only created a dependent artificial structure and no living rosebush. Perhaps my metaphor clarified the weakness in his work, perhaps because of this, it also lost value for him, anyway he pondered: „You`re right. Just a few days ago, I had considered of finally living for myself. But what shall I do with the Looni? I cannot leave them alone." – „Release them to freedom." – „Good Heavens, freedom! Didn`t you grasp at all, that people don`t want any freedom?" – „If you had educated them contrarily, they probably could have joy with freedom." He shook his head and accused me of being starry-eyed.

My discussion with Zazo became critical, when it was about the power of magic. For three months I had tried in vain to release his mental inhibitions Then, I realized, what blockaded him. He was caught by his own exceptional abilities. Someone, who is as mentally developed as Zazo is able to see things that simple people cannot. Reading thoughts and looking into the future are examples of such abilities. He had approached cosmic strengths and truths so closely, that he could overcome borders, limiting the simple individual. But he was pinned to the cage of power, and he reinforced the cage in cultivating his magic abilities. One morning, I knew that he thought of himself as a magician. He didn`t say anything on this subject, I simply knew it, by sudden intuition. Since my time in Tibet, sudden intuitions ran through my life like oxygen.

My question about his magical activities surprised him: „What put this idea into your head?" I explained to him that my own magical abilities would have given this knowledge to me. „But maybe even through the Ark of the Covenant, this idea came to mind. You had imposed magical strengths to it. Furthermore, it`s really astonishing how stubborn your blockade is, against the next step of consciousness." – „Astonishing, isn`t it?" Zazo became prickly. On the one hand, he liked the confrontations with me · after all, I offered him the rare attraction of a creative counterbalance · on the other hand he had expressed a few days before, living together with me reminds him almost of a civil marriage. The last time he lived so closely together, was with his parents. Now, in this closeness, I confronted him with his own weaknesses. Clearly, he was fed up with that. I put more pressure on him: „Indeed, amazingly stubborn blockades." – „Yes, that`s, what characterizes us. I called him to his face a chicken. Chicken! In his opinion the stupidest, I could give out. „You are afraid of losing yourself as soon as you lose your power." Suddenly, he shot back: „Ever since my youth, I have automatically become mightier from day to day. Nothing and nobody could prevent me from that. And only you come along and say, I am afraid to lose myself or my power. Is this supposed to be a rather ridiculous statement?" I had to laugh, because at the very same moment he had confirmed my opinion. He could see power and himself only in a symbiosis. „What would be, if all your power dissolved?" I asked him. Anxiously, he answered: „Nobody knows, maybe I would become a GU bum, just like you? But, you don`t seem able to understand. Your idea is off the point. Only in the course of time, I become stronger and stronger. Maybe, in a few years I`ll enter into competition with your Global Union." – „Now you can see, that you believe yourself not capable of much without power." – „Not capable?" dangerously, he hissed at me. I knew, that he was about to throw me out, but that didn't matter to me. I was free, free from goals, free from desires, free from fears. Whether he would throw me out, or

194

give me his Looni power as a present, it didn't matter to me. My serenity made him even grimmer: „What I`m feeling capable of, my dear friend, you cannot imagine in your wildest dreams." – „You`re confusing self-confidence with courage." – „So? I´ m really doing that? What, in
your opinion, would happen if my courage, unnecessarily would be added by self-confidence?" – „Presumably you wouldn`t stand in need anymore, to stuff yourself full of power." Annoyed he indicated no. I supplemented: „Think about it, power and magic are of no advantage to your soul, they are only of use to your transient small ego." Grumbling he left the room. On the same evening, I didn't see him again, not even for the Zazen sitting.

A few days later, he came back on the topic >magic< : „So, you also have magic strengths?" – „As you know." – „If one is given the chance to live such abilities, wouldn`t it be stupid, not to do so?" – „It would be stupid to cling to such a level." – „The level is sufficiently high. Most people become rather dizzy up there. And honestly said, it`s also high enough for me, at least in this life." – „The next step is only a small one. You could take it easily." – „Come on, explain it to me!" I asked him, where according to his opinion, magic comes from. „Maybe from your Creator, but perhaps also from the Fallen Angel." –„A falling angel, becoming the king of all magicians, nevertheless remains a part of the creation. And even if the angel of power and magic is very tempting, it never arises to the creator of itself. Its actions and itself remain dependent on the one, who created it and imbued it, like everything else." – „Then tell me, why did God let the angel fall and let it play bad games." – „The angel has the freedom of choice just like us. It lives in a world of decisions." · „Do you think even the Fallen Angel can find his way back to love or God, or whatever you call that thing?" – „Each soul got the chance to find unity and especially those, like an angel, had once already lived in it. By the way, your fallen angel is supposed to be the sum of all fallen souls, and not a single fallen angel." – „So I´ll probably join the sum of fallen souls, right?" – „Exactly! Prisoners of power belong to it." – „Prisoners of power! A nice term!" – „Yes. By the way, do you know, how prisoners of power can be recognized ?" – „No !" Zazo really seemed to be on the edge for the answer. „By not really being able to laugh." – „You think, I`m not really able to laugh?" –„You can only laugh at things. Zazo stopped short. He got an excellent red wine from the cellar, 1999 Chateau L`Eglise. Silently we drank and enjoyed the earthy fruity liquid. Suddenly, he said: „Who knows, maybe there is even a small ounce of truth in, what you`ve said."

In the following weeks, Zazo devoted more and more time to the question, how could he get out of business life in the most clever way. He had no desire anymore, „to waste life away" with permanent work. The problem was that he had no successor, and the way, he had organized the Looni, he would never be able to find one. To me it was clear, that he had to alter the entire organization. He had to lead his Looni into independence. It was really strange. I had already tried to bring closer to him exactly the same thing. At that time, I had been an idealist and a meaning-creator of the Global Union. Today, idealism drove me no longer. I was only interested in genuineness and truthfulness. If Zazo would remove the shackles from his Looni, this action would be genuine, for him and for the Looni. He would give up control and his baby would learn to run. I suggested to deprogram the mind-machines. „A freedom training program would not be so bad." With a pain-racked grin, he gazed at me. He didn't want to sacrifice his life's work.

With a certain mercilessness, I persisted with him: „Even though on TV and the Internet manipulations are usual nowadays, it would be a truthful liberation action, that only could be helpful to you. For the first time, I had frankly addressed him, regarding mind-machine manipulations. He would easily have been able to block me. He knew that I

196

wasn`t able to prove anything. He didn't know however, when I would give up,.... when I would stop the attempt of converting him. Maybe he was afraid, of staying in the power trap for the rest of his days. Maybe he thought, I would go, if he weren`t honest now. Anyway, he didn`t deny anything. „Okay, since you have your own magical abilities anyway, denying serves no purpose. Let's say, there thoroughly could be the possibility, to manipulate the Looni towards freedom with the help of some mind-machines. But, Good Gracious, Ronda, what would freedom mean to them? Say nothing! I already know it! Their chance, to find themselves in the universal consciousness. We had to laugh.

I tried, building him bridges: „If your new mind-machine programs would free the people, the Looni could administrate themselves. You would have less toils and your work would survive. Nobody had to necessarily know about any mind-machine manipulation.
Zazo indicated no: „Look at the normal free human being. Normally he is a commu-junky and fritters his valuable freedom in front of the computer tube. Of course, there are also other addicts. Sports-junkies or job-junkies. I´m probably a member of the latter, although my work addiction at least still brings in something. He spoke of power and money. Or the young generation, mating addicted, constantly on the search for partners. What remains as creative potential? Not much! On the whole, by and large, humans don`t have much on their minds with things like this. What do you believe, how many people would be keen, in building up a free, self-administrating Looni organisation?

He was right. All that persuasive power, I had reached day by day in the last weeks with Zazo, and even more, I would have to spend, in order to arrange the people`s sense of freedom and their own creativity. Individually, each had to be motivated. A Sysiphos work, that I had achieved in small means as a meaning-giver in Paris. I still knew exactly, how few were willing to exchange comfort for activities. Who really wanted to constantly broaden his own mind, just like Zazo? Who had so much power? To who was their own development more important than distraction? Who sat down and meditated instead of being provided in the living room with tension and entertainment through the computer tube?

Zazo and I made a deal: we both wrote. He a new program for the mind-machines and I a book about my journey to the truth. As soon as my book was finished, he would have the program run through. Each Looni would get my book as a present. It would be up to me, to write it so that as many people as possible felt the wish for an active shaping of their own lives and arranging creative things.

Now, that my book is finished, whoever wants, may find ideas in it. Who likes the idea of the Global Justice, may support the GU or the GJPs of their own country (some Web addresses are found here in the book). Whoever wants to give space to his soul might sit in silence twice a day. Whoever believes, running behind wild Mu cows could bring one closer to heaven, should not be held back. Whoever wants to be brainwashed by the computer tube, should do it. Whoever wants to run after money, power and leaders, should enjoy this way. Everybody makes his own soul. That is the freedom, we have.

www.ingramcontent.com/pod-product-compliance
Lightning Source LLC
Chambersburg PA
CBHW080906020726
47502CB00008B/2363